PATROLLING FOR LOVE AT SILVER RIDGE

CLAIRE CAIN

To pancakes.

____

CHAPTER ONE

Danny

Nonchalant. No big deal.

That's me.

I dragged my knuckles along the top of the library circulation desk and let my attention wander back to the woman now chatting with a small group of parents and kids.

Definitely not staring and unable to tear my eyes away because...

Whoa.

Not just unfamiliar, but... notable. Pretty. *New.* An unusual occurrence in the off-season in Silverton, Utah, particularly in a place I frequented.

More than that, though. But *whoa* was about as articulate as I could get. Because... *wow.*

Now this? This was an unfamiliar sensation. I hadn't *noticed* a woman in... well. A minute.

Her dark hair fell to her shoulders, one side pinned back to show a delicate neck disappearing down into a white collared shirt.

Delicate neck? Who are *you?*

Full lips curving into a smile that, I kid you not, made me feel a little faint. Knees weak. Mind hazy, like looking at her made my blood confused and forget how to find my brain.

I shook my head and broke out of the daze this woman's shiny dark hair and smooth laugh had put me in. True, I hadn't been on a date in... a while. But I hadn't wanted to. I wasn't hard up for female interest or friends, but I just... I'd been busy.

Jake, the summer intern for Mrs. Stanton, our librarian, approached. I gave him the old chin nod greeting, resisting the pull toward the embodiment of beauty floating there at the corner of my peripheral vision.

"Hey man! Great to see you! You here for some books?"

Jake spoke like he ended every sentence with an exclamation point. He'd never have been my first guess for the library internship, but when he asked for a recommendation, I happily gave it. He worked for us at Silver Ridge lodge as a lifty at midmountain and had assisted with ski patrol as much as he could considering he was still in school.

"Grabbing one of Grandpa Will's holds." I swung my keys on the ring like a pistol, aiming the small library card attached there at him so he could scan it.

"Cool! Love it! Let me grab it!"

Sweet kid.

I turned the other way, back to the place my mind hadn't moved on from, and surveyed the library's new set up.

"Huh." The sound left my mouth, making me feel like an idiot, because the whole place had been rearranged. The stacks created a kind of weaving path around the front room, herding patrons through several sections before reaching the circulation desk. I'd taken the direct route from door to desk that divided the building in half, but now could appreciate the layout.

Creative. Interesting. Probably something that would push patrons into wandering by shelves they didn't frequent.

Soft chuckles and friendly farewells pulled my attention to the other side of the room.

The woman turned to send the group off with a wave, and her dark eyes snagged on me because, like a weirdo, I was apparently standing there watching her again despite having decided I wasn't going to keep doing that. Her eyebrows arched in question, and then her attention dragged back to a child who'd approached.

A little heat crept into my cheeks, and I marveled at that. Just a flash of that eyebrow and she had me swallowing hard and looking for a reason to keep watching her.

"Got it! Looks good man! Tell GW I said hi!" Jake swiped the book, my card, and hit me with his best customer service smile.

I couldn't stop the chuckle. Jake's nickname for my Grandpa Will was classic Jake—he abbreviated whenever possible. "Will do, man. Come see me in the fall if you want to work your Christmas break again this year."

His head bobbed in an overenthusiastic nod before I'd finished talking. "Definitely! Thanks Dan! You're the best!"

I held the book up in farewell and took the winding path through the stacks, fingering book spines along the way. Suspense, Romance, Literary Fiction, History... I already had a few books checked out and no time to get lost in the titles, so I forced myself to stay focused on the task at hand—get Grandpa his book, and get home. Before pushing out the door, I turned back—*just one more look.*

Her head ducked back to her computer just as I looked up, and she caught her bottom lip between her teeth. Gorgeous, pink lips...

Get a hold of yourself, man.

Maybe she'd check me out next time I came in for a book.

CHAPTER TWO

Mia

I'd seen Daniel Morrison now no fewer than twenty times since moving to town weeks ago, but this was the first time he'd seen me see him. *Awkward.*

Or, maybe not. It'd be fine. We'd meet eventually—surprising we hadn't, really. Silverton was a small town, and though the people had welcomed me so far, they weren't exactly going out of their way to make me feel like a part of the community. Maybe that came from the nature of a resort town. The way Mrs. Stanton had described it made it sound like the people who lived here year-round didn't begrudge seasonal workers because they needed the help during ski season, but the residents knew they were temporary. Everyone else was seen as passing through.

Where did that leave me? I clearly didn't fall into the category of seasonal worker as I'd arrived just *after* the ski season ended, and I'd taken a very non-temporary job. Mrs. Stanton, the now-retired librarian, had worked at Silverton's tiny library for forty years.

Perhaps that played into it too—not many people knew Mrs. Stanton had spent her last day amongst the stacks this past June after I'd worked by her side for over a month. She'd quietly stepped aside, no fanfare, and now spent her days at Silverton Springs, an assisted living and retirement home right here in town.

The place was homey. In fact, much of the elderly population lived there, likely due to the harsh winters being nearly impossible to navigate as one aged—again, according to Mrs. Stanton. While I hadn't met Daniel Morrison officially, I'd seen his grandfather Will one day while visiting Mrs. Stanton, just after his grandson had left.

I'd done my best to pay attention to the kids chatting with me, bubbling over with excitement about the summer reading challenge and their progress while their parents asked if I'd thought about doing any extra children's programming for the month of August.

Truthfully, I hadn't. I'd planned to keep the status quo for a while until people felt comfortable with me. I'd been so afraid there'd be a revolt of some kind—people shackling themselves to the library doors in comically over-sized chains in protest of my arrival and their beloved senior librarian's departure.

No such thing occurred. I'd been welcomed by the regular patrons, and the only minor scuffle I'd had so far had been a verbal one with a book club leader who'd assumed I wouldn't order her books in time. Apparently, Mrs. Stanton had been a bit on the slower side, so when her July book arrived on the very date promised, her complaints had died on her tongue.

The point being, the people who'd come to the library had been kind. Welcoming. Eager to hear my ideas and plans, particularly the parents with young children and who seemed desperate for ideas to entertain their toddlers. I remembered the feeling and promised I'd come up with a few events to help fill out the summer until the school year began.

By the time I bid them farewell, Daniel had nearly reached the door. As he walked away, I let myself admire his broad shoulders, his easy gait, and the fiery tint of his hair, even though I could only see the little bit left uncovered by his hat in the back.

Miraculously, I knew he'd turn back before he did and tore my eyes away just in time. I bit down on my lip—had to—to keep my cheeks from flaming at him nearly catching me admiring him.

He left, and I let out a breath.

For some reason, Daniel Morrison made my stomach drop. I had never spoken to the man, but he left me feeling completely unsettled whenever I caught sight of him. It made no sense. He'd never so much as smiled at me. Our first time making eye contact—which as a side note had been mildly devastating because his eyes were astounding even under the brim of his hat—had happened moments ago.

Yet, I'd seen him time and again, and *every* time, even when I had no idea he belonged to the town's beloved Morrison family, I'd felt... funny. Full. Aware.

I'd been systematically *unaware* of men since... forever. Okay. *Lies.*

I'd been aware of one man one time at eighteen, and I'd come out of that... *awareness*... with my son Kai. Kai was the best thing that had ever happened to me, so no part of me begrudged that one man, even though putting even more space between us had been part of the reason I'd moved from Salt Lake City and found refuge in this tiny, odd town.

So why now? Why this red-haired ski bum? I mean, I didn't know he was a ski bum for sure, but he had that look about him. Always wore a hat, his hair a little too long out the sides and back, permanent goggle tan—or at least, that'd been there when I'd seen him the very first time in the spring. Lately, that'd changed, probably since he wasn't wearing goggles daily. *Whatever*.

If I had a type, Daniel Morrison was definitely not it. And that was beside the point, since I'd never so much as spoken to the guy, nor did I have plans to put myself in his way. He seemed nice enough, sure, but my job now demanded focus. I'd planned our move in detail, had done everything I could to prepare Kai for his change in schools, but in the end, we needed time in the saddle here. We needed to simply *be* in Silverton. Eat at the restaurants, shop in the stores, show up at church, do the things the locals did so we'd fit.

I wanted to fit here. I wanted Kai to fit. At six, there were few places he didn't feel immediately and fully comfortable, and though I appreciated that about him, I felt none of his ease. For all of his lack of self-consciousness, I'd been nearly silenced by mine.

I knew Mrs. Stanton, a few library patrons, and parents of kids who attended weekly storytime. And I'd met one woman about my age, Bel Paxton, who'd wandered into the library on a day I'd been training. When I learned she helped design flyers, I'd asked if she'd help advertise the library's programs around town, which she'd agreed to do pro bono. I'd spoken with her a small handful of times and had yet to be able to do so with ease. Guess I wasn't fitting in as quickly as I'd wanted...

I kissed Kai's curved little cheek, felt a pang at the ever-present realization that the curve was smaller as he became more a *kid* and less my little boy, and sat back down with my laptop, ready to pay bills while he left to enjoy a play-date at a friend's house. I sat there for no more than two minutes before the call of the mountains won out. I raced around the house gathering supplies, then charged out the door in my shirt, shorts, and hiking boots, only a small pack on my back—and a fully charged cell phone because I'm not a complete idiot—and jumped into my car to get to the trailhead.

I loved the library, but between getting settled in the house and working, I saw the inside of buildings more than I saw sky by a long shot. Nothing wrong with that, except part of what I wanted when I chose Silverton—though admittedly, in many ways it felt like it chose me—was the proximity to the mountains.

And now, here I sat on a rugged little stump at the side of the trail, gripping my ankle and praying I hadn't broken it when I rolled it moments ago. I wouldn't cry, no, because I'd given birth and nothing would ever compare to unexpectedly birthing a child without medication on the pain scale, but I clenched my jaw and had to blink away the moisture gathering at my bottom lids as I pictured a fissure in the bone of my foot and a doctor frowning at me saying, "It'll never be the same."

Perhaps I had an active imagination. I liked to think it

aided me in my job, my parenting, and also in my rather lonely interior life.

I ducked my head and breathed through my nose, then attempted to flex my foot. The sound that emerged from my mouth could only be called a yelp.

I shut my eyes and tried to calm my rapid pulse, the panic rising in me like a gushing fountain. If I couldn't flex my foot, then I couldn't walk down this path, even though I was only a half-mile or so from the bottom. I'd hiked for hours up and back down with no issues, but here at the end, the solo trip was catching up to me—*of course*. I'd be the ridiculous new woman in town who had to call 911 because she rolled her ankle.

I attempted to pull in a slow breath, but a sob interrupted it. I clamped my mouth shut, unwilling to give in to the panic, knowing it didn't give a crap whether I had plans to give into it or not.

"Whoa, you okay?"

My eyes flew open at the sound of a man's voice, and then, there he was, *him* of course, crouching in front of me, shucking his pack, lifting his sunglasses to reveal those brutal blue eyes.

"Ma'am?"

I didn't cringe at his calling me ma'am. Never mind that he had to be close to my age—he'd likely been trained to address people formally as a ski patroller. That I knew exactly who he was and he clearly didn't know me... well. Story of my life in Silverton thus far.

"Uh, yeah... hurt my ankle." I could hear the pain in my voice as it eked out, thin and watery.

"Okay. Can I take a look? I'm a ski patroller, trained for this kind of thing. I work for the lodge. If we can stabilize it, I can help get you down."

Those lovely blue eyes assessed me head to toe, then zeroed in on my mutinous left ankle.

"Sure. Of course."

He kneeled and placed a warm hand behind my calf, his large palm soothing and a little rough. If I hadn't been in this particular situation, I might have been captivated by his touch sliding along the curve of my leg, though there was nothing sensual in his movement. Just this contact...

I winced and stifled a gasp of pain when he shifted my booted foot to one side.

"Sorry." His face showed he meant it, his dark brownish-red eyebrows knit together, a frown on what I could now appreciate, even in a ridiculous amount of pain and no small measure of embarrassment, were surprisingly full lips. "Just need to get a sense of what we've got here. I'm hoping it's just a sprain and not broken—shouldn't need an evac."

I nodded, not sure I could find words as a bolt of fear rocketed down my spine at the word *broken*. I didn't have time for a broken ankle. I didn't think my insurance would cover much more than basic X-rays, and it certainly couldn't be cheap to have an *evac*, whatever that was.

He eyed me as he moved the foot one way, then the other. When I jumped, he nodded like it was good thing. "I'm sorry. But this is good. Pretty sure it's just a nasty sprain. Best thing to do is keep it in the boot to stabilize it and head down. You're going to be fine."

I wondered what it'd look like to get down this mountain, but couldn't pretend I didn't feel hugely relieved not to be on my own with this.

He shuffled a few things in his pack, took a swig of water and suggested I take one from mine with a nod toward where it sat next to me, then stood and set his pack in front of him. Every one of his movements was certain, steady. "Okay. We're going to get you up. It's going to suck, but if you can give one good jump, I'll do the rest."

"Uh—"

He leaned over, his face alarmingly close to mine. "Arms around my neck, and when I stand up, put your weight on your good leg. Then I'm going to turn, and I need you to hop if you can, and I'll get you up."

"Uh—"

He placed my arms around his head, and my hands seemed to know to lock at the back of his neck where they met.

"Okay, now."

He stood, and I pressed up on my thoroughly exhausted good leg and found myself flush against Daniel Morrison.

"Okay?" He searched my face, and I nodded, breathless from exertion and definitely not his proximity. "'kay, I'm going to turn, and you're going to jump, then I'll grab you under your legs and hike you up."

"Wait. Wait." I tightened my arms around his neck so he couldn't turn. "You're going to carry me?"

"Yeah. Piggy-back." A sweet little smile and wide eyes showed me he had no idea why that might be surprising to me.

"You're going to carry me the entire way down the mountain?"

"Yeah. Or did you want to take the car?"

Oh, good. Sarcasm. "No, I don't—that's fine, but I'm pretty heavy."

His gaze flickered over me again, and he shook his head. "Nah. We'll be fine. Ready?"

I couldn't tell whether my heart felt like it might pound out of my chest because this guy I'd never even talked to before planned to haul me on his back and hike down the rest of the mountain with my full, dead weight draped across his impressive shoulders, or if it came down to the pain still pulsing in my foot and the mild freak-out I'd been having when he arrived.

As much as I didn't relish being *carried* down, there wasn't another option unless I wanted to one-leg it, and I didn't. I swallowed and took a deep breath. When he bent down into a deep squat, I hopped up as best I could. His hands held my bare legs at my hamstrings and he sort of jumped me up to get a better grip. I silently winced at the jostling of my leg.

"Sorry. Just want to make sure I have a good grip." Then he reached down and somehow, in a move I didn't comprehend nor could I really see from my vantage point at his back, looped his pack over his chest. "Ready?"

"Yep. Just let me know if I get too heavy." I ran my hands along his shoulders searching for a place to grip—his very muscular, defined shoulders. Could I actually hold on without hurting him? I pulled my hands back quickly, then dove in and grabbed on since essentially caressing his muscles probably wasn't the way to go here.

"It'll be fine. You maybe should tell me your name though. I'm Danny."

Danny. *Adorable.*

"Right. I'm Mia. I work at the library. I think I've seen you a time or two."

"That's right." He let go of one leg for a minute to snap his fingers, like he should have known. "I saw you a week or two ago when I stopped in. Meant to come say hi but you were surrounded by a group of people."

He trotted down the path like I weighed nothing more than his pack.

"Why would you say hi?" My voice bumped along with

my body, my chest hovering a few inches away from his back to save us both from that discomfort, even if it made me feel like I might fall off. I tried to keep my core strong so I wasn't too useless, then wondered if stiffening up like that might make it harder for him. My cheeks burned as I tried to keep a sturdy grip on him without strangling his neck where I held on.

"Why not? You're new in town, and you're taking over as the new head librarian, right? An important woman to know."

I wished I could see his face. I could hear a smile in his voice and would've loved the distraction. His clean, woodsy scent calmed me as if this whole being carried by a stranger with a busted ankle thing didn't still threaten to push me into panic.

"That's nice. Not many people think that way." It would've been ideal if more people did. I felt awkward introducing myself and forcing my way into the community, but so far, I'd done it when I had to.

"Silverton isn't a terribly insular place, but I admit people are a bit slow to welcome newcomers because of all the seasonal workers we get. But you're here for a while, I'm guessing?"

Hmm. *Insular?* Was he trying to impress me, or was that just him? A little flare of attraction shot up into my mind as I recognized how naturally he'd said it and the odds of him having a good vocabulary if he read a lot, which it sort of sounded like he did. "Yes. Indefinitely."

He moved quickly down the path, slowing to tiny steps on steeper grades, taking larger strides where the trail inclined. We stayed quiet for a while, only the sounds of the mountain and his breath, just occasionally audible, our soundtrack.

"So... do you hike alone a lot?" he asked as we hit the last narrow, rocky decline of the path.

"No. Not usually. Not after today, for sure." Relief that he'd come along swooped in. How foolish I'd been, especially now that I knew my phone didn't have service up there.

"But... do you normally?"

I could hear the concern in his voice—not judgement, just wariness on my behalf. "No. Really. Before I moved, I had a group I went with when I could make time. I just don't really know anyone who's into hiking here."

Good thing he couldn't see the humiliation on my face.

I felt silly enough for getting hurt and needing his help, and let's not even talk about the fact that he'd now been carrying me for close to twenty minutes *on his back*. But admitting I didn't have anyone to hike with—essentially admitting I didn't have friends? I shut my eyes against the embarrassment.

He looked to the side—like he wanted to peek back at me, but since I clung to his back directly behind him, he had no way to see me. "Not hard to find people who like to hike around here. But you're new—you've only been here a few weeks, right?"

"Uh, more like two months."

"Really? How have I not seen you yet? This town is tiny." He sounded genuinely baffled.

I chuckled, forcing myself to project a lighthearted tone even though my ankle had begun to throb and my thighs felt raw where they rubbed against his hips and the waistband of his shorts. Where he gripped under my legs would be red, maybe even bruised, though I could tell he held me as lightly as he could.

"It is pretty small. I've been behind the computer or in

the back office at the library the vast majority of the time I've been here, so that's likely why, even if you come into the library fairly often."

Those first weeks of transition had been full of accounting reviews, volume reviews, funding request reviews, schedule reviews... so many things to review. I'd had a headache every night for weeks after staring at the computer, no doubt hunched like an old crone over the keyboard, neglecting good posture, hydration, and any effort at eating normal meals during the workday as I tried to meet Mrs. Stanton's deadline for her exit from the job.

"Guess that explains it. I definitely would have noticed you." An audible swallow—not quite a gulp —followed.

Did he realize he'd said that—and...

What?

My mouth opened like I meant to respond, but I had nothing. What did that mean? Did I look that obviously out of place? Sure, I was new to town, but I'd lived in the valley, was born and raised in the state. It wasn't like I'd transplanted from the east coast. My heart sped up for the umpteenth time in the last hour.

"I must not be blending in very well." My words were thick in my mouth.

He cleared his throat, did that futile backward glance thing, and hiked me up on his hips, then mumbled, "I doubt you ever could."

"*What?*"

He couldn't be referencing my race, could he? Utah wasn't a particularly diverse place, but Salt Lake had a decent cross-section of culture and I knew a fair number of fellow Filipinos. I was only half, technically, since my father was white—maybe one reason we hadn't been tapped into the community and I'd been left alone when my parents passed.

That's enough of that.

I'd worried Silverton would be a little pocket of homogeneity, especially based on the town's roots with German- and Irish-American settlers, but so far, I hadn't felt out of place or like I stood out. In fact, the bigger problem, maybe, was that I didn't. Or so I thought.

"I said, 'seems like you're doing good.' I just mean it seemed like that group of kids and parents were really happy and excited to be talking to you the other day. And Jake was psyched as ever to be working with you."

I smiled at that. "I think Jake is psyched about everything."

"All the time. Yep. He's the most roundly enthusiastic person you'll ever meet." He nodded even as he walked.

We settled into that quiet again, with me focusing on breathing through my nose. Jostling around behind Danny had given my brain a scrambled egg effect, bearing the strange thought I'd like to lean against him and rest my head against his—luckily, I wasn't that desperate. He'd probably think I was a crazy person.

We reached the parking lot where I directed him to my car. As he squatted down to get my good foot closer to the pavement, I slid down his back in a rather intimate way considering I'd only met him an hour earlier—less—and yet, I'd been riding on his back for close to a half-hour, so I supposed we'd crossed at least one normal physical barrier already.

I balanced, one hand on his shoulder, one hand on the roof of my car, and he spun around, grabbing my wrist to steady me as I wobbled, my feet pinging with the pins and needles sensation after dangling so long.

"You okay? Let me get your keys."

He reached for my backpack and helped me remove it, then found the keys where I'd hooked them inside the front pocket. He unlocked the car, and as I hopped to the side of the door, he reached around my waist and lifted me out of the way.

It would have been an entirely inappropriate move, again, if I hadn't just been *on* him. But I couldn't get used to his ease with hoisting me about, despite the recent trek.

"Elevate, ice, anti-inflammatory. If it swells a whole lot more than it is when you first get home, head to the ER. If your foot gets cold, head to the ER. If you just can't stand the pain and the ice and elevation and meds don't help—"

"Head to the ER, got it." I gave him a close-lipped smile.

"Good. Yes. I'm really sorry I can't escort you home and get you set up myself, but I have a meeting that started about ten minutes ago."

Horror struck. "Oh no. I'm so sorry to make you late."

He smiled wide, and his brow furrowed as he touched my wrist gently. "I didn't say that to make you feel bad. I just wanted you to know I'm sorry I can't help you."

I let out a laugh. "You have helped me—you've gone above and beyond. Really. Thank you."

"My pleasure, Mia."

His blue eyes pinned me there, made me forget, for a minute, how bad my ankle ached and how miserable the weekend would be as I tried to keep Kai entertained on one leg. He seemed so purely genuine and capable and happy to help. That paired with those sky-blue eyes sparkling back at me, that smile, that scruff-covered jaw...

I shook off that train of thought, refusing to acknowledge the butterflies flitting around my belly. "Thank you.

Again. Please go so you're not any later than you already are."

He smiled a moment longer, then nodded. "See you around soon, Mia. Take care of that ankle."

CHAPTER THREE

Danny

I read eBooks. It's just easier. I toss my ereader into my pack and have a hundred books at my fingertips without the additional bulk and weight of a paperback. I love a good print edition, but in the end, for practicality, I read eBooks.

But I'd been trying to figure out a reason to go see my new librarian friend for two weeks. I'd been busy cutting trails and checking in on my parents by phone and Grandpa Will in person, and before I knew it, weeks had passed. I'd meant to check in sooner, but thought better of it—didn't want to come on too strong.

I hadn't been interested in a girl—woman—in years. Not since I'd tried with Bel years ago during college, which had been a colossal failure if there ever was one. Bel Paxton had been my best friend growing up, a standard in my daily life both thanks to her absentee parents and our genuine love for each other. And by love, I meant the friendly, almost sibling-level kind. I'd been in love with her since I could remember—I'd place the point of shifting from loving her as a dear friend to loving her as a *girl* at around the sixth grade when all the kids in the school seemed to go girl-crazy, and many of them were crazy about Bel. As soon as one of my friends joked about how much he wanted to play spin the bottle with her while we changed for soccer practice, I'd felt it. He couldn't kiss her. No—she was mine.

There lay the problem—she wasn't. Nor did I dare tell her how I felt. That remained my leash and ended up being the very thing that shot me in the foot. I'd known my love for Bel was that epic, life-long love. I also knew that kids who got together in junior high or high school rarely ended up together. My plan had been to approach her toward the end of high school and enter college in a committed relationship. Done.

Bad news and long, ridiculous story short, she fell in love with my older brother. *Ouch*, right? I could admit the brutal lesson of missed opportunities had haunted me in no small measure. When I tried again with Bel in college and she said yes, I got hopeful, but even I could tell there wasn't a spark between us, and especially not by then. Her heart was never in it, and I think I'd tucked my heart so far in the back of my mind, I wouldn't have been able to give her much of it, even if she was the one I wanted to have it.

It'd been about four years since then. It broke me all over again when we mutually called off the dating and then drifted apart. And since then, awkwardness, distance, painful politeness when she came to family dinners or showed up at things with Leo, my sister, who was now her dearest friend.

In truth, just like I had in telling her I loved her, I'd

been dragging my feet confronting the issue between us. It rested with me—I couldn't deny that. She knew she'd broken my heart and she couldn't change that. In reality, she'd done nothing wrong—she'd been open with me, and probably the worst part had been when she'd told me she had no idea how I felt about her and she'd been wishing to be with me for years... until Jamie came along.

The thing about me I could freely admit—I'm an easygoing guy. I love the mountains, love my family, and prefer to leave it at that. Eventually, I'd like to love a woman who loves me back. I'd avoided making waves by shackling myself with the responsibility of serious office jobs or facing down the horrors of online dating—why would I want to spend my time that way?

But now, my resistance to confronting the matter left everyone in our fairly small town certain I was in love with Bel *still*. On top of that, it made me uncertain about how to approach Mia primarily because I had no idea how to be interested in anyone but Bel. And that'd been fine with me, even the distance we'd lived with for years. But now, I wanted that case closed. The time had come for me to clear the air and let us both move on.

"Thinking pretty hard there, littlest big brother."

Leo's voice cut through my musings as she stomped down the wooden deck stairs behind the lodge and sank into a seat next to me where I sat looking up at Silver Ridge Peak.

"I was, as a matter of fact." I gave her a sweet smile, which she inevitably met with a raised brow.

"You okay? Did it hurt real bad?"

Her look of concern seemed genuine, and I couldn't help my answering grin. "Nearly broke something. Thanks for saving me from myself."

"Happy to do it."

She smiled, teeth and all then, and if I hadn't been so comfortably wedged into the lounge chair, I might have hugged her. When she had her hair in braids, no matter how curmudgeonly, she reminded me of five-year-old Leo who'd demanded I tie ribbons in her braids. I'd learned to tie really pretty bows by age seven for that reason.

She held out a steaming mug and I took it. My coffee had grown cold while I spaced out. Almost time for me to get going. Something about the way she watched me sent up a spark of warning. "What?"

"You know Jamie's coming soon?"

Icy shame shot through me. "Yeah. Liam mentioned it."

She eyed me, those intense blue eyes, just like mine, pouring over me. I hated that she had any cause for concern, but she did. Jamie and I hadn't been normal since he'd left to become a Rockstar, Bel's heart in his pocket, whether he and I liked it or not. That anyone had reason to worry about us was embarrassing enough. Leo seemed particularly sensitive to all of this despite her pretending to be impervious to feelings and drama. But she loved her family fiercely, so ultimately, no surprise that she wanted us to get along.

"It's time we all moved on."

Her gaze moved back and forth between my eyes, deciphering my words. "Meaning?"

The blush crept up hot and tingly into my cheeks. Being pale and red-haired did me no favors at times like this. "I'm done with the strain. I'm going to find a time to talk to Bel and get it over with, and I'll do the same with Jamie too."

Her brows shot up, and she sat back in slow motion.

"Why do you look *that* surprised?"

The smallest smile. "I love you Dan, but you're not one to talk about stuff like this. *Ever.*"

I let myself take a breath and drink in the sun cresting over the peak before answering. "True. Maybe I'm trying to grow up a little."

"Okay then. I like it."

I chuckled and rolled my eyes, sipped the rapidly cooling coffee she'd brought me. The only negative to the mountains—coffee cooled off way too fast. "Glad you approve."

She patted the table between us. "I'm off. I know you are too. I'll catch you later."

Off she went, probably to meet Bel for a run, and I shoved out of the chair and stretched. Time to get to work so I could finish before the heat of the day.

"Do you have a minute?" I asked Bel as she stood there behind the *Rise and Shine* cash register. Terrible timing, but I didn't want this to be a huge deal. In some ways, it was—sure. But in the end, so much time had passed, it could also just... not be.

"Uh, sure." She swallowed and tucked a stray lock of hair behind her ear, her gaze sliding over my face and then landing back down on the note she'd sketched on a pad to the right of the register. I couldn't read it from where I stood.

I took a quick inhale. "So... I'm just going to say it."

She stiffened, and her focus flew to my face, but she didn't speak.

Okay. Here goes.

I tucked my hands into my pockets since they were

useless to me. I could feel Leo and her new friend Wells watching. "I'm sorry. I'm sorry I've made everything awkward for the last few years—really, since school. It's on me."

She blinked, her face frozen with her mouth open just enough to tell me she had no words. No problem—I had more of them.

"I loved you. Yes. But I'm not still in love with you. There's no reason we need to punish ourselves by insisting on this weirdness. I'm genuinely not pining for you anymore, Bel—a long time coming, I know." I gave her a smile and self-deprecating laugh.

A smile broke through, and relief whooshed through me.

"I'm sorry it's taken this long. But I want us to be friends. I know you've got Leo and we're different people, but this stand-off, this *nothing* is stupid. Let's be friends—friendly, at least. And let's forget that I've been a relational idiot for the last decade. Let's just be... normal."

Her face glowed with emotion—relief, joy, a bit of humor. "I'd like that."

I let out a dramatic sigh for effect, and we both laughed. "Good. That's settled."

A rough slap on my back and then Liam gripped my shoulder. "Should I be worried here?"

Never the one to be subtle, especially when it came to anything with his family—and Bel was likely included in that thought—he'd bulldozed right in there.

Bel and I smiled at each other. "Nope. We're good."

"*Finally.*"

I shook my head at Liam as we left, waving to Bel, Leo, and Wells as we headed to his car. I knew it'd cause suspicion, but I had to bow out of the drive to the airport to get

Jamie—Liam could handle that himself. As much as I needed to deal with the problems between me and Jamie, I wasn't about to do it in the car with Liam, and even though I considered myself to be in damn fine physical shape, I had miles to go on the emotional endurance. One giant peace-making conversation per day seemed like an appropriate boundary.

Plus, it was high time I visited the library.

CHAPTER FOUR

Mia

I spotted him the minute he walked in the door.

The pile of paperwork I'd been sorting through for hours and the ache in my lower back from slumping in my chair had become hallmarks of my days lately. That, paired with the total exhaustion that came from small talk with patrons trying to get to know me a bit and parents making suggestions for upcoming storytime reading, usually left me with little energy at the end of a long week.

Not today.

Because when Daniel Morrison—Danny, as he'd introduced himself weeks ago when he carried me down the mountain—blazed through the library doors just before closing on a Friday, my whole body perked up. My mind sharpened, taking in his dark, short-sleeved T-shirt, olive-colored shorts, and sneakers. I jerked my eyes away just as he pulled off his sunglasses.

My office looked out at the circulation desk through clear glass windows. The desk itself sat about a hundred feet from the entrance. Last time he came in, he'd taken the direct route from the door to the desk and Jake had helped him. I'd watched his every move, only returning my attention to the group of parents surrounding me when one of the moms physically blocked my view of him.

This time, no. He meandered through the stacks, his head ducking out of sight from time to time, likely to dip down and get a closer look or read a title on a spine. Whatever he was up to, it drove me insane. I hadn't seen him since that day, and I wanted to at least thank him again.

I had gotten over the embarrassment and frustration, my ankle back to its normal size and function, and I wanted to tell him how thankful I felt. It had nothing to do with the fact that the surprisingly handsome and incredibly likeable man didn't make me feel uncomfortable, even in the very unusual moments we shared. A rare feat, indeed.

But now, he roamed, evidently in no hurry to check out. I attempted to busy myself with the same pile of papers that had occupied my attention completely before he walked in. No luck. My mind kept jumping back to him—now in Horror, now in Romance, now in Non-fiction. Did he really want to look at every genre? Most people had their section or two, but no one wandered the *entire* library like Danny seemed to be doing.

My knee bounced in my seat under the desk, and finally, I couldn't wait anymore and decided I'd make an excuse to be out at the circulation desk rather than in my office just in case he hadn't planned to get my attention and talk to me. I couldn't stand the thought of waiting for him to wind his way up here and then *not* talk to him.

"How's it going up here?" I asked Jake as he folded up his satchel.

"Super, thanks for asking! I'm taking off if that's okay! Looks like it's just Danny left!"

I nodded, smiled. "No problem. See you Tuesday."

Jake took off with a wave, hollering a "see ya, Danny!" as he left. Danny's eyes shot to Jake at the door, then to me where I stood, staring back at him.

"Hey, Mia. How's the ankle?"

He strode to the front, directly now instead of winding through the stacks as he had been, not leaving empty space for me to feel anything but glad he'd said hi.

The small, shy, nervous part of me had expected him to ignore me. I'd thought he'd look at me, look away, maybe even follow Jake out the doors. Instead, he approached, a warm smile brightening his already friendly face.

"It's good. Thank you. I owe you—I really don't know what I would have done if you hadn't helped me." I ran my hands over the countertop, brushing away nonexistent dust.

"You don't owe me. I'm glad I could help."

He grinned at me, and I couldn't resist my answering smile. Just lots of... smiling at each other.

After a few moments, he blinked, seeming to recognize the lengthy pause in conversation and cleared his throat. "So, uh... can I still check out a book?"

I wiped a hand across my mouth to smooth away the smile. "Of course. You have—" I checked my watch, "—eleven minutes before we close."

"Plenty of time. Let me grab something." His gaze toured my face, sliding over my hair, nose, mouth, then lower, before he whipped around and walked to a display table with new releases.

"I'm just going to wrap things up in my office—I'll be back in a minute." I took one more glance at his broad shoulders and saw his answering nod, then watched his brow furrow and head duck to read the back of the book he'd picked up.

I fumbled through shutting down my computer—Fridays, we shut things all the way down since we were closed weekends. I hoped eventually we would open Saturdays at least—it seemed a shame to only open weekdays during working hours as that meant anyone with a regular nine-to-five job could only visit if they left work, but the town and budget were small enough, there wasn't a great way to make it happen. Add to it that I liked having time with Kai on weekends and it simplified my childcare situation immensely, so my motivation to change the library's hours hadn't hit critical mass just yet.

Slow and steady on the changes would work out best for everyone.

Gathering my purse and keys, I shut and locked my office door, then set my things down and resisted the pull to watch Danny skim pages, which I ultimately failed to do. To my shock, I saw him turn to the last few pages of one book and linger, then shut the book and set it down. I couldn't look away as he did it again—perused the back cover, then opened the book and thumbed to the back.

I felt it coming—no way to stop it at this point. *Sacrilege.* "Are you serious?"

His head popped up and tilted to one side in question. "About..."

"Are you standing there reading the endings?"

His brows dropped low, and a mischievous glint filled his eyes. "*Maybe.*"

He picked up a book without breaking eye contact and walked toward me, his attention not wavering for a moment, until he stood directly in front me. He set the book on the countertop and slid it my way. "I'll take this one."

I took the book, but couldn't continue the unbroken staring contest as I scanned the barcode. He held out his card and I scanned it.

"Do you make it a habit of reading endings?"

One side of his mouth kicked up. "You ask that like you're asking if I normally eat human hearts for breakfast."

I didn't particularly like satisfying the stereotype of a persnickety, prissy librarian, but this wasn't something I could pretend not to notice. "Both are heinous acts committed by madmen."

His head dropped back, and he let out a loud laugh. He then leaned on the countertop and dipped his head in a gesture both friendly and somehow intimate, despite our barely knowing each other. "I like you."

Something in my chest fluttered, and I released a disbelieving breath. "I called you a madman, and you tell me you like me?"

He grinned, nodded, said nothing.

I studied his handsome face—cut jawline, smiling mouth, strong nose, those ridiculous blue eyes. "I like you, too."

"Good." He took his book, card in hand, and stepped back from the desk. "Shall we? Can you shut down a few minutes early?"

I checked my watch— three minutes to five. "By the time we get to the front and I lock up, it'll be five anyway."

He waited for me to round the desk, and we walked side by side up the center aisle to the doors. I felt his eyes on me as I followed the procedures of closing the building and found him openly staring at me when I turned around. "Yes?"

"I'm wondering if it'd been ten minutes to five when I asked if you could leave early if you would have."

I pulled my purse higher on my shoulder. "Probably not, to tell you the truth."

"And why is that?"

We walked slowly toward my car—the only one in the lot.

"Because the library closes at five, not ten 'til. What if someone came in those last few minutes to just grab one book, or something they'd reserved? I'd feel terrible depriving someone of a great book, especially right before a weekend."

I scanned the lot again—entirely unnecessarily since it consisted of a whopping ten spaces and clearly had no other occupants—just to make sure there wasn't some poor soul pining after a weekend read even now.

"That's sweet," he said, like he was mulling it over still. "But I don't think that's it."

I opened the driver's side door and chucked my purse across to the passenger seat. "What do you think it is?"

He leaned a hand on the roof of the car, a few inches from my shoulder. He did that thing again, the one where he dipped his head to tell me something, like a secret just between us. That gesture made me feel a little dizzy, and I swallowed while watching him, wondering what he'd say— why he even had an opinion about this.

"I think it's because you follow the rules. All the time. I think you have a hard time breaking them, even when no one would know." His face still held that kind, joking expression, but something in my stomach sank.

"The whole concept of rules is that you follow them whether someone is watching or not. That's how the world functions. Back to your heart-eating example, if someone decides they can murder people because no one is watching, we'd be in big trouble. And in fact, those people do get in trouble." I crossed my arms and blew out a slow, steady breath.

He cocked his head to the side, gaze darting to my arms, my face, before he said, "Why did that bother you so much?"

"It didn't."

"It obviously did. You're really bothered by the fact that I said you follow the rules. It's nothing to be upset about. I just think it's—"

"I'm not upset," I snapped, then huffed. He just said what he meant all the time—didn't try to be polite or tactful, though he wasn't exactly rude. He just...said what he meant. So I decided I would too, even if this didn't rank as something I'd ever talk to an acquaintance about, much less a man I barely knew. "I have... I've been accused of being like that—all work, no play, a stick in the mud, whatever— and I don't like it."

He moved the hand that had been on my car and touched my shoulder lightly before pulling back. "I'm sorry. I don't mean it like that at all. I think it's..."

I tried not to gulp or jump to any conclusions, thankful the look on his face seemed genuine. "You think it's..."

"*Cute.*"

It hung there, that word, surprising and totally foreign. My heart sped up, and later, I'd think back on it and feel annoyed at how easily it'd been riled up into a rapid beat by that one silly word.

"Oh... okay." I couldn't think of anything else to say.

He stepped back, scratched at his neck which seemed a little red in the early evening light. "I'll let you get going—sorry for keeping you."

I watched as he turned toward the walking path, and despite the strange interaction, or at least how our time together came to an end, I didn't want him to go. "Do you need a ride?"

He turned around, but kept taking small, easy steps backward. "Nah. I'll walk."

CHAPTER FIVE

Danny

"What are you doing?"

The voice jolted me out of the single-minded focus I'd sunken into while whittling the end of a large limb. I looked up to find a kid—maybe five years old? Hard to say since I didn't spend a ton of time with little kids, much to my sister's chagrin. She constantly guilted me about not helping out more often with lessons for the *kinderski* school, but I didn't have the time. Kids were fun and I could enjoy them when I taught them—but I preferred being on the mountain, dealing with problems that popped up, and generally just skiing wherever I wanted in search of people who needed a hand until Rod radioed to tell me where to find one.

"I'm whittling."

"What's that?" The kid approached the fence of my small back yard and leaned against it. He had dark hair cut short, olive skin that'd likely spent hours becoming darker in the summer sun, and curious brown eyes.

I held up the stick in one hand, my pocketknife in the other. "I'm trimming off pieces of bark with the knife. I slide the edge of the knife along the wood and eventually I can shape it how I want it to look."

He leaned over the fence and craned his neck to see better, though he stood only ten feet from me. "Why?"

"I'm carving out the top of a walking stick for a friend."

I'd started doing it as a hobby a few years ago, and turned out I had a knack for it. I'd carved some pretty ornate sticks. The first step was to remove all the bark and that work's mindlessness always satisfied me. Perfect activity for sitting and mulling over the more idiotic moments of my conversation with Mia earlier.

The boy leaned farther over the fence, his top half hanging over the short, wooden door that I found myself thanking God was securely latched shut or he'd be on his face in the dirt by now. "That's cool. What will it look like when you're done?"

I chuckled at his curiosity and his complete lack of concern with talking to me, an adult male he didn't know. Speaking of... "Where are your parents?"

He raised his brows, still leaning on the fence, or maybe at this point balancing on it entirely. "My mom's at home— we live here. Just moved in."

Huh, good to know. I hadn't seen any moving vans in the neighborhood but I was rarely home during normal daytime hours in any season, most especially summer when I was trail cutting for work and hiking for fun. In winter, I made it to the mountain a half hour before the lifts opened, if not earlier.

"And your dad?"

The boy scrunched up his face. "He's in prison."

I ducked my head to keep him from seeing my face as my eyes flared in shock at his open statement. But why shouldn't he say that freely—he had nothing to be ashamed of. Kids dealt in facts, and that was clearly the fact he could share about where his dad was.

"Ah. Well. Sorry about that," I said dumbly, not sure what one should say to a kid whose parent was in prison.

"Why are you sorry? I'm not. He's the worst."

I let out a chuckle. "What's your name?"

"I'm Kai." He held out a hand from his posting at my fence and teetered, his balance off-center now that he'd stretched out his arm.

I hopped up and jogged to take his hand, shook it. "I'm Danny. Nice to meet you, and welcome to the neighborhood."

"Nice to meet you too. Can I have a turn whittling?"

I smiled at his asking, enjoying the childlike willingness to just ask for what he wanted. "I'm happy for you to help, but I bet you should ask your mom if it's okay, right?"

His eyebrows shot up, then plummeted down in concentration. Then his little head shook enthusiastically. "You're right. I should. I'll run ask her and be right back."

He was off and running before I could stop him. "I'm actually leaving—"

Futile. He'd already rounded the corner and disappeared before I could tell him I had to go and he could try another time.

I slumped into a chair on my deck and took a swig of beer—Liam's beer, in fact. My big brother had been more and more stressed lately, and I had no idea how to help him. I didn't have much to offer him other than making him lunch, which he seemed to appreciate. And I always drank *his* beer, as a show of support.

The day had been odd. I'd gotten into an argument with my parents, which was completely unheard of. They'd been traveling over the summer and helping my mom's parents get settled in Arizona where they'd recently moved. And today, they'd told me they weren't coming back until *maybe* Christmas, and they wanted me to take care of the house for them.

No problem. I could do that. The argument part came when they wanted to pay me to do it. I didn't need money to take care of my own parents' house. They insisted, and I refused, back and forth, until Ma said it. *"I just know you can't make much at your patrolling job, honey. I want you to be able to have a home, start a family, and if this is how we can help..."*

I was a laid-back guy, but shame and fury had burned through me at that. I'd made clear I didn't need their money and that they didn't need to support me, and that was that.

But I felt terrible. I didn't do conflict. Not my thing. I stayed far away from it—as evidenced by my avoiding Bel for years and my own brother for much longer than that, despite the fact that there wasn't even really conflict there. Fighting with my parents felt fundamentally wrong, but their assumption that I didn't have money, that I needed help...

I'd bought this house several years ago. I'd started out renting the basement apartment, but when the owner wanted to sell, I asked if I could buy it, despite my relative lack of assets. We agreed on a rent-to-own kind of situation until I'd been steady with the rent payments for two solid years, and then she let me have it. I'd lucked out, also because I'd been able to rent the basement place to seasonal workers at a decent rate, and I owned it outright.

I might not earn much patrolling, but I lived simply. Other than college loan payments, I had no debt. I owned my small truck and had very few bills. In the end, I was actually doing quite well, I thought. The fact that I hadn't shared this with my parents—possibly an oversight. But some part of me refused to do it just so they'd see I wasn't a total screw up.

I knew what everyone thought. And I could admit my tendency to avoid responsibility was real, and maybe even a problem. But I'd been working on taking on more, and that had started with the house a few years ago. Admittedly, that's all I'd done in a while, until I'd talked to Bel. Sometime—someday really, I swore it—I'd talk to Jamie. He'd been busy all during his visit here a few weeks ago doing who knew what, so I didn't push him to make time for me, and we fell into our years-old habit of stepping around each other.

"You going to whittle again tonight, Danny?"

There he was, my little curious neighbor. Kai had stopped by every evening since the first visit a week ago. He'd promised me his mom said he could whittle. I really didn't know if it was okay to let a kid his age—which I'd discovered was six—use a pocketknife. Seemed like I'd gotten one around that age, but I could've been off by a few years and not realize it. So we'd compromised and I let him sand one of the sticks I'd already cleaned up. He seemed, if not completely satisfied, at least happy to be a part of the process.

"No buddy, not tonight. I'm so tired I can hardly see straight."

Truth. I'd spent the early hours on the trails, then headed in to talk with Rod about getting people organized for the season. We still had six weeks 'til everyone would return to the mountain, but we needed a few new recruits since some of our staff from last year weren't returning. At least we had our old reliables. I hated finding new patrolling staff, but such was life. This all fell under Rod, but he usually consulted me since I knew most of the people in town who might be a good fit for the jobs.

And after that, the awesome phone call with my beloved parents, which had probably worn me out more than anything else.

"Aw. Too bad. Are you going to that alma tree thing tomorrow?" He leaned on the fence again, though I'd told him he could come in the yard whenever he wanted.

I smiled. "It's *almabtrieb*, but close. Yeah I'll be there. Never miss it."

His eyes lit up even as he asked, "What is it?"

"My friend Wyatt owns a bunch of cattle that graze way up in the mountains—higher than here, even. This time of year, things start to freeze, so he brings them down the mountain through Silverton, and then to an area he owns farther down where they winter. He decorates them with flower crowns and stuff—it's cool."

Kai raised those expressive brows. "Huh."

I chuckled. "I promise you—you'll enjoy it. And if not, you can come find me and I'll buy you a caramel apple or something."

That perked him right up. "Okay, deal."

CHAPTER SIX

Mia

Mrs. Rosemary Stanton positively glowed today.

"You look lovely, Mrs. Stanton."

She smoothed a hand over the hair pulled back into a bun at the nape of her neck. "Thank you, Mia. I'll admit I love dressing up when I go out, even if I don't wear the traditional garb like some around here do."

By *traditional*, I'd learned, she meant Bavarian. The town's cow festival, modeled after the Alpine traditions of parading cows through towns on the way to lower elevations before winter, was a really big deal. There was even a small section at the library dedicated to it—histories and some personal accounts of the tradition. I'd seen the flyers advertising the event, but only today had I discovered it was a *must see*.

"Do people really dress up?"

Mrs. Stanton raised a tastefully penciled brow. "Do you

think I'd be going like this if no one else dressed up? They do. We missed the Oktoberfest this year because of budgets and whathaveyou, so this will mean even more to the community. The Irish and German roots here run deep, and the celebrations rooted in those traditions brought by the original founding families are very special. You'll see."

I hadn't been planning to attend. Thanks to being sick for the last week but not feeling I could opt out of work, it was all I could do to make it home from work and prepare Kai dinner without passing out in my soup. Thankfully, he'd been playing with a neighbor boy and hadn't needed me for much except to practice his reading before bed. I felt like a lazy parent, but sometimes, especially as a single mother, you had to accept that doing your best was keeping him fed and clothed and in school. It wasn't the flu, but it might as well have been for how terrible I'd been feeling.

Until yesterday. And finally today, I'd been up to visiting Mrs. Stanton as I tried to do every few weekends. Her children and grandchildren had moved away years ago, and since she was basically the closest thing I had to a friend here, I made a point to keep the connection. Plus, Kai didn't have a relationship with his grandparents. My parents had passed years ago, and his father's... well, not an option, to put it simply.

"I don't have anything to wear. I definitely don't have a German dress."

Mrs. Stanton wore a smart looking suit-style combo with a skirt and little jacket, a blouse underneath, and fine jewelry. She looked elegant, sophisticated. I wasn't sure it quite matched up with the images I had in my head of German traditional wear—*lederhosen* was all I really knew —but she seemed pleased.

"No no, don't worry. You don't have to wear a *dirndl,*

dear, but you may want to get one sooner than later so you have something for next year. There's a small boutique here that sells them though they're very expensive so it's worth planning ahead."

I blinked, not sure what all that really meant other than that I could safely attend the cow fest this year and not worry about wearing a *dirndl*, thank goodness.

"Okay. Well, I've got to run pick up Kai from his friend's house and we'll get ready. They're bringing you all together, right?"

The Silverton Springs Assisted Living Home was remarkable—I hoped I could live in a place like it when I was old enough to need to move out of my own home. They kept their tenants active and getting out—they brought a bus to the library once a week and offered shuttle service all around the town regularly. They'd shuttle anyone who wanted to go to the festival in a few hours.

"See you then, Mia. Tell Kai to come find me and say hi."

I promised I would, and left her room, tapping a message to tell Carrie, mom to Kai's closest friend Michael, I'd be on my way, when I bumped into someone.

"Oh my goodness, I am so sorry!"

I looked up to find Danny Morrison smiling down at me, his hand steadying me at my shoulder.

"Well hello to you too, Mia."

"I'm so sorry. I shouldn't have had my face in my phone. I'm so glad you're you and not—"

"Not someone more dashingly handsome, like his grandfather?"

My gaze slid to the man next to Danny who had the very same color of gorgeous blue eyes. "Well... yes. I would have been swept off my feet."

The man's eyes twinkled back at me.

"I'm afraid *I* would be the one swept off my feet." Before I could respond, he stuck out a hand. "William Morrison, Daniel's paternal grandfather and greatest fan."

I took his large, warm hand in mine. "Mia Parker, Silverton's new librarian and Daniel's newest acquaintance."

Mr. Morrison's brows raised, and his head tilted to the side. "Ah, you're Genevieve's replacement. Big shoes to fill, but I hear you're doing well. I haven't made the trip myself but I hear good things."

Warmth flooded my chest. "Thank you. I'm so grateful for all of the help she's given me."

He nodded, like he expected no less of Mrs. Stanton than she'd be helpful to her replacement. "And Silverton? Are you settling in well? Liking the place, the people?"

His eyes slid to Danny, then to me. Meanwhile, Danny smirked and looked down at his shoes, but not before I noticed his cheeks brightening.

"That I am. It's a great little spot and I'm enjoying the small-town life. Eager to meet more people, but that comes with time." My phone pinged at me, notifying me of an incoming message, which I quickly glanced at. "Oh, and speaking of, I actually need to get going so I can get ready for the cow festival."

Mr. Morrison clapped his hands together.

"Excellent. That's the way to do it—dive in head first. Keep an eye out for this one—I've been told all my grandsons fill out their lederhosen quite well." He raised his eyebrows a few times, those eyes sparkling.

Danny let out a cough and set a hand on his grandfather's shoulder.

"That's enough of *that*, Grandpa." His voice was stern but his face was all smiles and now deeply flushed.

Oh my, adorable.

I chuckled as we reached the exit and Danny held the door for me. "Thank you. Nice to meet you, Mr. Morrison. I'm sure I'll see you again soon."

I checked out the shop Mrs. Stanton had mentioned that sold the Bavarian *trachten*—the traditional German dresses called dirndls and the more widely known lederhosen. They were all handmade with the highest quality fabrics and leathers, and so far out of my price range it wasn't even funny. I'd expected the shop owner to look down her nose at my stepping foot in there —I always felt sure the people helping me could tell my purse came from Target and my haircut cost less than a hundred bucks, but Melodie Bryson provided nothing but kind, attentive care for the five minutes I wandered her shop.

When I left, she'd helpfully suggested I visit the store *Odds* where they often had some "festive wear," as she'd called it. I hadn't been in before, but *Odds* was aptly named. It had one of everything, it seemed, in its confusing but charming mix of antique and brand-new stock. Some of the items placed right by the door centered on the cow festival's theme, including T-shirts that looked like the suspenders of lederhosen and cow bells. I purchased shirts for me and Kai and hoped nice jeans, boots, and sweaters would suffice.

I surveyed my reflection one last time, then grabbed my purse and keys. The crisp October day made me feel giddy and refreshed, and when I asked Kai if he'd like to walk downtown instead of drive, he happily agreed.

He looked adorable in jeans, warm little brown boots, his lederhosen T-shirt, and a cardigan. I sighed a little at the way his pants looked about two inches too short out of nowhere—he must have had a growth spurt. He'd just turned six, and it killed me as much as it delighted me that he was growing so quickly.

He noticed my stare, or maybe that look in my eye I got when I felt mushy and sentimental about him, and opened the front door to our basement apartment wide. "Ready? I don't want to be late. I want to be able to see the cows."

We left the house and chatted as I locked the door. I was rifling through my purse to make sure I had my wallet when I heard Kai holler at someone.

"Hey! What are you wearing?"

I turned to see who Kai spoke to, and any breath in my lungs disappeared because there stood Danny Morrison in the full German-style get up. He wore a navy and white plaid shirt with fancy embossing on the right breast, and yep, there they were—lederhosen. The leather was a medium brown color with lighter brown and blue stitching details around the pockets and along the suspenders. They fit... well. On his feet, he wore brown leather shoes with woolen socks to his mid-calf.

I took all of that in as fast as possible, ignoring the thought that Grandpa Will had spoken true, praying my face wouldn't flame up and hint at the thoughts in my head. He looked good, and I never would have thought I'd find leather pants attractive on a man.

"Mia?"

"Hi." All I had—just *hi.*

"You know my mom?" Kai asked Danny, just as I connected that he'd been speaking to Danny—that my son knew him.

"Uh—your mom?" Danny's eyes switched between me and Kai, the resemblance unmissable.

"You know Kai?" I asked Danny, drawing his attention to me.

"Yeah, he's been coming by my back yard to hang out after school the last week or so." His voice was cheery, but his face still held that perplexed look.

"This is my friend, Mom! The one I told you about!" Kai held up a hand to Danny and Danny gave him a high-five.

"Oh. Wow. I don't know why I assumed your friend was a kid..." No small amount of horror shot through me. I'd assumed Kai had been playing with another kid around his age. The way he talked about him... nothing hinted that the friend he'd been hanging out with was a grown man. I ducked my chin and eyed Kai. "Kai, you have to tell me stuff like this."

Never mind that I should have gone to meet this new neighbor friend—that my six-year-old son's friend was an adult and could have harmed my extremely outgoing and trusting child. I'd been sick and desperate, but that didn't excuse this. My heart kicked, then raced, and my breath quickened into pants.

"It's okay, Mom. He's not creepy. He's really nice." Kai's wide eyes, his sweetness, calmed me, even as the thoughts of what could have happened raced in my mind.

Danny stepped closer, put a hand on my arm. "Are you okay?"

I pulled in a shuddering breath, then eased it out. "I'm just... I should have come to meet you. I've been pretty sick and I thought—"

"It's okay. I get it. We hung out in my back yard—I let him sand some walking sticks I'm working on. We didn't go in the house nor did I let him use the knife to whittle. I live just right here so you guys must be close."

Knife. Knife. Oh. Good. He didn't let my six-year-old use the knife... *wait.*

"You live right here as in... there?" I pointed to a house across the street from where we stood on the sidewalk next to the house where we rented the basement apartment.

"No, no. I'm just here." He nodded to the house immediately next to us. *Our* house. "Where are you guys?"

I opened my mouth, but no words escaped. Danny Morrison lived on top of me.

Okay. Weird way to put that.

"We live in the basement of your house," Kai explained simply, and something about that told me he'd known it for a while, though of course he did if he'd spent time in Danny's back yard.

Impossible that I'd never seen Danny Morrison going into or out of his house, except I'd never seen anyone going into or out of the house. The entrances were completely separate.

I looked at the house built into a small hill. It had never occurred to me that we didn't see the front entrance to the main house, and Danny would never have seen us coming and going since our door was practically around the corner from his entrance. The resident of the top of the house would rarely, if ever, interact with the basement tenant.

"You live in the basement." Danny's eyes assessed me now, sliding from the top of my head to the toes of my boots.

"Yes." I watched him, wondering if that upset him—wondering if having a child in the house bothered him. Wondering if he owned the home. "How long have you lived here?"

"Almost five years. Rented it first, then bought it a few

years back." He tried to stuff his hands into his pockets, but the lederhosen didn't have any so he smoothed his palms down the leather and then propped them on his hips. "I feel really bad I didn't even come to meet you. I mean, especially now that I know you're... *you*, but, still. I don't normally do that because I usually have seasonal people in, and I have a management company do all this for me..."

His cheeks reddened, and another slice of that anxiety building in my chest eased. Those blushing cheeks were fast becoming my favorite thing.

"No apology, please! It's not... there's nothing wrong here. We love the place. I mean... or, is there?"

He cocked his head while Kai chased after a leaf, evidently uninterested in how world-rocking the realization that I lived in Danny's house had been for me. "Is there... what?"

I swallowed back the welling feeling choking me. I liked our place. I didn't want to move. "Is there something wrong? I'm sure the lease allowed for kids and I didn't know—"

"Whoa, definitely not. It's great. I just feel like a jerk." He ran a hand over his short hair, glancing around before returning his attention to me. "But... are you okay? You seem upset."

I shook my head quickly. "No. Not at all. Odd, and crazy that I've never seen you anywhere near here, and you must not have seen me, but I love the place. I don't want to move."

"Good. Don't." He grinned at me, a small show of reassurance.

Kai ran over. "Can we go now?"

CHAPTER SEVEN

Danny

I walked next to Kai and Mia. Kai's mother. His *mother*. But she couldn't be much older than me if she even was older than me, which I wouldn't have guessed. Not by much. She must have had him young.

Since the moment Kai had asked if I knew his mom, I'd felt fuzzy. I'd been interested in Mia... interested in a woman other than Bel for the first time since pretty much ever. But here she was with a kid.

Granted, an awesome kid as far as I could tell. But... wow. Her husband, or maybe not her husband since she didn't wear a ring, but Kai's father lived in prison. Single mom, and my chances evaporated off the planet because no way a woman who had a kid and all kinds of responsibility would pair up with someone like me.

Right.

Okay.

Good to know.

I spent the rest of the evening trying hard to shake off the sinking sensation in the pit of my stomach, to not be disappointed. But I knew how this went—no way could I be enough for a woman with a kid, let alone be a father figure to anyone. Maybe I'd gotten ahead of myself there, but in reality, that's more and more what I wanted. I wanted one good woman, and I wanted to be a good man to her.

But Mia and Kai?

For someone who eschewed responsibility like he got paid to do it, that pair had a flashing red *warning* sign above it. Never mind the fact that there was no way they'd want me.

The problem with all of that doomsday thinking? I kept coming back to how much I liked them both. I really enjoyed Kai—he was hilarious and curious and probably the cutest kid I'd ever seen. And Mia...

I let out a slow breath as I watched her lean down and hand Kai a caramel apple. During the parade, his eyes hadn't left the cows. It seemed so simple—just cows, right? But there was something kind of magical about them parading through the streets all decked out in celebration of the end of summer, in anticipation of the colder months. It heralded my favorite time of year— ski season, and the snow couldn't come soon enough.

Most of the cows had marched through, their bells clanging, hooves clomping, flower crowns adorning their heads. Wyatt's cows were the best in every sense, and this day confirmed that. The town brimmed with visitors, and I heard Wells Bryant say her inn had filled up for the weekend. Good news for the town. Maybe it'd help Liam calm down a bit—he'd been increasingly stressed about the lodge's season being the best ever.

"Thanks for showing us the ropes," Mia said as she wandered back toward me and caught my eye. Kai darted after a friend to climb a stack of hay bales.

"Glad to. Did you like it?"

As she got closer, I realized just how small she was—bit of a dumb realization considering I'd given her a ride on my back the first time we met, but at that point, I'd been focused on keeping the jostling to a minimum and making it down quickly without falling on my face and her with me.

"You know, I thought it'd be all hype, but it's actually really awesome. I have no idea why cows walking in the street got me so excited, but it really was fun." She beamed, glancing back at the street where clean-up crews would have their work cut out for them. "And I liked seeing everyone in their fancy German clothes."

I could have sworn her dark brown eyes slid down my torso before they jumped back to my face.

"Yeah? You going to get a dirndl for next year?"

The thought of her in a dirndl... appealing. I wouldn't want it to be what we all wore all the time, but there was something fun about dressing up for Oktoberfest at this festival. Sometimes, we held other fests and everyone who wanted to wore their *trachten*. We hadn't done much but this one in a year or so, probably because Wyatt had to bring his cows down anyway, so we might as well make a big deal of it. A few vendors put out food, a few food trucks came up from the valley, but overall, it meant more business for the town and very little effort in the way of set up. Only the clean-up crew had much to do, and considering the expense and effort some of our other events took, no one could complain.

"Unlikely, based on the price point. But I appreciate that everyone else does."

"Happy to set the scene for you."

She laughed—a light, lovely sound—and shook her head as her gaze surveyed the now-empty street. "I really do like this town. It's just weird enough, but not so odd you can't get comfortable if you're new."

"I like to think so. Obviously, I've never been the new kid here, and all of our traditions seem great to me since I grew up with them, but we've had transplants before and there's no sense of separation between the founding families and people who moved here. Once you're here and you want to be, that's it. You're in."

She flashed a bright smile, then sobered. "So, about Kai..."

"I'm sorry you didn't know he was with me. I—"

She stepped to me, hand on my arm again, her touch soft and fingers cool against my skin. "No, no. That's my fault, and wouldn't have happened if I hadn't been so sick. I just wanted to say I'm sorry if he's been bothering you. He has no filter, no sense of a stranger, particularly here where everyone feels so familiar even after just a few months."

I glanced over at the boy in question, currently waggling his caramel apple back and forth like the second hand of a grandfather clock in front of his friend's face like he'd hypnotize him. I couldn't help the chuckle that escaped.

"He's great. And while I'm not usually one to hang out with six-year-olds, I've enjoyed it. I just hope I haven't done anything wrong—my little sister is only eighteen months behind me, so I never had the babysitting experience some older siblings get. I'm pretty clueless about what's right for this age."

The smile that lit her face then was all warmth and beauty. Truly—her face seemed to glow. Whatever I'd said, it was right. I took in her deep brown eyes, her smooth olive skin, her small nose and pink, curved lips. A little makeup, but not a ton, so I could tell I was actually looking at her face, really seeing her. Her simple clothes and the dorky T-shirt were an appealing change up to the business casual she'd been wearing at the library.

A pang of attraction hit then like a punch to the gut. Mia Parker embodied beauty—she owned it. I had no idea if she tried for it or not—nothing wrong with it if she did. But something told me that with all she had going on, she didn't. She just...

"He's a great kid. I'm glad you can see that." The words came soft and low, like a secret between us.

"I can." I studied that face again, one I now felt an incredible desire to touch—just run a finger across the curve of her cheek. I swallowed against that impulse, tamping down the desire building in me just standing there talking about her kid.

Right. Her kid. Pull it together.

"There's my littlest big brother," a voice said from behind me.

I turned to see Leo smiling at me, full traditional getup in place. Her hair was braided into a golden crown on her head, and she wore a blue and white themed dirndl-style dress with modest covering at the chest, thank God, and bright red Converse All-Stars on her feet.

"Hello Leo. Have you met Mia Parker?" I gestured to Mia, who studied Leo next to me.

"I haven't." Leo's hand jutted out. "Leo Morrison, Danny's sister."

Mia took the offered hand and shook it. "Nice to meet you. I'm the new librarian."

Leo's eyes lit up. "Awesome. We've needed someone in

there. I'd heard Mrs. Stanton had a replacement. Sorry I haven't been by."

"It's a crazy time of year," Mia offered, giving Leo the out.

I wanted to scold Leo—how dare she not go welcome our new resident, the new librarian? But I hadn't—not many people had. Even though she walked with me and I'd introduced her to everyone who said hi, clearly only a few library regulars and parents of Kai's friends knew her.

"I'm off to check on Bel, then Liam." Leo tossed a thumb over her shoulder then stepped back slowly in the direction of the coffee shop.

"Bel's hanging in there with the crowds. Liam should be having a rare and welcomed break from his stressing." He'd been getting worse, but today should make him happy.

Leo nodded, then waved goodbye as she turned.

"Liam is..." Mia asked.

"My oldest brother. Jamie's the middle, then me, then Leo. Do you have siblings?"

She folded her arms and pulled her sweater close around her. It'd started out as a fairly mild day, but the full effect of fall had arrived as the sun set.

"No. It was just me."

She didn't sound sad, but I couldn't help but think it was. I couldn't imagine life without my siblings, though in some ways I lived like that now, only seeing them when I ran into them on the mountain, never prioritizing them.

"And Bel? Is that Bel Paxton?"

We wandered toward where Kai sat on a bench with two friends, both arms gesturing wildly, his face animated as his friends looked on, captivated.

"An old family friend. She works at *Rise and Shine*—

you know her?" Something about that felt... weird. Had she heard about the drama with me and Bel—about our history?

"Not really. We've talked a bit about her doing some work for the library in the new year—nothing big. She's really nice."

I nodded, some stupid part of me wondering if I should just tell her, right now, that I'd been in love with Bel but it wasn't an issue anymore. But that would be the work of a crazy person, and fortunately, I kept my mouth shut. Mia and I weren't dating—she didn't need my emotional or dating history.

Despite the internal warnings, I couldn't talk myself out of spending the rest of the evening with her and Kai. We grabbed tacos at the *Guac* carry-out stand. We got cow-shaped cookies from *Rise and Shine*. I walked them home, even walked them to their door. Kai sent me off with a high-five, then ran to do... whatever he had in mind.

"Thanks for showing us around today."

Mia stood at the threshold of her house. Her black hair hung straight and looked so smooth. I wondered if it'd be cool from the air. I wondered what it'd feel like sifting between my fingers.

I cleared my throat, mentally rolling my eyes at how out of control I was.

"Glad to do it. Anytime you need a tour guide, I'm your man." I smiled, stepped back before I could do something stupid, and turned. "See you around sometime soon."

CHAPTER EIGHT

Mia

The knock on my door confused me.

Might seem odd, but other than Kai trying out the doorbell a few dozen times the first day we moved in, no one had come to our door but the pizza delivery guy. So at seven o'clock on a Sunday morning as I stood in my sweatpants and baggy shirt, my hair knotted on my head, glasses framing my eyes and my first cup of coffee barely poured into my mug, I couldn't wrap my mind around it.

Must've been hearing things.

But no, there it came again.

I shuffled to the door and peeked through the hole to find Danny Morrison standing there. *Huh.*

I'd spent more than a little time thinking about him last night after tucking Kai in bed. Danny had been charming and sweet all day. He'd been great with Kai. He'd been...

generally great. Just like every other time I'd interacted with him. I wanted to spend more time with him... I hadn't felt that way about anyone in a long, long time.

I pulled open the door to find an adorable, warm half-smile on his face.

"Hello." Not many words available until after my first cup of coffee. I'd only had a few sips. Plus seeing Danny unexpectedly gave me a nervous little flutter and I couldn't talk around that.

For his part, he seemed entirely comfortable to be standing on my porch—well, technically his porch—at seven on a Sunday. "'Morning. Hoping I can talk you and Kai into sharing breakfast with me."

"Oh... uh... now?" Eloquence came easy to some. I did not fall into this category.

Danny gave me a funny look. "Yes? I saw your lights were on when I came back from my run earlier—I'm making pancakes and it's always more fun to share. But listen, I don't mean to barge in or make you feel like you have to. I just thought—"

"Pancakes! Yes!" Kai shouted from somewhere in the house.

How could he hear our conversion from several rooms away and yet couldn't hear me when I asked him to put his laundry away or his plate in the dishwasher? *Amazing.*

I couldn't help the chuckle that came and knew I couldn't refuse Kai. "Do you mean *right* now, or do I have time to put on shoes?"

Danny's grin widened, and he nodded. "No rush. Batter's ready but you guys wander over anytime. I don't want to rush your Sunday morning."

I took a sip of coffee and closed my eyes at the warmth of it, the sharp, comforting flavor. When I opened my eyes,

Danny's attention centered on my mouth. I tucked my lips between my teeth.

"Er, sorry. I don't function well until I've been up for a bit and had some coffee."

His cheeks reddened. "Didn't mean to catch you so early. Your lights have been on a while—I assumed you'd been up a few hours by now."

"Kai has, for sure. He's an early riser, and now that he's six, he can hang out and play and get himself cereal without waking me, which has been a blessed development I thank God for every weekend."

A truer statement had never been uttered. The advent of Kai's morning independence had changed my ability to function on a primal level. Getting to sleep an extra hour and not having to spring out of bed as soon as my very morning-minded baby woke had been my favorite developmental milestone aside from talking.

Danny told us to come when ready and wandered back toward his house, leaving me to ponder why he got up so early and wonder what made him invite us. Whatever the case, the little zing of anticipation at not only eating pancakes, but seeing his house, and being near him this morning, told me I'd definitely been charmed by Danny Morrison.

Danny's adorable house included a welcoming, retro-style kitchen—a complete surprise. Not that I knew him well at all, but I never would have expected this style.

"You look surprised," he said, biting his lip against a smile.

I smiled back and realized that's one thing I already

liked about this guy. He smiled *all* the time. He had this sunny, sweet way about him. Entirely the opposite of my ex, who'd functioned in a once-thrilling but ultimately mostly exhausting place of intensity, anger, and danger. What eighteen-year-old me had wanted in him—adventure, the thrill of someone wanting me the way he had, at least at first—had taken me to a fairly dark place. I thought I'd found my forever person in him, and he'd found a baby mama he had no intention of supporting. That his family turned out to be so toxic, even after I won sole custody and he ended up in prison, was just one more thing that had me running for the hills—literally, here to Silverton.

I'd parted ways with Mason Delacruz six years ago—hadn't seen him since he'd walked out on me, and I'd generally given up comparing people to him when he'd ghosted me a week after Kai was born.

But something about this moment, seeing Danny's bright kitchen, watching him survey my face with that friendly grin tugging at his lips, his holler at Kai to grab orange juice from the fridge if he wanted it, dumping a ladle full of pancake batter on the stove... my mouth dried up.

My heart sped up.

My eyes, the fools, became watery.

I clutched the mug of coffee Danny handed me after he showed us into the kitchen, and I felt certain if I didn't get a minute to myself, I'd end up blubbering there in his idyllic kitchen and scare him away forever.

"I'm not—I just—can I... I'll be right back." I shoved my mug of coffee at him and marched back through his living room and out the front door, a great gust of air bursting from me once I reached the cool October morning.

I closed my eyes, breathing carefully through my nose and out my mouth, then grit my teeth against the frustration of having a mild emotional breakdown in an acquaintance's kitchen because he was nice and I hadn't had a man be nice to me in years.

That certainly held a bit more pathetic, pity-inducing flair than I meant, but it accurately reflected some of the feelings that overwhelmed me. I couldn't ignore the fact that I liked Danny Morrison—I liked pretty much everything about him that I'd seen so far. And standing in his kitchen as he made me and Kai pancakes after barely knowing us but being nothing but kind... it floored me. It quite literally blew a circuit in my ability to process the situation.

It made me *want*.

It made me want a life with Kai and a man who could be a father to him. It made me want a man who would smile at me and make me want to smile back. That might not be Danny Morrison—I wasn't an idiot in a fairytale, and I barely knew this guy—but he certainly got credit for being the one to open that window for me.

I took one last giant breath and let it out. Tucked the tears away, calmed my heart, and slowed my breathing. Straightened my spine and pulled back my shoulders, prepared to go have a perfectly lovely breakfast with a nice man who would not induce another panic attack about making me want things I'd told myself I'd never have.

CHAPTER NINE

Danny

Mia Parker was... unique.

No, that's not quite the word. She was... intense. But not—not like Jamie where he'd get all broody and dark and I couldn't stand to do anything but break the silence with a joke. No, she had this internal gravity to her, like she weighed and processed everything around her.

And evidently, something about my kitchen had struck her enough that she had to excuse herself. When she shut the front door, I reanimated after freezing when she'd stumbled through excusing herself. I looked to Kai, who just shrugged, those dark eyebrows shooting up with as much confusion as mine must have held, and went back to pouring orange juice.

She returned just a few minutes later, cheeks red from the chilly morning but nothing else remarkably different.

Still intolerably pretty, of course, but nothing amiss that I could tell.

"Everything okay?" I asked, flipping a pancake on the griddle.

She gave me a small, close-lipped smile, but it didn't seem forced. Maybe I didn't know her well enough to know if it was, but it looked real.

"Yes. How can I help?"

"So what do you do? You're always just hanging out in your back yard." Kai mopped up the last of his syrup with his final bite of pancake and waited for me to respond.

"Well, in summer, I'm in charge of maintaining all the hiking trails in this area. And in the winter, I'm a ski patroller." I settled back in my seat and sipped the coffee in my cup, blessedly warm since Mia had given me a splash when she got herself some more.

And, side note, I enjoyed that. I liked having someone there with me, and I especially liked that she hadn't shied away from getting herself more coffee, or offering me some. We'd just started the process of getting to know each other, but she felt comfortable enough to help herself, and I took that as a win.

"So you just like, hike all summer and ski all winter?" Kai's eyes were wide.

I chuckled, because yeah. "Basically? Yes."

Kai fell dramatically from his seat. "Oh *man* that's amazing. That's what I'm doing. I'm doing that, Mom—seriously." He eyed his mom, waiting for a reaction, and once he saw her shoulders shake in laughter, let his head roll to the side and his eyes closed. "I'm dead."

I found Mia shaking her head, her eyes shining with delight at her son. Something in me ached at that sight, but then she said, "I'm sure it's not *that* simple, is it?"

"Pretty much is, actually. I've managed to keep life pretty simple."

She raised her brows, making a face like I impressed her with the idea. I collected the plates and took them to the sink.

"I think we should clean up because you cooked."

Mia set a hand lightly on my back and I nearly jumped —we hadn't touched much. Since giving her a ride down the mountain, there had only been one brush of my hand at her shoulder before I realized it might've been unwelcomed after we talked at the library, and once when she put a hand on my wrist yesterday.

"No, definitely not. I invited you guys—you don't get to clean up."

She looked mildly perturbed as she crossed her arms, and I wished that response hadn't caused her to pull away.

"Fine. We'll clean up next time."

I liked the sound of that—next time.

"Can I show her our projects?" Kai waited at the back door.

"'Course. Just be careful opening the shed." I kept the walking sticks and supplies in a small shed out back, and after a week of coming by to help, Kai knew his way around. His mom would keep him away from the more dangerous items.

I rinsed plates and utensils, loading the dishwasher, all the while thinking about my words. *I've managed to keep life pretty simple.* That same sense of dissatisfaction I'd felt more and more recently crept in. Did I truly love that I essentially hiked and skied for a living?

On one hand, yes. Obviously. Of course.

On the other, no. Honestly, I could say I'd lost some of the satisfaction I used to find in that being all I did—basically doing what felt good, what I found to be fun, what I *liked*, and nothing more. Nothing that required me to stretch myself or stress out about a deadline or take on the usual drudgery of paperwork or even really having a boss. Of course, I had people in charge of me, but they generally left me to do my work because I did it well.

I used to feel smug about avoiding anything that felt like work, but more often than not, I wondered if that evasion didn't have something to do with the sense that something was missing, and whatever it was had been pressing in behind me lately. Up and down the mountain, early or late, it came hot on my heels and didn't let me relax into the bliss of the sloping pines or the blue skies in the same way I used to.

Maybe my jobs weren't the only parts of my life to blame. I'd never had an actual relationship. I'd never cared to pursue one if I couldn't have Bel, some lame part of me holding out hope she'd finally see me even though I knew after we attempted dating in college that we weren't meant for each other. Just like work, perhaps, it let me avoid having to commit and be tethered to something, someone. It let me avoid disappointing someone.

I rolled my shoulders as I wiped my hands and moved to the window looking out at the back yard where Kai pointed to different parts of a walking stick and Mia made a show of oohing and aahing over his work.

There were two people I could very easily disappoint— maybe I already had. She didn't seem completely disgusted with my lack of professional ambition, but it very clearly didn't mirror her way of doing things. Had she hidden her thoughts well, or did she not care?

Despite my inviting them, I couldn't do this. Here sat another example of the ways I didn't match with them.

And that thought process is yet another perfect example of your spiraling out of control. We'd never even dated. We'd done *nothing* other than chat amicably, and now I'd fed them pancakes. Friendly stuff, and here I was brooding about whether I could join their little duo, something I obviously didn't actually want anyway.

Better to just do my thing, and let them do theirs.

____

CHAPTER TEN

Mia

I'd seen Danny twice in November outside the library —once in passing at Silverton Springs when I visited Mrs. Stanton and he'd just finished a visit with his grandfather, and again when he stopped by to invite me and Kai to breakfast again, which we sadly couldn't make because of an early playdate for Kai.

Because his role as volunteer at the library meant he read to the kids so I didn't always have to, I used storytime once a week to do other things. Consequently, I didn't get to do much more than wave or say thank you before something pulled me away.

The days flew by, and Silverton continued to charm me, especially as the holiday season arrived. They strung up pine garlands, wreaths, and lights on all the light poles. Each store decorated its door, and the main streets of town felt so cheery, I loved walking around even without a destination. The town's Christmas tree towered over the small plaza just across from the library so I got to enjoy those lights whenever I gazed out at the snow-covered mountains.

Winter wasn't the time for socializing—all the locals were incredibly focused on capitalizing on the ski season. It made sense. It also meant I hadn't done much of anything but work and hang out with Kai at home.

So when I saw Danny stringing lights on the front of his house one December afternoon in the dim wintry dusk, I couldn't resist the chance to talk to him.

"Need any help?" I stood at the base of the ladder and held the legs, though it seemed to be planted securely.

He rotated a bit, and I saw the flash of a smile before he quickly turned back to the roof.

"Hey! Um... no, I'm okay. But I can't turn around and look at you because I've recently discovered a very specific fear of heights."

I could hear the chagrin in his voice. "Really? Well... looks like you've gotten a lot done already. Almost there."

"Yeah. Almost. I'll be down in a minute."

He worked there for a few minutes, and after silently praying he'd be safe and make it down without incident, I huddled into my down-filled jacket and shuffled side to side to keep warm. Winter had arrived and didn't seem like it planned to leave. This dusky time of day without the sun brought temperature drops—why had he waited 'til now to do his Christmas lights?

When he descended the rungs of the ladder, I braced the base again to give it more stability. "You know, you're really supposed to have someone steady the ladder for you. Doing this alone is dangerous."

He hopped off the last step and turned to me, his cheeks visibly ruddy from the cold, even in the dull gray light. "If

I'd known I could have had a lovely assistant, I certainly would have."

"All you have to do is ask."

He looked at me like he hadn't seen me in weeks, and I did the same for him. He wore a knit hat and made it look adorable. He sported black ski pants, heavy snow boots, and a sweater—no jacket. He had on slim gloves which couldn't be warm enough to keep his fingers from freezing. By the time I realized I'd been openly surveying him and looked to his face, I found him smiling at me, and a bolt of anticipation flashed through me.

"I will ask next time, then." He closed the ladder and walked it into the garage, glancing back at me in invitation to follow him.

Something about that made me wish he'd ask me for more than just help. Though we'd hardly seen each other the last month or so, I'd thought of him often, and I'd come to realize there were many things I wouldn't mind giving Danny if he asked for them.

"Good. You should." My voice came out thick, like I'd loaded all those thoughts into my lame reply.

He glanced at me as he secured the ladder, and I took a moment to admire his tidy garage. Not spacious, but he'd carefully organized myriad tools and had storage bins stacked on shelves from the floor to the roof. A kayak hung from the ceiling, as did two bikes. A work bench lined the far side, and a stack of his walking sticks piled there—either completed or waiting to be, I couldn't tell.

"How've you been?" he asked over his shoulder as he shucked his gloves.

"Oh, good. I've really enjoyed seeing the town decorated."

"It's great. I feel bad I haven't gotten lights on the whole house—I can get some up for you guys on Tuesday afternoon, probably." He glanced to the side, staring nowhere, then looked back at me. "Yep, Tuesday works. That's my day off. Do you think Kai would want lights around the door too? Do you want to tell me where you want them?"

If my cheeks hadn't been already red from the cold, they would have brightened. "Are you seriously offering to hang Christmas lights for us?"

He quirked a reddish brow. "Of course."

I had to look away. I liked too much about this guy for not knowing him at all. I surveyed his workbench, the various tools, until he approached and stopped just far enough away.

"I'll get out of your hair. I just wanted to come by and say hi." I pressed my lips together, hoping my smile seemed natural and not nervous like I now suddenly felt with him next to me.

He set a hand on the bench next to me, effectively blocking my way. "I'm glad you did. It's so crazy once ski season starts, I feel like I don't see anyone until spring."

"I'm learning that's true of a lot of people around here. Kai's going crazy waiting for school to let out so he can ski." He'd been driving me insane, and he only had four days left.

"Has he skied before?" Danny leaned in a bit, his voice warm and low.

My neck grew hot as I looked back into his eyes, which were remarkably dark in the low light of the garage. "Only a little. The *kinderski* program is a dream come true for him. He's so excited to be so close to the mountain."

"Kid after my own heart. He'll love it." He nodded approvingly.

Then we stood there. Just stood. For a beat too long. I twisted my hands behind my back and finally registered I should be the one to leave since I'd walked into his garage—he had nowhere to go.

I slid my hands into my pockets and stepped back. "I'll let you get back to your evening. Just wanted to stop by."

"Stop by any time, Mia."

"Okay."

All I could manage—*okay*. There were so many things I might have wished to be in that moment. Graceful. Charming. Mysterious, even. And then me, with okay. At least my voice hadn't wobbled after hearing him say my name all sweet and smooth.

I scuttled back to my house as fast as I could without slipping on ice and cracking my head open—the walkway to his side of the house had been cleared, but a layer of ice covered the pavement. I'd salt it next time I walked over to help me not die on the short walk—not that I planned to visit Danny's garage again. But just... for safety reasons.

I shut the door against the cold and encountered the full force of butterflies rising up in me. Danny often seemed friendly, sweet, perpetually nice, but tonight, his attention had felt downright hot. And I liked it. Hopefully, it wouldn't be weeks until I saw him again.

CHAPTER ELEVEN

Danny

Rod speared me with a look as I hung my helmet, jacket, and gloves on a peg near the door of the small patroller hut at the top of the mountain. "Time we talked," he uttered.

"Yeah? Hit me."

I'd listen to anything Rod Smith had to say. The man had been a friend and mentor all my life—he'd worked for Silver Ridge Lodge forever, or at least as long as I could remember. He'd been my boss since I started ski patrolling right out of high school and all through college. He also embodied the idea of a man of few words, so when he chose to speak, I listened.

"You realize you're doing my job?" Rod leaned back, his weathered face stern as always, his feet stretched out and balanced on the heels of his ski boots so the toes pointed to the log-cabin ceiling.

I chuckled. "Sure I am, Rod. Sure."

He sat up, leaned forward, and rested his hands on his black ski pants-clad knees, his gray eyes on mine. His expression bordered on severe on the best of days, only breaking into a smile when he skied powder or lately, twitched a grin when he spoke of his new girlfriend, Angelica. Just now, his face sent a flight of warning up my neck.

"You okay, man? What's going on?" I grabbed a seat next to him at the table where we ate, sat around and talked, sometimes held meetings for whoever was on duty.

"I'm fine. No—better. Ang asked me to marry her, and I said yes. I'm leaving end of this season, sticking with her there through the next. Time for you to step up." He raised his dark brows, his forehead creased with expectation.

"You're getting married? Congratulations, man!" I stood and offered him a hand which he took and shook, that grin softening his face for a moment. It looked good on him, that softness. I truly never would have thought he'd want to get married, but hearing him borderline gush about Angelica the last year or so... it made sense now.

He nodded. "Thanks."

"So awesome. Finally getting hitched." I leaned back, my shins pressing against the front of my boots. That reminded me—I had scheduling to work on for the last half of January since I'd put off doing it before Christmas, and since I wouldn't be going anywhere, I unbuckled my boots.

"Yep."

I offered him a big smile, genuinely feeling the joy for this development. Years ago, I would have felt sad for his loss of skiing year-round. At one time, I even thought I might do the same as him—work seasonally in the southern hemisphere and live the year-round skiing dream. But I found it impossible to think of leaving Silver Ridge for months at a time because as much as I loved skiing, I loved the summers too. I loved the thaw in spring, watching the run-off build the tiny streams into something worth calling a river, seeing the wildflowers come to life on the same steep land in the back we'd blasted for avalanches just months earlier.

"Gonna be sad to say goodbye to the life?" Would he resent Angelica once the newlywed phase wore off? He'd done his own thing for... well, I had no idea if he was closer to forty or fifty, but at least a few decades.

"As I told your brother, I've been waiting thirty years to have a good reason to say goodbye to it."

"Huh. Good for you." I crossed my arms and leaned back in the chair, wondering what it felt like to meet someone and love them that way. To be loved back, and give up the thing you valued most like it was a relief and not a sacrifice.

His eyes smiled more than the rest of his face, but they sobered, and he took a breath. He wouldn't let me avoid the other part of his news, and I had to respect that.

"As for the job... I don't know." My answer whenever someone me asked about taking more responsibility.

I don't know. Like there was some mystery about whether I would take the job rather than just me feeling like I didn't want it but couldn't outright say it.

Though this time, it felt different. My answer came unbidden, automatically, but something in my gut felt different when I said it. This time, I really didn't know.

"You do, Danny. You're ready. It's time. No one else can do the job like you would." He leaned back and grabbed the handle of the coffee mug on the table in front of him.

"I don't know," I said again, quieter this time, as I

scratched my neck and swallowed against the terrible feeling of truly not knowing how I felt.

He took a drink of his coffee, took his time swallowing it down, then pinned me with the same look he'd given me the time I'd shown up too hungover to buckle my boots—after Bel and I had broken up, coincidentally. Not a look I ever wanted to receive again, but there he sat, stinging me with it.

"Look, I promised Liam I wouldn't say anything. He wants to talk with you about it in a few weeks. He's got other issues to deal with, and so I said I'd wait. But I'm coming to you as someone who knows you out here—" he looked around the cramped cabin, chairs, small desks and tables in the far corners, hooks and pegs on every wall, first-aid kits and toboggans waiting for the call just inside the door, "—I know you on this mountain, with these people. You're it, and you know it."

I didn't have a response. Saying I'd think about it was pointless—he knew I would. He didn't say another word, and I didn't either, not as Shauna and Kevin stumbled in two minutes later or when Jeff asked me to shuffle his schedule for the third week of January.

I settled into the worn plastic seat in front of the computer and opened the document, then stared unseeing at the screen. I'd been sitting in this seat more and more over the last two or three years. I'd spent every working hour of the winter months since I'd turned eighteen either in this cabin, the small hut mid-mountain, or on the snow.

Silver Ridge embodied home for me in more than one way. What Rod suggested wouldn't change that, but accepting the responsibility of managing—people, the mountain, the policies we dealt with for emergency response, the blasting schedule... it mattered.

I could admit the idea of stepping into Rod's role both appealed and repelled me. I'd have to narrow down which feeling had the stronger pull.

CHAPTER TWELVE

Mia

Leo Morrison's eyes were like beautiful, star-spangled Alaskan glaciers, and I couldn't look away from her.

"He's doing really well. He's got a lot of natural athleticism and he's a great listener, especially for a kindergartener." She patted Kai's helmet, and he smiled up at her.

"You're a great teacher, Miss Leo." Kai smiled at her, and I could already see the hearts in his eyes.

"Thanks for being a great student." She smiled, her teeth glittering like the bright snow all around us, and Kai's answering gap-toothed grin broadened at her words. "I'll see you next weekend."

We waved as she turned to another parent and child and began talking to them. The *kinderski* program had started a few weeks ago and Kai's life was now complete, or so he said. He loved skiing, though he didn't actually know how to do it very well—or hadn't known until he joined this program. We'd skied a spare few days last year because a very kind friend of a friend had gifted us lift tickets. The resorts here priced their day passes so high, I never felt like I could justify going with Kai, and didn't see a way to have just him go, except that once.

Silver Ridge and, I'd discovered, particularly Leo Morrison, had decided they didn't agree there should be such an economic burden, especially for local kids. Their *kinderski* program let kids ski every weekend of the season after Christmas for a ridiculously low price, as long as they attended one half-day lesson each weekend. As though that wasn't the best part of the deal.

Kai had lucked out with Leo as his age group's teacher and had talked of nothing but Leo Morrison since. I'd met with her once after the first lesson, and then today she'd provided some feedback and a little check-in on how things were going. It all sounded good.

I couldn't believe my eyes when I saw Kai racing down the mountain, recognizing him easily by the flame stickers on his helmet. He made turns and came to a stop, in control the whole time. I marveled, but Leo smiled and acted like it was par for the course.

"She's a remarkable instructor. Your son is lucky to have her."

The voice to my left surprised me. I looked to find the owner and saw an extremely tall man, arms folded over his chest, in a slate gray ski jacket with black pants, sunglasses covering his eyes, face unsmiling but remarkably attractive.

"Ah. Yes. I can tell... or, I assumed. I don't know much about it, but he's loving it. Are you a parent?" Not that this towering man had a dad vibe with his immaculate clothing and no small children tugging at his legs, but he seemed to know what he was talking about.

"No. I work with the lodge staff."

A trace of an accent, maybe? Something. Definitely not from here. Also, no introduction.

"Oh, nice. Well... have a good one." I offered a small smile as I fumbled a bit with Kai's skis and reached for the handle of the large wooden door leading into the lodge.

A hand landed on the door just before mine.

"Let me get that for you." Danny's voice greeted me just as Kai said, "Danny! You're here!"

"Sure am! I heard my sister say you're killing it. Good job, buddy."

Danny's smile matched his sister's, and I worried for myself if he took off his sunglasses.

He wore a blue fleece zip-down sweater on top of black ski pants. His hair looked wild and charmingly mussed, probably from his helmet. He pulled off his glasses—gulp—and squinted at me. "How are you guys? You chatting with Jonas over here?"

"We're good. And, uh, I think? We didn't actually intro-duce ourselves." *Awkward.*

"Apologies. I'm Jonas Bauer. I'm consulting with the Morrisons, though I'm here unofficially. In fact, Mr. Morri-son, if you'd forget you saw me, I'd be in your debt."

Danny quirked his head in question, but Jonas made no move to explain, so he nodded.

"No problem." He turned to me, a smile sliding back across his face. "Can I help you with these?"

He stepped close to me, inches away, as someone passed by us to get through the door, then set his hand on Kai's skis just above mine, so the bottom of his hand touched the top of mine. That contact, as minimal as it was, made me suck in a breath.

"Sure. Yes. Thanks."

Instead of taking them and moving ahead, he waited a minute, another one of those over-full pauses like we'd shared in his garage as his gaze swept over my face, then nodded to Kai. "Come on man, let's go!"

Kai jumped and skipped next to him all the way to the parking lot, chatting the entire time, Danny talking right back.

I walked behind them, and every once in a while, Danny would glance back to check on me, or reel Kai in closer with the hand not holding the skis. He shot me a smile after grabbing Kai's jacket when he stumbled over the curb, lifting him bodily with one arm before he face-planted on icy pavement. Danny flared his eyes at me as if to say *that was close* and the only thought in my mind must have telegraphed across my face: *you just lifted my fifty-pound child dressed in ten pounds of ski clothes barreling at twenty miles an hour with one arm.*

My red-haired, blue-eyed, ski-patrolling hero.

I rolled my eyes at myself once he turned around and continued to the car, admiring the look of his arm at Kai's back, and if we're being honest, admiring the back of Danny's everything. He was tall and muscular. His shoulders looked especially broad, his hips narrow where his sweater fit over his ski pants. Even the way he walked in his ski boots made my pulse tick up a bit.

I could admit it. I had more than a little crush on Danny Morrison. Problematic for more than one reason.

How many? Let me count the ways. One—he owned the house I lived in—messy kind of mess if we tried dating and something went wrong. Two—Kai. Kai clearly loved

Danny, and again, if something went wrong, the thought of hurting Kai... There we had one main reason I hadn't dated. Well that and no one had appealed to me even remotely. Until Danny.

But back to the reasons my crush would remain a crush and go no further? Well, perhaps the biggest reason rested in Danny himself. He'd been nice, and solicitous with his breakfast invite and his Christmas light hanging and his occasional standing too close, but so far, he'd done nothing but be nice. I didn't want to be the woman who thought any man who showed her kindness was interested in her romantically—how pathetic. And because I'd come from a tempestuous relationship in which the man very rarely showed anyone kindness at all, I knew that might just be my Achilles' heel.

Back at the car, I opened the trunk and Danny loaded the skis in while I helped Kai out of his jacket so he could crawl into the back seat. As Kai climbed in and got settled, Danny approached, and I made a concerted effort not to notice how adorable he looked with his cheeks flushed from the cold, or how even a fleeting look at his eyes showed me they were even more astounding than his sister's, especially when paired with his red-brown eyebrows and lashes and inviting, smiling lips—

"Is he liking the program?"

Danny's grin looked suspiciously pleased, and I prayed he hadn't noticed my glance at his lips. *Fine.* My study of them.

"Loving it. He's doing super well from what Leo says."

"He looks good, for sure. I spotted him coming down on the last run." He ducked into the car and gave Kai a high-five. "I've got to get back, but I'll see you at the library next week, right?"

"See you then."

He patted the top of my car the way people do when they're saying *goodbye*, or *we're all done here*, or *off you go*, and I hauled myself into the driver's seat to keep from saying anything else or standing there and continuing to appreciate the departing view.

CHAPTER THIRTEEN

Danny

I'd been volunteering at the library for two months. Part of me wanted to keep that to myself, not tell the family, but at dinner a few weeks ago, it just came out. Since then, Ma had tried to get me talking about why I'd been volunteering, and I'd refused.

That niggling feeling of frustration snuck in more and more recently. Did my family really see me as someone so self-focused they were *that* shocked at my volunteering?

Of course, I had told Liam about having seen Mia, about being interested in someone for the first time *ever* since Bel, and he'd easily discovered my volunteering at the library stemmed from my interest in the new librarian.

But I didn't want Ma wandering in there checking out Mia next time she came to town. We'd never even been on date and Ma wouldn't be subtle—I shuddered to think what she'd say if she stopped by. The biggest problem with all of this rested in the fact that I had no time or energy to ask Mia out. I worked constantly during ski season—up long before the lifts opened to take first runs and check things out, sometimes blasting for avalanches in the back areas, sometimes dealing with personnel issues if Rod didn't make it in as early.

And there was the other thing plaguing me. Rod. Rod, my mentor, friend, and *the* man, the boss and manager over patrollers, planned to ride off into the sunset and get married to some woman in New Zealand.

Fine. Not just *some woman* if Rod, the quintessential ski-loving snow bum who sought snow all year round by alternating winters in the US and then in NZ when it was summer here, would surrender his seasonal lifestyle to settle down and endure summers *and* winters in one place. Because he wanted to. He'd *waited for an excuse* to. Mindblowing.

But the real curve ball? He'd suggested I take his job.
Me.
Truth be told, if Rod had approached me about the job this time last year, I wouldn't have given a second thought to saying no. I'd have told him to find someone else who wanted the responsibility. But his words from a week ago had been ringing in my ears since he'd spoken them with that Sam Elliot voice of his. *"I know you on this mountain, with these people. You're it, and you know it."*

He had a point. And as much as it pained me to think about, many people thought of me as an overgrown kid or someone who had actively avoided growing up. I knew why —because I had. I could admit that now—something about being over twenty-five had done it, maybe. Perhaps my *quarter-life crisis* in this last year or so had been confronting the reality that I'd never taken on anything that required much more than physical health from me, and I hadn't planned to.

Whatever the case, I'd heard Rod when he said I'm it. I felt it too. Time to grow up, as ridiculously obvious and belated as that sounded.

I'd even taken some steps toward that end by making peace with Bel, by letting myself be open to someone new, to engaging with Liam and attempting to be more supportive of his hardships with this mess of the lodge running out of money.

My knee-jerk response had been my old line—*I don't know*. But at my core, I did know. I wanted nothing more than to work at Silver Ridge for the rest of my life in one way or another. This job clearly fit both my skills and interests.

But if I took the job, I'd be in charge. I'd be the one hiring and firing, dealing with problems, calming hysteria, making the decisions. A part of me shrunk down, huddled in my bed with blankets over my head, wishing I didn't have to do that bit.

I didn't have to decide now. No point in rushing it midseason. Rod would be here until the end, and then we'd have all summer to hire someone else.

And I didn't have to do anything about Mia. I could keep seeing her at the library, even if just waving or sharing a few words in passing had become tiresome. I wanted to know more about her, *know* her, and I wouldn't get to do that if I didn't do something to develop the relationship.

But right now, I didn't have time, and she probably had a crazy schedule too, so I'd wait. It could all wait.

She looked especially pretty today.

She'd pulled her hair into a ponytail which made her long neck seem even more graceful. She wore a collared white button-down shirt tucked into an extremely appealing fitted black skirt I couldn't tear my eyes from when I saw her talking with Jake as I walked in—I didn't always see her standing up during my visits. And as though she could satisfy the fantasy, she wore glasses today. Dark rims highlighted those gorgeous eyes, her smooth light brown skin looking somehow warm and lush even in the dead of winter.

Not to be a jerk, but Mia absolutely qualified as a sexy librarian.

But that probably did make me a bit of a jerk, so I ducked my head back to the first book I planned to read, *The Day the Crayons Quit.*

I sat in the wooden chair with posters of various classic children's book covers tacked to the wall behind me and stacks full of the best of children's lit brimming in winding shelves at either side. A group of bouncing kids varying from cooing babies to about five sat, or sat on parents, waiting for me to begin the first book of the day.

Twice a month since November, I did storytime. It started as an excuse to visit the place without seeming like the only reason I came by was to see her, sure, but I liked kids. I always had. And maybe if Liam could take a break from freaking out about the lodge and confess his undying love for Wells, it would only be a matter of time until I had nieces and nephews. Right? But really, I liked working with kids—I'd taught lessons at ski school on and off through the years and got a kick out of my students.

Now that the season had started, that meant I saw Mia approximately twice a month, except on the happy occasional run-in. But honestly, that hadn't happened as often as I would've thought, considering I literally lived on top of her. My hours were weird, and I only took one day off a week, at most. Sometimes, I filled in for people who couldn't make it, and sometimes, I skied for myself those days, so I still wasn't at home.

But this year, twice a month on my days off, I wound up here at the library for about an hour, reading as many books as I could in the allotted thirty minutes of story-time. I always arrived early to make sure we had good books chosen—and we always did since Mia picked them out—and I stayed after to chat with parents, re-shelve books, and ideally, grab a moment with the woman in charge.

Having a chance to talk with her had happened exactly zero times in the previous four times I'd read. Today made number five, and I was determined not to leave the library until I got to say more than just a greeting.

I shared a few high-fives with little readers, shook hands and exchanged a few words with the less harried parents, and made my way to the front desk to find her.

"So nice of you to do this, Daniel." Mrs. Stanton beamed at me from a chair in Mia's office where she spoke entirely too loudly for a retired librarian and beckoned me to come to her with giant waves of her bejeweled hand. She wore something that looked like a cross between a 20s flapper dress and a mother of the bride suit—right in line with what she usually wore.

I chuckled under my breath as several people's heads jerked toward the too-loud voice. As library regulars, they were no doubt familiar with Mrs. Stanton's volume, but it still jarred me. Jake nodded and opened the swinging door so I could pass by the circulation desk and back into the small hallway where Mia's office and a few other rooms were located.

Once I reached the doorway, I caught Mia's eye where she sat with her hands resting on her desktop, then responded to Mrs. Stanton who sat closest to the door, watching me expectantly. "I'm glad to. Mia's built a great program. Happy to be a part of it."

Mrs. Stanton lifted her chin and stark penciled eyebrows in way that offered approval.

"She has indeed. I never had the manpower to do so many things for the little children during the school year." She turned to Mia, who'd been watching with the faintest smile on her face. "You were smart to recruit this one. He's a charmer with all those toddler moms, I'm sure. Easy on the eyes, too."

Mia's smile grew. "Oh, certainly. But he approached me, Mrs. Stanton. And I can't thank him enough for being the one to do that. I wouldn't have been bold enough to ask."

Her dark brown eyes found mine now, and something about that look made me swallow. Were we talking about the volunteering? I thought so.

I mean, we were, right?

"A man who takes initiative is worth keeping around, as you know."

Mrs. Stanton winked at me, and a rush of heat flared at my neck—maybe this would be the one time in my life my fair skin and red hair didn't stage an ambush to telegraph my thoughts to anyone watching.

"Indeed."

Mia's response didn't give much away, but I could see her press her lips together, a small twitch in her cheek, and what could only be described as a twinkle in her eye.

I shifted on my feet. "I'm, uh, glad to do it."

Because that was worth saying out loud.

"I'm sure you are. Libraries are the lifeblood of their communities. Volunteering here is actually good for your soul, if you didn't know it yet, plus you get to gaze longingly through the window at this magnificent creature between books, so I'm sure you're very pleased." Mrs. Stanton batted her eyelashes and nodded one sharp, final nod, then looked back to Mia. "As we were saying, I don't think I can..."

Mrs. Stanton kept speaking, and with that, I'd been dismissed. Mia bit her lip with a regretful smile, and I held up a hand for a silent goodbye, enjoying the shared moment with her, even if I didn't get to actually talk to her. Better than the days when I only saw her through the windows. Better than the days I didn't get to see her at all.

I grabbed my coat from the rack just inside the library's entrance and exited into the freezing January day. Failure to grab a moment with her today meant I wouldn't see her again for two weeks if the last month meant anything. I couldn't wait that long.

CHAPTER FOURTEEN

Mia

Valentine's day.

Not a day I'd enjoyed, probably ever, until I had Kai. After that, even though the first came a few months after being left by Kai's father, still loathing any pants with a waist, and generally feeling coated in either milk or spit-up, I loved that first day. I didn't need chocolates or romance, because I could celebrate my littlest love, just me and him.

And so every year since, Kai had been my Valentine, and I couldn't ask for more. I genuinely didn't feel sorry for myself or lonely—at least not on February 14th.

Because more and more, and frankly more than I'd ever felt when Kai was tiny and it was just me and him, I'd had moments of self-pity I wasn't proud of. Like when I had a flat tire and wished I had someone to call—though fortunately, my grandfather had shown me how to change a tire when I got my driver's license.

Or when I wanted someone to commiserate with after a long day at work or after one of Kai's moody spells that left me feeling irritable too.

I didn't need someone to save me, but I wanted someone to myself. Someone I didn't have to force to eat his peas or wear pants or beg not to smear his bright blue toothpaste all over the sink because, apparently, putting toothpaste on a toothbrush without getting said paste all over everything *every time* had become an impossibility in my son's life.

And in truth, I knew who I wanted that to be—at least who I'd like to try out for the job.

As Kai and I walked back from downtown, our bellies full of the glories from *Basta*'s gourmet holiday prix-fixe menu—well, that for me and plain noodles with butter for Kai, of course—I savored the feeling of my little boy's gloved hand in mine and breathed out a prayer of thanks for the moment. No additions required.

We hustled across the street and into the neighborhood, up our road, and finally into the house, stomping our boots on the mat just inside the door. Kai chattered away about his sledding playdate scheduled for the next day as we shucked our layers, and then he ran off into the living room just as a knock sounded at the door.

I braced for the gust of chilly air that would assault me when I opened it. I'd worn fleece-lined tights and a velvety long-sleeved cranberry-colored dress to dinner. The walk home, despite my long jacket, hat, gloves, and scarf, had been brutally cold.

"Oh, hi." Definitely unexpected to find Danny Morrison, rosy-cheeked and huffing a little, at my door.

"Hey." Huff. "Mia." Huff. "So glad I caught you." He

gulped in air, then let it out again and leaned one hand on the door frame.

"Uh, are you okay? Do you want to come in?" I pulled the door open wider.

His face brightened and he nodded, evidently still recovering from whatever had caused his heavy breathing. "Yes. Thank you. I ran over here to catch you."

I stepped back so he could enter and get out of the doorway, watching as he carefully stepped around the minefield of Kai's boots and the melting snow puddles he'd tracked into the entryway moments ago.

"Also that may have sounded creepy. It's just, I've stopped by two other times when you weren't here, and when I pulled into the driveway a few minutes ago, I saw you guys coming in the door and figured I'd catch you and you couldn't be in the middle of anything, so I booked it over here." He put his hands on his hips and looked at me as he took one last large breath.

"Is something wrong? With the lease or something?"

"What? No, definitely not. Why would you think that?" He tilted his head to the side like he'd figure me out more easily from that angle.

I crossed my arms and leaned back against the wall. We hadn't moved quite all the way into the house. "Uh, because you said you'd try to get ahold of us—"

"*Right.* No. I just... I wanted to talk to you. And I'm never home when you're home, I'm realizing. It's insane that I basically only see you at the library, and even then, I barely see you."

His forehead wrinkled in what I would have called frustration, but that didn't make much sense.

"That's true. And Mrs. Stanton provided excellent color commentary for our last interaction, didn't she?" I tried to hide my smile as I thought of his blush after Mrs. Stanton had both mentioned he was *easy on the eyes* and called him out for looking at me between books.

She'd nailed him on that, and part of me had been genuinely pleased by her calling me—even if it was a bit far-fetched—a *magnificent creature*. I didn't know if Danny had been more embarrassed by her insinuation that there were toddler moms in his audience who had crushes on him or that she'd noticed him looking at me, but either way, I'd loved it.

He did look at me between books. I could count on seeing his head pop up and his gaze casually work its way over to my window, or wherever I stood. But I only knew this because I frequently found myself watching him. He brought so much animation and humor to the readings—he didn't shy away from doing silly voices or making big facial expressions to engage the kids, and they loved him for it. Few of my other volunteers matched his reading enthusiasm.

He looked down, then up at me, a smile tugging at one side of his mouth. "Yes, she did. I particularly enjoyed how she called me out for looking at you between books."

My eyebrows popped up in surprise—I didn't expect him to admit that. "I enjoyed that part, too."

His face sobered, and the energy shifted in my small hallway, the friendly blue color looking darker and more intense, the air somehow thickening. "She's right though. I do that."

I swallowed, swaying toward him just a bit. "I know."

"You do?" His voice sounded particularly rich.

I nodded.

"Any idea why I do?" He stepped closer, now standing

in the middle of the hallway, only a foot or so from where I leaned against the wall behind me.

I shook my head, suddenly a little breathless. I'd never felt this kind of intensity from Danny. My insides grew fluttery, my mind slow.

"Because you are a *magnificent creature.*" He flared a brow, and a wide smile broke out on his face. "She wasn't wrong about that. It does add to the pleasure of the volunteer experience immensely."

I rolled my eyes at that. "Sure, sure."

"No, really. I like looking up and seeing you studiously avoiding me like you weren't just watching me, too." He inched closer, even as he chuckled.

Embarrassment flooded me, but something warm spread out over my chest. He'd noticed me watching him. He didn't seem upset about it, either.

"I admit I like to keep tabs on my readers. You may not get paid, but you technically work for the library. I have to exercise some measure of quality control." I lifted my chin to show I wasn't fazed by this little interaction, even though my pulse raced.

"Oh is that it? Good to know." He nodded, then his brow furrowed. "Well, I hope it's not a conflict of interest, then."

"You hope what isn't a conflict of interest?" I leaned back into the wall, pressing my hands behind me against the cool paint, locking my arms in place to keep from reaching out and touching him. I hadn't realized I wanted to until just that moment.

"What I've been trying to track you down for. I'd like to take you out. But maybe if my volunteering makes me some kind of library *employee*, that might not—"

"—No, that's okay. That's not... that's not an issue." I pressed my lips together to keep from speaking any more.

A spark lit in his eyes. "Good. Then, Mia Parker, would you be interested in going out with me sometime?"

And then, he did this thing that I never would have thought happy-go-lucky, super-nice, friendly as a puppy Danny Morrison would do. He smoldered at me. I could have sworn his eyes darkened and his whole presence sort of... expanded, or something. He took up more space, but not in an intimidating way. More like an appealing, sensual way.

What is happening to me?

"Uh, yes. I do. I would. Be interested."

The spell broke when he smiled, his perfect teeth bringing that friendly, much more familiar Danny back. "Good."

I agreed. "Good."

"Can I get your number? I'm sure you and Kai have things to do since you just got back, but we'll need to figure out a good day." He pulled out his phone, unlocked it, and handed it to me.

"Mom, can you tuck me in?" Kai wandered in wearing his favorite Spiderman pajamas, looking half-asleep already.

"Of course, buddy. Let me say goodbye to Danny and then—"

"Danny! Hey! Why are you here?"

Danny

Kai had to be the cutest kid on the planet, and with his Spiderman PJs? Killer levels of cute.

"Hey buddy!" I high-fived him. "I was just saying hey to your mom. Love the jammies."

His dark eyes—exactly like his mom's—lit up. "Do you like Spiderman too? He's my favorite Avenger. Probably my favorite superhero, though I do like Superman too."

"Superman's cool, I can agree there. Though I'm a bigger fan of Wonder Woman, I have to say."

Kai immediately jumped up and down, then spun in a circle. "My mom is Wonder Woman! Or, well, she was last year for Halloween! Mom, you should go get your costume so Danny can see!"

Horror slipped across Mia's face before she hid it behind a neutral mask. "Not tonight, bud. It's time for bed."

Her gaze jumped to me, and I let her see the full force

of my amusement. And maybe she could see the interest that burned behind my eyes—I had no doubt Mia would make a fine Wonder Woman.

But back to the moment at hand...

"Do I have to?" Kai asked, as though he hadn't just asked her to let him go to bed.

Mia chuckled and ruffled his hair. "I think so, especially since you just dragged in here announcing it was time. Danny's about to leave anyway, so you won't miss anything."

I nodded, though a twinge of regret at her pronouncement made itself known. Part of me had been hoping maybe we could share a beer or sit and talk now that I'd tracked her down, but this was probably better. Adrenaline still jolted through me in the wake of asking her out and even more so, her response.

"Really? Didn't you just get here?" Kai frowned and crossed his arms, looking truly upset.

I knelt down in front of him, bringing us eye to eye. "I just came for a quick stop, but next time, I'll make sure we get a chance to talk, okay? I got up really early so I need to get to bed too."

"You go to bed at the same time as I do? Don't adults go to bed later?" One eyebrow rose in question and stayed, waiting for my response.

I laughed at that. "I guess some do. But I wake up really early and my job wears me out, so I tend to go to bed early."

Kai's eyes grew wide and he nodded, his whole head jerking up and down. His level of animation made me laugh every time I got to see him.

"Okay. That makes sense. Well, Happy Valentine's Day, Danny." With that he turned on his heel and scampered off around the corner, just as a pit grew in my stomach.

Valentine's Day!!?

I completely forgot. A few people had mentioned it this morning, but by the end of the day after paperwork for a broken leg evacuation and rearranging the end of month schedules, I'd spaced it.

Mia called after him. "I'll be there in a sec. Brush your teeth!"

I inspected her as she stood there, taking in her hair pulled up behind her head, the makeup, and her notably fancy dress. *Oh.*

Oh. No.

Had I really just come over and asked her out on Valentine's Day? And after she'd gotten home from what looked like an important date, if her outfit said anything about it.

I ran my hand over the back of my neck, an inescapable itch of discomfort there. "Uh, I totally forgot it's Valentine's Day. I'm—I didn't mean to interrupt your evening, or anything."

She narrowed her eyes at me. "Interrupt my evening?"

I forced a laugh. "Yeah, you know. You're all dressed up, and you just got home..."

She pressed her lips together, which only drew my attention there and caused a pang of awareness before I looked back at her eyes.

"We did just get home. It was a really good date."

My spirits sank. "Oh, um... that's good."

Her grin grew. "Yeah, the guy talked non-stop—great conversation. He hogged all the breadsticks, ordered from the kids' menu, and held my hand on the way home."

Uh, what?

She laughed then—a sound free and light and incredibly appealing, her lips shaping into a teasing smile.

"Kai was my date, Danny. We go out every year. Didn't you see him when you pulled in?"

I shuffled my feet. "Uh, yeah. I did. I just—I don't know. Thought maybe the dude was in the living room waiting for you to put Kai to bed and then I interrupted, or something."

I tucked my hands into my pockets.

"The *dude*, huh? So this dude took me *and* Kai out for Valentine's day, in your version of things?"

She bit her full bottom lip, which I actively chose not to let my attention stray to, and waited for me to respond.

"If a guy is lucky enough to take you out on Valentine's day, I figure he's smart enough not to make you get a babysitter. And if he's smart, he gets that Kai is a big part of your life."

Her face sobered, no trace of that teasing smile left. "That dude would be smart, but he doesn't exist."

I searched her face. Had I upset her? Drawn attention to the fact that she hadn't had a romantic date? That didn't seem to be something she cared about, certainly hadn't mentioned wanting to date in any conversations we'd shared, though it would've been unusual if she had talked to me about that, I guessed. But I couldn't read what changed in her at my comments.

All I felt, selfishly, was glad she hadn't been out with another guy. I finally plucked up the guts to ask her out a few weeks ago, but it literally took two weeks to track her down. Now that I had, I wanted to spend time with her and already didn't like the idea of someone else getting to.

"I... *good.*" I inwardly cringed. If I had just upset her, that probably only added fuel to the fire.

I watched her face as one corner of her mouth twitched like she might smile.

"*Good?*"

"I just mean, I'm glad you were free to say yes to me. That I wasn't too late, or you aren't involved with someone else—I mean, I guess I assume you aren't—"

"I wouldn't have said yes to going out with you if I was seeing someone else." She crossed her arms and leaned back against the wall again.

I shook my head, feeling the exhaustion of the day settle on my shoulders. "Okay, that sounded bad. But I'm just glad we can go out sometime. And I'm now going to take myself home and put myself in bed before I say anything else stupid, and I'll text you soon."

"Are you going to be able to make the trek back up the icy sidewalk safely?" she asked as she followed me to the door.

I opened it, stepped through, then leaned back in. "I've got thoughts of you to keep me warm. I'll be just fine."

I hit her with an exaggerated wink and turned to go. I heard her loud laugh behind me as the door shut and I trudged my way back to the house in the truly frigid wintry weather.

As soon as I made it inside, I got ready for bed. I quickly made a sandwich and wolfed it down as I stared at the back-splash in my kitchen, mentally reviewing the things I had next week. Lunch with Leo—I'd promised, under threat of death. A call with my parents, who were still hiding out in Arizona, enjoying the warm winter there. Hopefully, Mia could go out on Thursday night. Thursday was my day off and though not ideal, I didn't want to wait any longer to get to know her. Every interaction we had made me like her more.

The way she talked to Kai. The way she laughed and smiled so freely. And tonight, a glimpse into the fun, teasing side of her.

Not to mention, she seemed to get prettier every time I saw her. I knew that couldn't be true, but each interaction we had brought one more lovely feature to mind—her glossy black hair, her smooth skin, her full bottom lip, her straight teeth, her graceful neck, her figure.

I laughed and snorted, accidentally inhaling the last bite of my sandwich. *Figure.* Who said that? But really... hers was nice.

I stuffed my plate into the dishwasher and grabbed a glass of water to take with me to bed. Everything about her was nice.

I'd kept it together at Mia's—well, for the most part, though I probably only felt that way because I got a laugh out of her in the end—but the tiredness had seeped into every part of me. I managed to text her since I said I would before I passed out.

CHAPTER SIXTEEN

Mia

I set the book down and sighed. Yes, audibly sighed in the pure satisfaction that comes at the end of an excellent book. *West with the Night* by Beryl Markham made me feel a kind of expanding possibility—a hope that, at many times since my grandfather died, I hadn't been able to find. I'd reread it a few times in the last few years, especially when I needed to be reminded what amazing people can do.

I wouldn't liken myself to Beryl—not even close. And I was certain if I'd lived in her time, I wouldn't have stepped foot in one of the airplanes she loved to fly. I had a hard enough time not breaking out into a sweat on the Silver Ridge gondola when I skied, and since moving here, I'd ridden it at least twenty times.

Women's history month presented an opportunity to showcase some of my favorite female figures through history and the many amazing books written by and about them. I couldn't wait to set up the display next week. This bonus day off before the madness of March, which always seemed to be when people reemerged into the world of the library, even when I worked in Salt Lake, was a welcome reprieve. Kai was more than happy to go home after his half-day of school with a friend before an extra session of *kinderski* this afternoon.

My head rested against the back of the armchair that had traveled with us from Salt Lake. The apartment came furnished, which had been a huge blessing, but this chair, Kai's rocking chair, and my bookshelves—no house ever had enough of them—had all made the move. The fire crackled and jumped in the stone hearth a few feet from me, and I wiggled my toes in my fuzzy socks.

Small, quiet moments like these filled me up with such peace. My chest expanded fully, and I sighed again.

Then I rolled my eyes because *that* sigh had been a wistful one, and also, since when had I become a sighing woman? I shook off the fleeting thought that I wished I had someone to share this quiet with. I had been content with being a single mom for so long, and we were just barely coming up on our one-year anniversary here in Silverton next month. I didn't like the niggling feeling that I wanted more. I *had* more. I had everything I needed.

The doorbell rang sometime later. I stretched and pulled myself out of the afternoon haze I'd fallen into as I scuttled to the door. "Danny?"

"Hey! You ready?"

"Is it time?" I asked looked down at my watch, bewildered.

Oh.

Sure enough, the watch said five o'clock. I'd finished my

book at half past three and must have fallen asleep. I didn't remember nodding off or waking up... I assumed we had a package delivered or something like that, not that Danny had shown up for our date *right on time.*

His gaze flitted over me, taking in my sweatpants, over-sized T-shirt, and landing on my makeup-free face, a clear contrast to his button-down white shirt, dark jeans, and stylishly mussed hair. "You're not ready?"

I clasped my hands together and bared my teeth in a regretful grimace. "Come in. I can be ready in ten minutes. I'm *so* sorry."

"It's no problem. Are you sure you still want to—"

"Yes. I do. I didn't mean to fall asleep, and Kai's been at a friend's after school so I didn't have him to bang around and wake me. I didn't realize I was so tired but I shouldn't be surprised." He followed me into the living room. "Have a seat, and I'll be out in just a minute."

He plunked down on the couch, and I smiled warmly as I walked out of the living room, then ran on tiptoes to my room and shut the door.

Ten minutes later, I'd changed into my nice jeans and an off the shoulder cream-colored sweater with leather snow boots—no chance of using more stylish options this time of year. I pulled my hair into a ponytail and added a bit of eyeliner, mascara, and lip gloss. That's as good as it's gonna get tonight.

When I returned to Danny, he sat leaning back on the couch looking comfortable, maybe even at home, while he thumbed through a stack of storybooks Kai had checked out from the library.

"Ready," I said from the doorway of room.

His attention popped up to me. "Awesome. You really meant ten minutes, didn't you?"

I chuckled. "I've perfected the art of the costume change in no time—having a six-year-old means I rarely have time to get ready or do anything that requires much time unless it's before he wakes up."

He set the book back on the neat pile, then approached me. "You've definitely perfected it."

His bright blue gaze lingered at my lips before he met my eyes.

Did his voice just drop a bit? Were his eyes twinkling? Had I ingested fairy dust while I slept, which made everything seem a little hazy and magical right now?

"Uh... hah. Thanks. Should we go?" I turned and moved to the entryway, and he followed. I layered up as he slipped gloves and a hat back on. "Sorry I never took your coat."

"No problem at all. We're going to drive—it's freezing out there." He pulled keys from his pocket and got the door, then moved to his car, which he'd parked just outside my front door, and opened the passenger side.

I hopped in, and he closed the door behind me. *Woof.* He didn't lie—it must've been in the teens if not colder. Kai had his last weekend of *kinderski* with an extra session thanks to the half-day for the schools, and they wouldn't have canceled it without calling, nor would Cindi, his friend's mom, have kept me out of the loop. He must've toughed it out. I silently let out a prayer of thanks for the long johns I'd made Kai wear the last few weeks—no way could he have survived today without that base layer.

"Did you work today?" I wondered aloud as Danny navigated the snowy town and entered the small parking lot at the far end of Elk Street.

"I did. I'd hoped I could trade someone to get today off, but I ended up having to cover for the guy who took my shift because he got a nasty cough." He parked the car, then looked over at me. "We're just going to *Basta*, if that's okay? I thought we could use some hearty pasta and bread on a freezing night like this."

I rubbed my hands together, wishing for warmth through my gloves. "Perfect."

"Good. So... now we have to go outside of this car, and get to the restaurant without freezing in place. Are you ready?"

~

I liked this guy. Probably too much. This marked our first official date, and I'd already mostly screwed it up by not being ready, by which he wasn't fazed, and now we sat across from each other, savoring the last bites of our dinners, and I couldn't escape the reality that I really, really liked Danny Morrison.

Why did this feel like a bad thing?

I couldn't figure out why the feeling of liking someone— really liking them—had created a distant patter of panic in my chest. I'd been looking forward to our date and had been disappointed we weren't able to find a time to go out sooner than we had, which ended up being nearly two full weeks after he'd showed up on my door on Valentine's day to ask me out.

The last time I liked someone, and to be honest, it might not be called *liked* because whatever I had with Mason had never been that simple, it'd ended terribly. The man who'd promised to marry me left me just as soon as I felt better after having our baby, and then I'd had to pick up the pieces of my life *and* raise a baby without having any idea what I was doing.

But I got Kai. And for that, I'd be forever grateful to Mason, even if thinking of him and our time together led to jaw-clenching and headaches and mild heartburn.

Obviously, Danny was as much like Mason as the streets of Silverton were like the slums of LA. They weren't alike, weren't related, and nothing about Danny reminded me of Mason. But what might've been most concerning was that I already felt a tenderness toward Danny I had no place feeling.

"I don't know what I'll do. I see the chance to be a leader, do some good, take care of the mountain, and have a job I can see enjoying... at least most parts of it. But it's not something I planned on." Danny set his utensils on the side of his plate and wiped his mouth with his napkin.

"Did you grow up thinking you'd do something else?" He'd been talking about a job he'd been offered—manager of the ski patrol, which seemed perfect for him from my view, but I'd only just started getting to know him.

He grimaced. "You know, that's the weirdest part of all this. I don't know if I ever had much ambition beyond being on the mountain and having a family I can take care of."

That warmth I so often felt when I spent time with him suffused my chest. *Having a family I can take care of.* What a beautiful thing to hear a beautiful man say.

And that should be stated for the record—Danny may have been charming, sweet, and sunny, but he had an outdoorsy, capable beauty to him. His handsomeness sort of crept up on me. I thought he was cute the first time I saw him, and of course I could tell he was in peak physical condition as he carried me down the mountain. I liked that he visited the library, that he volunteered, that he got along with Kai.

But lately, he made me feel trembly and nervous and

eager in a way I hadn't since the first few times I'd talked to Mason, and even then, I didn't ever *like* Mason the way I naturally liked Danny.

Speaking of, he sighed. "I guess in the end, I've always approached stuff like this with the attitude that it should be someone else to step up."

He stopped, but he'd left something unsaid.

"But...?"

He huffed, and a half-smile crept to his lips. "But I'm wondering if the feeling of dread that sits low in my gut at the thought of taking this job... I wonder if that's less about feeling it's not right for me, and more about the thought of taking the job and failing the people who work for me, and maybe more acutely, the lodge and my family."

For someone who seemed to avoid responsibility, he'd taken a lot on there. "That's an understandable fear. Everything we do comes with a risk. I guess the question for you is, is it worth the risk?"

CHAPTER SEVENTEEN

Danny

Dinner went well, despite my best effort to self-sabotage by laying bare all of my biggest weaknesses right there at her feet before we had dessert.

She didn't seem particularly put off by my admission that I didn't know if I wanted the job or to take the risk. But why should she? She had no investment in me thus far, and this was only our first date. We were friendly. I liked her kid. We shared a meal. Easy.

But as we drove the half-mile home after a truly great meal together, I wished it hadn't been so brutally cold. February sat squarely in the *winter* category for Silverton, but couldn't it have been an unusually warm night so we could've walked and I might've grabbed her hand? Other than a quick moment here or there in passing, we hadn't touched since I'd carried her down the mountain. At that point, I'd locked down any attraction so I wouldn't be the creeper giving her a piggy-back and getting all turned on. *Not* a good look for a man.

I wanted to touch her with a kind of desperation I'd never felt until we got in the car and I realized I couldn't reach for her hand. We both wore gloves because even in the car with heat blasting, we needed them. The car wouldn't be warm until we pulled into my garage as it was.

"Do you mind if I park in my garage? I'll walk you to your door."

"Of course not—not at all." She tugged her knit cap down over her ears. I smiled at the giant fuzzy pom-pom that crowned it.

"Meant to tell you I like your hat," I said as I steered into the garage and turned the car off.

"Thanks. Kai picked it out for me a few years ago, and I've never seen him so consistently happy with a present he's chosen. He comments on the fact that he gave it to me every time I wear it."

She pulled the door handle to climb out, and I winced at the recognition I should have jogged around and opened it for her, but too late now.

"He has good taste," I said, meeting her at the back of the car by the entrance to the garage. *Now or never, man*, I told myself, even as nerves swarmed in my stomach. "Any chance you can come in... for a drink or something?"

She glanced at her phone and winced. "I wish I could. I promised Kai's sitter I'd be back by eight since she shuttled him home from ski school. She has something else to get to tonight."

I should've said something to that—show her I could be easygoing and understood about life with a kid. I didn't, of course, but I certainly got that she had to keep her babysitter happy. But I couldn't bring up any words now that I realized we were about to have a doorstep scene, and if I planned to make a move, the time had come.

We strolled down the driveway as my heartbeat picked up pace, then we turned at the sidewalk leading to her small driveway entrance. My palms sweated in my gloves, and I could feel little coils of stress on either side of my neck.

The outrageously stupid thing I hadn't thought about until *this* moment, despite having thought about how much I liked her, and wanted to be around her, and wished I could figure out how to spend more time with her, was that I hadn't kissed a girl in over a year.

A year.

And even then, that hadn't been... well, let's just say I hadn't been nervous. It had been a peck, a kind of friendly farewell after a blind date I went on to appease a buddy—there was never a chance of me seeing her again.

Mia slowed her pace as we approached her porch, and before we reached the space in front of her door, she swung around to face me.

"Thank you for taking me to dinner."

Her dark eyes glittered up at me, and my heart downright *thumped.*

"No problem. I mean, it was my pleasure." My voice sounded stupid low, and I wondered if she could tell how nervous I felt.

She looked down at her boots and scuffed her feet across the salted surface.

She's looking down. She doesn't want you to kiss her. Pretty clear signal there, guy.

Just as I began to accept that thought—that she had no interest in anything but getting inside, she looked up at me and stepped closer—closer than we'd ever been face to face.

"I just want to say again that I'm sorry I wasn't ready. I've been looking forward to spending time with you, and I..." she trailed off, then exhaled, her breath swirling in the air like smoke slipping out her perfect pink lips. "I don't want you to think—"

I kissed her. Right then.

Honestly, I kind of pounced on her, just sprang at her like a crazy person, because it felt like the only option. Her soft sincerity, those eyes looking into mine, the torture of wondering if her lips would be cold, and what it'd feel like to taste the warmth that lay beyond them...

And because there is a God and I know now all the more He loves me, she kissed me back. She stepped closer, right into me, the puff of our respective coats keeping us separated by about six inches. Her gloved hands came to my chest, but she leaned into me, arching against me, deepening the kiss.

I pulled back before I lost my head completely and drew in a long breath as I eyed her. She gifted me a wide—and if I did say so myself, pleased—smile, then stepped close again to place a kiss on my cheek.

"Thanks for a great night, Danny."

I convinced myself I wouldn't be crossing a line by showing up at her door a few days later to offer them Sunday morning pastries. I'd done it before, and I wanted to see her. I'd texted her yesterday to say what a great time I had. I should've asked her out then, but she didn't respond, so I thought maybe I'd made it all up.

But no, I could still see the movie of our kiss in my mind, and it hadn't been one-sided. And then, she came back to give me another kiss on the cheek—entirely super-fluous and no doubt only because she wanted to. The absence of a response was disheartening, but she had a lot going on. She had to pay the sitter and who knew what else.

I knocked on her door at a little past seven. I decided I could deliver pastries to her and Kai, ideally be invited in to share them, and still make it to the mountain with plenty of time. I wouldn't be early like I preferred, but it'd be worth it if I got to spend a few minutes with them before a long day. Plus, it gave me a chance to ask her out again.

I occupied myself with looking around—remarkably, it felt almost like spring. A storm front had come through late Friday, dropped a few flakes, and left warmer temperatures in its wake. Though a welcome change from the cold we'd had, it wreaked havoc on the base of the mountain and they'd had to make snow all night last night to compensate.

By this time of the year, a few warm days could change things quickly. They predicted another storm would be here by the end of the day tomorrow and estimated eight inches of fresh snow, which meant both that we'd be good for another week or two and likely able to extend the season past mid-March, and also that I'd need to blast the eastern face like crazy because it'd no doubt frozen into ice in the last few days. Nothing like some heavy spring snow fall to make all those delicate planes of ice give way to a life-threat-ening avalanche.

My rabbit trail of thoughts brought me back to Mia's door, at which point she still hadn't answered. I rang the bell, confident they'd be awake, especially since I saw lights on in the kitchen. Then I heard her voice from the depths of the apartment.

"Coming!"

I stepped back so I wouldn't look too eager standing

there crowding her threshold, but admittedly, relief whooshed through me at the sight of her.

"Oh, Danny, hey." She hung on to the door, holding the edge of it and slumping into it.

"Hey..." And then it registered—she looked exhausted. Dark smudges under her bloodshot eyes, her hair wild in a knot on her head, a ragged robe and sweats, but not in a comfortable, Sunday morning way. No, she looked bedraggled and raw. "Uh, are you okay?"

She giggled, a wild, borderline hysterical sound. "I am so far from okay, it's comical. But thank you for asking. Can I help you?"

I swallowed and edged back a bit, not sure what to do with myself but hold out my offering between us. "I brought you pastries."

Her tired eyes flickered to the canvas *Rise and Shine* bag, then back to me.

"Thank you. Thanks, that's so nice of you." She brushed a hand over her face and pushed a piece of hair that had fallen into her eyes behind her ear. "I'm sorry if I sound like a crazy person. Kai has a stomach virus. A bad one. He's miserable, and I don't think I've slept since..." Her eyes glazed as she focused on something to the left for a little too long, then her head jerked up. "Well, since that nap I took before our date on Friday."

"That's awful, Mia. What can I do? Can I bring you soup, or do you need medicine for him?"

"No, thank you. We went to the doctor yesterday and it's a ride it out situation. Just have to watch for dehydration. He's just now starting to keep stuff down, so I'm hopeful the worst is over."

I stepped closer, but she stepped back.

"No, Danny, don't get any closer. I wouldn't wish this virus on an enemy. You don't want this, trust me."

"I appreciate that, but please, let me help." Seeing her looking so strung out and exhausted made me ache a little. The acute need to fix it, to make it better, to see Kai and check on him, pulsed in my mind.

"That is seriously so sweet, but it's just a matter of this virus running its course." She pressed her lips together into a thin smile, likely all she could summon at this point.

I ran a hand over my head and extended the bag of pastries. "Will you at least take these? If you want them?"

She chuckled. "Sure. Thank you."

"*Moooooooooom!*" Kai's voice sounded desperate from inside.

She laughed outright then. "I better go."

I nodded in understanding and backed down, wondering at her relative calm despite the circumstances, wishing I had any knowledge about taking care of a sick kid that might help. But I didn't... I had nothing to offer her in this situation, and even though I didn't need that thought swirling around in my brain, it persisted through the rest of the day.

CHAPTER EIGHTEEN

Mia

It was now March, and I hadn't heard from or seen Danny in a month.

A month.

Not a great sign, actually.

He'd stopped by the weekend Kai was so sick and he hadn't seemed scared by it, which I found refreshing. I hadn't dated anyone since I had Kai, so I didn't know what I expected, but especially for a guy who'd only taken me out once, I didn't think he'd practically beg me to help.

The next day, he'd messaged to check on us and I gave him an update. Two days after that, he'd messaged again and I was happy to report that Kai had gone back to school and I'd made it in to work. And then after that?

Radio silence.

Nothing.

And I had no idea why.

I thought we'd had a great time at dinner. He'd kissed me and it had been a really, really good first kiss. I mean, hello, I'd almost gone back for more but talked myself into aiming for his cheek at the last minute since I knew I'd cut the time close with Kai's babysitter. And then, he came back with pastries a few days later, which had to be a good sign. It told me he probably liked me at least a fraction as much as I liked him, and he wanted to spend time with us.

All good things.

And yes... *yes*. I could message him. I could send out a little volley and see what came back. But the part of me that guarded myself—my life, my son, and my heart—that essential part wouldn't allow me to initiate.

Pride clearly controlled that place in my mind. I should suck it up and just message him, but every time I got my phone out and opened up our texts, I couldn't make myself be the one to reach out.

What I could do was corner him when he came into the library, and that had been my plan until I ran straight into him—literally—after talking to Bel Paxton at *Rise and Shine*. And you know? For not having seen each other in weeks, it wasn't quite as excruciatingly awkward as you'd expect.

I scrambled for words, then said I owed him breakfast. He'd brought us pastries, so that statement was technically accurate. Then he said I didn't owe him, and then, *See you soon, Mia.*

So for the last thirty-six hours or so, I'd been wondering what he meant by that. Did he mean in the general sense that people in a small town inevitably see each other all the time? Or did he mean he'd seek me out and make sure he saw me soon?

I hoped for the latter.

And today must've been my lucky day, because just then, as I stacked a cart with returns and began wheeling it out to shelve, in walked a rosy-cheeked, messy-haired, blue-eyed Danny Morrison.

"You're not in your office."

A warm smile lit his face, and my stomach turned over.

"The cold snap at the beginning of the month made people desperate for a good book, I guess. They all returned them this week." I ran a hand over the spines of the books, a lovely potpourri of genres and subjects.

Right there sat the reason I had such a keen sense of the passage of time. Library due dates. People checked out books and I knew when they were due. The usual suspects would return much more quickly, but they'd come in with stacks—my resident romance readers who gobbled up five to ten books a week, my non-fiction addicts, my crime novel lovers. But most turned them in right about when they were due—three weeks later.

"Anything good in there?" He craned his neck to see the titles as he stepped close to the cart.

A wave of nervousness cascaded through me. "Uh, yeah. Some good ones. *The Shining, The Hating Game, All the Light We Cannot See...*"

"All good, for sure." He tucked the tips of his fingers into his pockets and watched me.

I swallowed. "Um, yeah... *Wait*. Have you read those?"

"Of course. Probably my three favorite genres, though I love a good space opera too."

"You read *The Hating Game?*"

"Sure. It was great. My sister's big into romance, and that's one of her favorites." He nodded to a few parents coming in with toddling kids pulling at their hands.

"Huh." He constantly surprised me. Not that men

didn't read romances, but that *he* did... it fit. I wouldn't have guessed it before, but of course he read romance and historical fiction and horror and everything else. That was just *him*... easygoing and voracious, apparently.

I'd never been more attracted to a man in my life.

"Listen, I should get over there and get started, but will you be around after? Can we talk for a minute?"

Something about the way his blue eyes stared back at me before he nodded and walked to the reading circle made my stomach clench. I knew instinctively this talk wouldn't be small talk and basic catching up.

In my heart of hearts, I knew why I reacted that way— why my body seemed to brace against his words. I fully expected him to apologize for not being in touch and make clear he planned to continue not being in touch. He was a good enough guy not to blow me off completely, but at this point, I knew.

By the time Danny finished his half-hour of storytime, I'd finished shelving the returns and sat in my office clicking from one window to the next, not seeing the contents of the screen, trying to keep my leg from bouncing under the desk.

I did my best not to look up, not to watch him make small talk with parents and give high-fives to the kids in the circle. Of course I watched it all from the corner of my eye, but couldn't bear the thought of him looking up to see me watching him and then get what would likely be a very gentle let-down from a very nice man.

"Do you have a minute now?" he asked from the doorway to my office.

I tilted my chin but kept my eyes on the computer as I

clicked out of those nameless windows before giving him my full attention. "Sure, come on in."

Breezy. Casual. Totally not affected by the plain navy T-shirt and how it stretched across his chest and made his eyes look more vibrant than ever.

"Do you mind if I..." He set a hand on the back of the chair that faced me on the far side of my desk.

"Please." I gestured to the seat, my demeanor morphing into some weird version of professional librarian mixed with awkward, probably 'bout to be dumped.

Danny took the seat and smoothed his hands down his dark green pants. They were some kind of mountain man-ish utility pants that were both practical and also strangely well-fitted. I internally winced and rolled my eyes at the ridiculousness of that thought in the face of what I antici-pated him saying.

"First, I have to say I'm sorry. I didn't plan on disappear-ing, and then the longer we went without seeing each other or talking, the less... sure I felt about reaching out." He maintained eye contact through this, even as he let out a deep exhale.

I resisted cringing like I wanted to. "Okay."

He offered a weak smile. "I can tell I upset you."

I straightened in my squeaky office chair. "Upset? No, not at all..."

"I didn't mean to let so much time go by. I'm sorry I did, and I'm hoping you'll give me another chance."

He'd leaned forward, and since my desk was fairly small and my body was tucked under it in my seat, it brought us only about twelve inches apart.

My, my. Those eyes were astounding. "Another chance?"

He nodded. "Yeah. I should have kept checking on you.

We had some issues at work, some blasts go wrong, a round of the flu come through—there's always chaos at the end of the season. I've been wiped, and then I started... doubting."

He scrubbed at the back of his neck and his cheeks tinged red.

A little burst of feeling shot through my chest at the sight of that blush, at his words. "What did you doubt?"

"Uh..." His eyes darted around the office, then landed back on me. "That you'd want to hear from me."

My eyebrows shot up. "Why would you doubt that?"

He scratched at his neck again, and if possible, his blush intensified. I'd never met someone who blushed so brightly.

"I'm not sure, exactly." He studied the surface of my desk—a pen holder, a desktop calendar, an ancient but usable computer. "I guess all I can say is I don't have a lot of experience with this."

"Can you elaborate?"

Usually so direct, Danny's words were cagey. At the same time, I could tell he'd offered me something that made him feel vulnerable, even just by coming here. I felt oddly honored by that, even though I really didn't understand what he meant.

He blew out a breath. "I haven't dated much. I mean, I've dated, but not like... people I..."

I worked to hide my smile, but he must've caught me, and he gave me a chagrined look without continuing. "Please, don't let me stop you."

He chuckled, that good nature of his shining through despite his nerves and hesitancy. He looked down at his hands in his lap, then up at me in a way that pinned me in my seat.

"Look. I'll be honest." Those blue eyes held mine, and I wouldn't have looked away for a thousand bucks. "I like you. A lot. I have no idea if we make sense, or if you like me, or—"

"I do."

His grin came immediately. "Good. So… I'd like to take you out again. I'd like to hang out with you and Kai. I'd like to see if we go together. I've been through all the excuses and I keep coming back to wanting to know you better, and it just seems like we should."

My heart thumped slow, heavy beats from my temple to the sole of my feet. His words were pretty much what I'd dreamed of hearing from him, and not at all what I'd expected after his weeks-long absence.

"Okay. Good. Yes."

He jolted to standing, so I stood too.

"Yes?"

I confirmed with a nod, split between a dizzy, over-whelmed feeling that made me want to sit and the desire to throw myself at him and hold those still-pink cheeks in my hand while I kissed him.

I cleared my throat, hushing that wild desire since, only at the last moment, I remembered we were in my office at my job, and not some place where my physically attacking him with potentially too-soon affection would be more appropriate.

"Yes, please."

CHAPTER NINETEEN

Danny

Somehow, I'd salvaged my ability to speak in full sentences and not have my skin light on fire with the red creep that plagued me—thanks a lot to my Irish side of the family for the red hair and pale skin that signaled my emotions all too vividly in scenes like yesterday.

But Mia, as always, proved to be something out of a dream rather than someone I had to contend with. Maybe I'd grown used to Leo's way of things, or perhaps I'd become too familiar with alienating and unrequited feelings for Bel, so I'd never learned what talking to someone who liked me back could feel like.

Not that I'd never talked to a cute girl who clearly liked what she saw in me, but I'd never been *interested* in a girl like I was in Mia. Nice, attractive women, usually friends of friends on blind dates or in groups or parties, but never had

I wanted anything from them. I'd spent so long thinking I wanted Bel, but the farther from those feelings I got, the more I suspected that clinging to my desire for Bel had become a crutch over the long years we'd been apart.

If I liked Bel and I grasped at that like a dying man despite having tried and mutually agreed to the failure during college, I didn't have to wade into a relationship with someone who might reject me the way she had. Even years later, I couldn't pretend the crushing, collapsing weight on my chest when she'd tried to tell me she loved me, just not *that* way, hadn't shaded the following years.

I'd been pushed to the confession by Jamie, by their summer together, by her admission she liked my brother. My brother, and not me. "*It's not all that complex, Bel. I'm asking you to go out with me. I've been in love with you basically since I met you, which I guess you were totally oblivious to, but I'm telling you I'd like to take you on a date.*"

Even as I'd said those words, I could see her face blanch and crumple with such sadness and regret, I'd felt it like a punch to the gut.

"*Danny, you know I love you.*"

I did know it. I'd felt sure of it. So sure, I'd felt secure that someday we'd make our move for each other and we'd be together. I'd felt confident we didn't need to rush into some messy high school version of a relationship that burned too bright and fizzled before we hit college. My plans for Bel were lifelong, and knowing she loved me, I felt sure my being slow and steady would work.

In reality, and after much rehashing and cursing hindsight, that confidence and surety I'd felt crumbled. I saw her face, that sadness and maybe even betrayal. I saw my waiting for what it was: fear. I'd been terrified that if I told Bel how I felt, she wouldn't feel the same. Whether I'd really missed the window like I sometimes wondered when I thought of what might have happened if I'd stayed behind that summer instead of Jamie, I couldn't say. Whatever the case, she didn't feel the same. And for a long time—for years, in honesty, I'd felt the sting so sharply, it made me sure I'd never get over it.

When we did date—when she agreed to meet for coffee and then a date and then time alone... it wasn't just her. I'd changed too, and we didn't fit.

But instead of accepting that and letting myself move on, I'd held on. I couldn't loosen my grip on the idea of Bel. Or maybe, I didn't want to have to face the reality that any romantic relationship carried risk of rejection. Maybe I wanted to stay stuck with a familiar rejection and failure so I didn't have to deal with any new ones.

Enter Mia Parker.

I couldn't escape her. Couldn't stop thinking of her. Had no desire to.

And beautiful discovery, she seemed to feel the same. At least to some degree.

"*Yes please.*" That sweet phrase nearly had me pulling her to me right there in her office. If the library hadn't been brimming with toddlers and their parents browsing for books after my reading, I would have. But I suspected the sparks between us would ignite powerfully the next time we got close, and I didn't want that next time to be in her office at eleven in the morning on a Thursday.

So I managed to toss the last vestige of my cool on the table and said, "Saturday."

She nodded, her cheeks flushed pink. I leaned across the desk and brought a hand to her neck. I kissed her cheek and relished how she turned toward me, like she wished I'd kiss her lips.

Then I walked out of her office and kept going until I made it home, the cool early spring air floating along with me, because the case could be made I floated home.

I knew this meant I had no game. *No* game whatsoever. And I might've felt embarrassed except I didn't give a flying fox about having game if Mia didn't mind.

So here I stood on her porch again at eight in the morning on the Saturday after I manned up and confessed my feelings for her—at least to some degree. I didn't lay it all out—I hadn't said she was the first woman I'd been interested in since Bel. I didn't say her status as mom to Kai both drew me to her and terrified me. I didn't mention the whole bit about being fairly certain I had nothing to offer her.

None of that had changed. I hadn't found some deep stepfather-ly well of wisdom to share with Kai. I had a great dad and good brothers, both of whom I now had great relationships with—and believe me, I couldn't have been happier to say that. Jamie and I had been at odds for years. But he'd returned and he and I had finally cleared the air—primarily by me saying he'd be an idiot if he refused to pursue Bel who, almost certainly, was still in love with him.

With Jamie and I reunited, I had three strong men in my corner, not to mention Grandpa Will, Rod, and a handful of others I admired. But I didn't know how to be a stepdad to Kai. I didn't know if she could even want me that way. But what I'd come down to in the long weeks since our first date, through the nights of typing out and canceling texts asking her out again, through manic power-walks to her doorstep only to turn on my heel and jog home was this: I wanted Mia Parker.

I'd never wanted anything like I wanted her, and Kai, and even though it scared me, I'd started to wonder. Just like

I'd started to wonder about the patrol manager job, and I couldn't stop the refrain each time it came.

Why not *me?*

This thought had crept in so often in the last year. I'd started transitioning from *I don't know* and automatically pushing away opportunities and responsibilities and decisions to *why not me.* The cataclysmic shift had consequences. It meant I didn't fall asleep like an exhausted toddler, like I used to when I spent all day expending physical energy on the mountain and came home to worry only about me. It meant my thoughts were riddled with questions and visualizations of mental scales that pitted new opportunities with my old closet hermit tendencies.

It meant I started to want and hope and *dare.* Terrifyingly enough, at nearly twenty-seven, I found myself ready to try.

Kai's voice shook me from my thoughts. "You're here! What'd you bring? We have French toast. My mom makes the *best* French toast and you're going to eat so much you'll want to throw up your guts all over the table and—"

"Kai, buddy, let him in!" Mia's voice sounded from somewhere down the hallway behind her son.

Kai's brows shot up. "Oh. *Right.* Come in. Follow me!"

And then, he disappeared into the house at an all-out sprint, sliding on the hardwood in his socks and grabbing at the wall to stop his momentum and pull himself into the doorway that led to the kitchen.

I made no effort to contain my chuckle as I pulled their front door closed and hung my light jacket on the pegs mounted on the wall. I toed off my shoes—happily, just tennis shoes, now that the snow had melted on the sidewalks, though it still clung to the mountain.

Mia came out of the kitchen in slippers, sweats, a long-sleeved T-shirt, and her hair in a springy knot on her head. I watched as she craned her neck back into the room though her body continued moving toward me. "Make sure you hold that with two hands, please."

Finally, her eyes found mine, and we met in the hallway just before the entry to the kitchen. She held a finger in front of her lips just as I opened my mouth to speak, so my greeting froze on my lips.

And then, I watched in a kind of *Dream Weaver* slow motion as she rose to the tips of her toes while one hand came to the bicep of one arm and the other came to rest on my opposite shoulder. She leaned in and pressed a soft, sweet kiss to my lips.

As she began to retreat, my brain caught up with the fact that she'd just kissed me—she'd just gifted me another kiss, and I'd be an idiot not to return it with enthusiasm.

So I brought a hand to cup the back of her head and stepped closer into her space so our bodies brushed, then chased her mouth with mine.

CHAPTER TWENTY

Mia

Danny was different. Something about him had changed from our first date to the time he'd asked me out again.

It. Was. Fantastic.

Not that I would've complained to begin with, but his laid-back nature could be confusing. Clearly enough. I still couldn't tell whether he let weeks go by without contacting me because they just flew by and he hadn't thought of us, or if he really had doubted my interest. That seemed hard to believe—I'd kissed him after he kissed me. I'd told him I had a great night. I'd thanked him for stopping by when we were sick, and when he texted, I'd made clear how much it meant that he bothered to check on us.

That was precisely why I didn't feel like I could reach out again to him. But maybe he felt he'd put himself out there with checking in. He'd been honest and nervous and adorable at the library Thursday, so I hoped he'd continue. We had breakfast and he laughed and teased and engaged with Kai in such a lovely, sweet way, cozy warmth flooded my chest as I watched them.

Danny didn't hesitate to lean down and listen to Kai—not just in a way where I could tell he knew I was watching. I'd seen that before—men apparently interested in me trying to *seem* interested in Kai. No. Danny genuinely wanted to know what Kai thought of *The Lego Movie* 2. He honestly wanted to know everything about his time in the *kinderski* program and what he thought about Leo.

"Miss Leo is the best. She's the most beautiful, and she's the nicest, and she's the best skier on the mountain." Kai's eyes practically had cartoon hearts springing out of them. Leo Morrison had become his first crush, and she continued to be completely sweet and charming about it whenever we saw her around town.

"Is she? I have to beg to differ on the most beautiful part, and I guess I'm glad *you* think she's the nicest. But you may be right about her being the best skier."

Kai nodded enthusiastically, as usual. "Oh, she is. But she *is* the most beautiful—I dare you to tell me someone else."

Kai had recently discovered daring people to do things. Just last night, he'd dared me to drink the pickle juice from the jar. Somehow, I'd resisted.

Danny quirked a brow at me and smiled. "I'd have to say your mom, don't you think?"

My mouth dropped open just a bit, and an incredulous laugh escaped just as Kai said, "Oh, well yeah. I guess she is. Maybe not *the* most beautiful compared to Miss Leo, but she's up there too."

Danny chuckled and winked at Kai, then leveled me with a look that held all kinds of thoughts I couldn't read. His tell-tale blush didn't show—he wasn't embarrassed. Those eyes were heated, full of meaning, and they were aimed at me. "It's okay if you think Leo's the most beautiful. But my vote goes to your mom."

Different Danny had some intensity about him—*wow*. My belly dropped to my toes, and there came the heat to my cheeks right along with a fair amount of fluster.

Kai shrugged and patted my arm, which shook me from the trance Danny held me in. "I still love you though, Mom."

I released a gusty laugh then, letting out the pressure that had built in my chest along with it. "That's good to know, bud."

"Can I go get ready for Jared's?" Kai asked, already dumping his dishes in the sink.

"Sure. I don't think they'll be here for another hour or so though..." I trailed off because he'd already disappeared down the hallway to his room, and he wouldn't care if he had to wait. His friend Jared had a birthday this afternoon, and another friend's mom had offered to pick Kai up and take him so I could stay home. Bless her.

This worked perfectly, because Danny and I were going to have a few hours together before Kai got back, and I couldn't wait to get him alone and have an adult conversation without an audience.

"He's just a little excited, huh? I half expect to see a little cartoon dust cloud left in his wake."

Danny's chuckle as he looked after where Kai had disappeared charmed me. Unless I was reading him completely wrong, he seemed to really like Kai. This was one of a few reasons I felt comfortable having him in our home. I'd known him for just shy of nine months now. I had met most of the rest of his family including his grandfather, his sister, and his older brother Liam. I'd seen his other brother, gorgeous rockstar Jamie Morris, in town twice now—that didn't make me comfortable, but it certainly meant I knew who his people were.

As someone who didn't have people, it struck a chord deep in me. It didn't just make me long for that myself—no. Something about the way Danny navigated through town, smiling and chatting with everyone, offering friendly hellos and check-ups on their business, which he genuinely seemed to know, gave me assurance that what I saw with Danny was what I got.

He didn't put on a mask in town, with his family, or with me and Kai. It didn't take a PhD in psychology to see the link between my upbringing by my parents and then my grandfather, and my misguided relationship with Mason, to see why Danny being upfront and honest and nice and loved by many appealed.

"Do you have plans for after Kai leaves?" Danny asked, looking casual and comfortable in my kitchen.

He might have been casual, but I felt anything but. Hadn't we made plans to spend time together? "Uh, I thought we were hanging out?"

"Good. Yes, good. I was hoping you still wanted to. I mean, I know we talked about it, or texted about it, but I didn't want to assume that you didn't have something come up, or something...." He looked down at his hands, then gathered his silverware to his plate, avoiding my eyes.

I set a hand on his. "I said I wanted to spend time with you, and I mean that, Danny. I'm all yours today."

How could he go from that confident, heated look a minute ago to doubting I wanted to spend time with him?

We'd have to talk about that.

A slow smile spread. "I like you, Mia."

"I like you too."

CHAPTER TWENTY-ONE

Danny

Kai had left ten minutes ago, and Mia and I settled onto the couch in her living room, each of us taking a seat at an opposite end. I would make a move to sit closer to her, but it felt like a time to talk, not anything else... sadly enough.

"Have you thought any more about that job you mentioned?"

She'd snuggled into the corner of the arm and the back of the couch, both legs tucked and folded next to her, her coffee mug resting on one leg.

"Nothing official." I let out a breath. "I think I should take it, though."

Saying it aloud made my heart pump a little faster. I hadn't said yes, but Rod seemed to be acting as though I had. Since the time to close up the outer huts fast approached with the end of the season last weekend, we'd all have a nice long break. He'd be heading to New Zealand like he always did, but he'd promised to come back for a few weeks in early November to transition whoever took his job. He'd said this with a stern look at me like I should know exactly who that'd be.

And honestly, I did know. I knew who it should be, and I knew who I almost wanted it to be. I just wasn't ready to go for it.

I attended board meetings at the lodge. I seriously contemplated a high-responsibility job. I started pursuing a woman I had feelings for, and from whom I wanted things. As Leo had cracked the other day, I'd surrendered my Lost Boy card.

Not that she or Liam or Jamie or *anyone* knew everything going on, but no one could miss my willingness to show and help and even take on taskings for the Sommerfest. Though no one made a huge deal out of it, probably to avoid spooking me and causing me to run fleeing from my shadow, but still. They could tell, all-around. Jamie'd evidently shared his utter surprise at my owning my house with Liam and Leo, who both knew, but seemed to see that fact in a new light once Jamie had made such a big deal.

Whatever. They were right. And I felt good with the changes I was making. I just... I hoped I was ready for them.

"Why do you say *should*?" Mia tipped her head to the side in question.

I took a drink of my coffee—just the barest hint of heat left in it. "Time to grow up. I told you how I've avoided stuff like this job in the past. But I think it's time I get serious. I'm twenty-six. I own my own home and my car outright. I live simply. But other than a house, a car, and a mountain I love, I don't have much, you know?"

Her eyebrows rose, I guessed in surprise, so I hurried to

explain. "I don't mean that to sound like *poor me*. I mean, I think I'm ready for what comes next."

And suddenly, now that the words were out, I realized that clearly meant regarding the job, but also insinuated, or at least she might assume I meant, between us.

"And what's that?" Her voice remained calm, didn't seem surprised or anything other than curious.

I cleared my throat, sipped my coffee again. "Maybe just that I'm done sitting on the sidelines, which I'm realizing I've done for a long time now."

Before I could feel embarrassed, or like I'd spent the last few minutes oversharing considering this counted as *maybe* our second date, she spoke.

"I can understand that."

My gaze shot to hers. "You can?"

She gripped her coffee mug in her hands and cradled it next to her chest. I fleetingly wondered if hers could possibly still be warm—the way she held it made it look warm. Then I wondered why I'd become so obsessed with the temperature of coffee since we'd started this conversation.

"Yes. I felt that way for a long time professionally before I got here, even though I probably had unrealistic expectations for what working right out of my master's would look like. I worked for a really controlling boss at my last job and never shared my ideas, never did anything. It's one reason I was so ready to move, and was willing to move—"

She cut herself off and her eyes widened.

"Willing to move...?" I prompted, curious to know why she stopped.

She pushed a thick fall of hair that had escaped her bun back behind her ear and chuckled. "It's why I was willing to move up here into Nowheresville."

She bit her lip and shared an embarrassed smile which only made me want to kiss her. Instead of launching myself across the couch, I said, "You seem sorry to say that. Silverton is tiny and genuinely pretty isolated. That's not news to me."

I winked for good measure so she'd know her comment didn't offend me.

Her face lit, and she pressed her lips together. "That's good. I should say I've only ever lived in Salt Lake, so it feels really removed here, but so far, that's something I'm enjoying rather than disliking. I knew I'd like it initially but we're coming up on a year next month and I'm only liking it more."

I rested my elbows on my knees and set my coffee mug on the low table there in front of the couch. "I'm very glad to hear that."

Her lashes fluttered prettily, and she continued. "Anyway, coming here was a big step in about a hundred different ways, but professionally it was huge. Having my own library at this age, even if it's tiny, is unusual. I lucked out that no one wanted to move up here, and since I'd been looking for an out, I took it. And beyond the professional side of things, I've placed myself on the sideline since I had Kai."

Those words, said in her smooth, rich voice, swirled around in my head. She'd been on the sidelines for over six years, if she meant what she said. "Really? Six years?"

Her gaze shifted down, and she studied her coffee for a moment. "I was with Kai's dad for a year. Most of that I was pregnant and he was barely around. After I had Kai, he disappeared. He left me with a newborn, and not long after that, Mason was put in jail, which I only found out because the police officers who ended up arresting him came by the apartment to find him. I guess the address was still listed on some of his stuff."

"That's... insane."

"It was. He was. I didn't realize what a bad guy he was at the time, but in a way, his leaving us was the best possible thing. Who knows what we would've been mixed up in if he'd stayed around? After that, I had no desire to meet anyone. I had no one in the world left to me but Kai, and I decided the moment I met him I'd make a better life for him. At no point did dating and dealing with all the crap that comes with it seem like it'd improve the quality of life."

I must've had a stupid look on my face because she ducked her head to catch my eye and tilted her head in question. I shook my own head, still searching for words.

"So many thoughts. First, uh, I'm sorry that happened. I'm sorry he left you and I'm also amazed you've accomplished so much on your own. And my other thought is, I can't believe *you* didn't date in that time, though I get your reasoning. And then I want to know what happened to make you all alone."

Her lips stretched into a sad smile. "My grandfather raised me. My parents died when I was young and he was my only surviving relative, so I went to him. He loved me and pushed me to do well in high school. I took early college classes as a way to get credits without paying for them, things like that. But he passed my senior year of high school, fortunately after I turned eighteen, so I never had to deal with foster care or anything."

My heart clenched at the thought of her losing the only family she had. I couldn't imagine my life without my family—any of them dying would hobble me. "I'm so sorry."

"Me too. He was a good man. My mom was from the Philippines and I have no information about her family there. My grandpa was my dad's dad. My parents died in a car crash when I was five, so I mostly remember what Grandpa shared with me and what I can see in pictures."

I moved then, couldn't stop myself. "I'm so sorry. Can I... hug you, or something?"

She huffed and shook her head, though her voice sounded warm when she said, "It all happened years ago, Danny. I'm fine."

"I'm glad you're fine." I took her coffee mug from her hands and set it on the table. "I'm not. Call me selfish, but I need to hug you after that."

I lifted my arms as she leaned in, and the relief I felt as she let me press her to me grew with each moment. I breathed in her scent—clean with coffee and maple. My heart pounded in my chest at her proximity, but also with the realization that this woman was easily the strongest person I'd ever met.

"Thank you," she said as she leaned back.

"Thanks for humoring me. Mia, I can't believe you went through that. How did you raise Kai to be so awesome and get through not only college but also a master's program?"

I could barely function day to day with the minimal responsibility I had as it was. I avoided decision-making and stumbled over it when faced with a choice. I couldn't fathom raising a child on my own, let alone going to school and pursuing a career.

"I had a good start from high school credits toward my bachelor's degree. And I had a scholarship. I missed a semester when Kai was born but caught up summers. Fortunately, a lot of what I wanted to do was offered online. Same with the master's, but by that time I could put him in childcare. I had a neighbor who lived next to my grandfather and she babysat Kai fairly often, bless her. It's not that I did it alone, but just not with relatives." She bent to grab her coffee mug and held out a hand to mine. "Warm up?"

I moved my mug from the table to her hand and nodded. I wanted to follow her, but wondered if she needed a moment to herself. Maybe I reacted poorly to her story—maybe she thought I pitied her. Nothing in her existence spoke to being pitiable—everything I saw and learned about her made me admire and like her more. Everything about her told me she was not only the most beautiful woman I'd ever seen, but also the strongest and most determined.

It intimidated the hell out of me, but damn if I didn't want her even more.

Mia

He hugged me.

He asked me if he could, then he hugged me, and it might've been the best hug of my life. At least from someone who wasn't Kai.

Sweet, comforting, charged with the emotion from sharing my life story, it settled me. Normally, being near Danny made me feel like someone had turned the light on in a dark room, but this felt like that feeling you get watching waves sliding up a sandy beach. Relaxing. A little mesmerizing. Full of hope and longing.

I ran a hand over my face then tipped the coffee carafe down and topped up our two mugs. I didn't often talk about my family, mostly because I didn't have many occasions to get into personal topics like my dead parents and grandfather or Kai's delinquent father. Mostly, that's how I preferred it. But sharing my history with Danny came naturally, and now all I wanted to do was share more, hear about his life and family, get closer.

I carried the steaming mugs back into the living room and handed Danny his as I sat on the couch. He hadn't moved back to his side, and seeing him sitting there in the middle gave me a small thrill. My tale of woe hadn't caused him to retreat.

"So you really didn't date all that time?" He settled back into the cushions and cupped his mug in his hands.

Side note, he had great hands. Strong, fairly large, trimmed nails, not pretty and smooth but not neglected. I liked them.

"Um, nope." I studied his face, wondering why this came as such a shock to him. "It didn't ever fit into my life."

"I definitely see that. You had plenty on your plate already."

I nodded at this. "I did. It's not that I didn't have opportunity, but I never met someone who made me want to try and figure out how it might work."

His eyes held mine then, and heat inched up my neck. "Never?"

I pressed my lips together, not wanting my smile to betray me. "Until now."

His answering look just about speared me. In place of a beaming smile like he so often shared, a minute grin tugged at his mouth. This had me swallowing, fully aware of what I'd just admitted.

"That's good news." His voice emerged a little rough, more textured and lower than usual.

When I couldn't stand the eye contact anymore, because it qualified as just about the most intense thing I'd done in a long time, I broke the quiet. "And you?

He straightened. "And me?"

"What about your dating life? You said you were hung up on someone, but have you really not dated? You seem like such an outgoing person, I can't imagine you not having quite a selection to choose from."

He'd been sipping from his mug as I spoke and consequently choked, sputtering a bit as he set the coffee down on the table. An embarrassed-sounding chuckle issued from him, then, "I did date. Here and there. Blind dates, friends of friends, stuff like that. But I was hung up on someone for a long time—way too long. That kept me from really wanting to be with someone else at first."

"And what about after?" Don't mind me and my shameless prodding. He wanted to know about me, so I figured he'd expect to share the same.

"I've realized recently most of that time was spent believing I was hung up on that person, but ultimately, I used her as an excuse not to be with anyone else." His eyes flickered to mine, then around the room.

I curled my legs to the side so they touched along his where he sat next to me. I wanted to touch him, feel the heat coming from him, but I didn't quite know how to engineer that. So I settled for first contact being me snuggling in next to him, facing him so my back was to the arm of the couch and I sat fully perpendicular to him. "An excuse for what?"

He paused a moment, like he couldn't decide whether he wanted to explain or not. But as I'd come to expect from Danny, he decided he would. He turned to me, angling his body to me and laying his arm across the back of the couch toward me. If I leaned my head to the side, it would rest on his arm.

"The girl I was hung up on... I'd been in love with her for years. When I finally told her, she shot me down." One side of his mouth hitched up in a devastating half-smile. Not sad, exactly, but something almost nostalgic. "It threw me for a loop because I was sure she loved me back. A few years later, in college, we actually tried dating and it was terrible. I mean just... not right. Clearly. Which was ultimately good, but still painful in that I couldn't face the dream of *her* being dead, I guess. So I clung to it, despite knowing we weren't a match after the experiment of trying. I didn't want to face being invested in someone and having that happen again, so it was easier to just stay hung up on her and have that be the reason I didn't ever move on."

"That sounds pretty awful."

He let out a pent-up breath. "It wasn't great."

He quirked a brow at me, and I finally got a full smile out of him, which sent my insides scrambling. I waited, eager for more but unwilling to force it.

He humored me. "When I did go out, it was usually as friends. If it was a date or whatever, it didn't lead anywhere. I don't think I ever liked anyone enough to ask them out for a second date, though I did go out with a few girls more than once here or there. No relationships, nothing... significant."

I couldn't summon regret or sadness for him, or those various girls he mentioned. Some selfish part of me felt glad he hadn't been jumping from relationship to relationship while I lived the single mom life. Not because I wanted him not to have that, but because I wanted it with him, and his evasion of relationships was likely the only reason he wasn't married or at least steadily dating someone. I wouldn't have had a chance, so I couldn't be anything but grateful he'd been hung up on some childhood love.

A thought niggled in the back of my mind. *What if he's still hung up on her?* But he seemed so clear about why he'd stayed focused on this girl and admitted they didn't work together. No point in getting worked up about that idea when here he sat with me.

"Well…" I started, but trailed off when I realized I didn't know how to ask. It felt too soon to say *"are we significant?"* and yet, that's what I wanted to know. I'd already given him that, in essence, but could I ask it of him?

"Well, Mia, now you know my history, or lack of. I've never had a real dating relationship. I don't know what I'm doing. But I want to learn how to do it with you, if you're interested." Blue eyes glittering, white teeth flashing, a warm hand gently placed at my wrist.

Could he feel my pulse there, where his thumb swept over my skin? Did he know how breathless just that comment made me? "Yes. I am interested. Very interested."

CHAPTER TWENTY-THREE

Danny

I wandered home slowly. The journey from Mia's door to mine took less than a minute, but I wanted the cool air of the spring afternoon. I wanted the breeze. I wanted the slanted mountain sun on my face for just a minute.

I could breathe out here, and I needed to breathe. If I didn't, I'd march back over to her door and knock, and when she answered, I'd continue the kiss we only barely tore ourselves away from in order to avoid Kai being dropped off to find me and his mom making out on the couch.

The day had gone well, if I did say so myself.

After our heart-to-heart this morning, we played Monopoly and kept talking. We ordered in *Guac* for lunch and talked and flirted, and I spent all day with a wobbly, light feeling in my chest. When Mia laughed, she threw her head back, then covered her face, like she wanted to keep whatever spurred the hilarity in mind as she enjoyed the laughter. She had no issues eating—shoveling—food in front of me, which I'd always found to be an attractive trait.

And the way she talked about Kai. Man, she was a good mom. She loved that boy, and he clearly loved her.

But that also meant that for the foreseeable future, she didn't want him confused by me being there too much. I could understand and respect that. Plus, since it was only our second date, it was time for me to leave and give us both some breathing room before the chemistry between us took over and we lost our heads.

Would've been easy.

Moments ago, she'd walked me to the door after her alarm sounded in warning that Kai would be home soon. She stopped me from opening the door, then pressed against me in a kiss that zinged to my toes. She pulled away just as quickly, and I nearly staggered out the door, drunk on the shot of her lips.

As I moved through the routine of shutting down the mountain the next few days, I couldn't keep my mind from Mia. Happily, I didn't need to. What a strange thing—to find my mind wandering to a woman and feel no hesitancy, no guilt, no longing other than that tight, sharp wishful feeling that comes when you want to be around someone all the time.

Relief. I savored this sense of relief that came—not because I knew what would happen between us or where we'd end up, but just that we both wanted to keep going, to get closer, to know more of each other.

Since I'd wussed out on following up and genuinely pursuing her over the last few weeks, I determined not to do that in any way. I texted her daily, sometimes holding conversations all day back and forth. I'd knocked on her door two nights in the last five just to say hi before I ran off to other things—dinner with Liam, close-out patroller meeting, drinks with my buddy Pete.

Things were hectic, but they were for Mia and Kai too. Kai had after-school activities every other night, it seemed like, and Mia ran a book club plus made sure to attend any town meetings or events just for the sake of showing up.

I liked that about her. She showed up. She didn't shy away from being a part of things, even though she still felt new. Granted, she'd been here nearly a year, but in a place like Silverton where many of the people who lived here could trace their roots to the five founding families' arrival over a century ago, a year truly was new.

"If I happen to mention Kai asking me to let him do gymnastics or fishing or anything this summer, please remind me I want to say no."

Mia's text had me chuckling. Two seasons of sports were overlapping, basketball and baseball, and she'd been run ragged with the schedule of season ending games and practices paired with new player orientations and parent meetings. I offered to take Kai to baseball and she said she might have to take me up on that. She must've thought I said it as an afterthought, but I meant it. Kai cracked me up, and I could see Mia could use some back up. Maybe it was presumptuous but I didn't mind being that person for her.

"I promise. I'll make a note—say no to Kai, no matter what."

This earned me a series of emojis indicating her enjoyment and exasperation. She confessed to me she had a hard time saying no to him because she felt he often missed out on so many things between not having a dad or even grandparents, and having to move from his childhood home.

For whatever it was worth, I assured her she was doing

great. Anyone could see that. Not that I knew much about raising kids—or anything—but her son was smart, vivacious, happy, and respectful. Oh, and completely hilarious. What else could you want in a child?

"Dan, man, where *are* you tonight?" Warrick slapped my back a little too hard, but only because that's how he did it—he never meant to be too rough.

The dude was six-five, had bear paws for hands, and weighed in well over two-twenty. By all accounts, he should be too big to be very good at skiing, but in the end, his athleticism and dedication made him just shy of amazing. He'd played college ball at the U, gotten drafted into the NFL, and made it three seasons before he busted his shoulder so bad he couldn't go back.

"Sorry. Sorry. I'll put it away." I held up the offending device in show to Warrick and Pete, then tucked the phone into my back pocket and took a drink of Avalanche pale ale —one of Silver Ridge Brewing's finest.

War smirked. "Who's on the other end?"

He elbowed Pete and nearly knocked his slim best friend, who always looked particularly slight next to his gigantic build, off the stool.

"My, uh... girlfriend, Mia." First time I'd said it aloud, and man, did that give me a not-small jolt of satisfaction.

"Girlfriend?" War's eyes lit up.

"Ohhh!" Pete's voice chimed in delight, his bass-voice always a mild surprise in the context of boyish face.

"What's this, now?" Liam approached and wrapped an arm around my shoulder, jostled me and released, just like he'd done another eight hundred thousand times before. He took the remaining empty stool at the high-top table.

"That seat isn't for you, fat head," I grumped, not

wanting Liam's teasing any more than I wanted War and Pete's.

"Too bad, little tiny brother. I haven't seen you in a few days. You've been slacking on lunch, running around like a chicken with your head cut off, and since that's normally my job, I had to track you down. A little birdie told me you'd be here tonight." He took my bottle of beer and inspected it, then nodded in satisfaction and replaced it.

"Would that little birdie happen to be an extremely annoying blonde we're related to?"

War and Pete cracked up, and War mumbled, "An extremely *hot* annoying blonde…"

I shot him a look, and his eyes jumped to the screen showing Bundesliga soccer, the whole reason we were meeting tonight.

Liam chuckled and stood.

"It might. Now that I see you're in one piece, I'll leave you be. But I want to hear about this girlfriend." He wiggled his eyebrows. "And I want to follow up with you on your ideas for Sommerfest. Lunch tomorrow?"

Relieved to see him go, I nodded. I had no problem telling my friends about Mia because they'd be happy and leave it at that. They didn't know the extent of my past hang ups, so there wouldn't be any careful questioning, any knowing looks. They'd just rib me a little since they certainly knew I'd never had a girlfriend, and then we'd move on and hopefully watch Bayern Munich destroy Berlin—I'd made a point not to look up scores so the replay would be fresh.

But I'd have to talk with Liam. He'd want to know about Mia, and he would want to know about some ideas I'd mentioned off-hand in the last board meeting, and he'd probably ask whether I'd decided to take Rod's job or not.

I couldn't blame him for that—for any of it. He took his role as big brother and de facto in-state Morrison patriarch seriously, and he did it well—especially now that he was a few months out from his nervous breakdown about the lodge.

Thanks to Jonas Bauer, and Liam's hard work, and Wells' wisdom and calming effect, the lodge had a future much brighter than it did six months ago. Liam would feel better about letting go of the reins if he knew I'd step up in Rod's place. And the more I thought about it, the more it made sense.

Except that gnawing sense of doubt about myself. I'd never had that much responsibility. I'd never been in charge. Did I really have it in me?

CHAPTER TWENTY-FOUR

Mia

The last few months had flown by.

Danny had been a fixture in them, too, much to my delight. We'd grown close, and I dare say so had he and Kai. Sometimes, the sight of the two of them huddled together whittling or laughing or playing video games left me no choice but to squeeze my eyes shut and let the overwhelming wave of longing, joy, and fear pass.

I began seeing a life for us—the three of us. And once that started, I couldn't unsee it. I tried burying it under books—any and all books I could get my hands on, though carefully and concertedly no romance, just to make sure my imagination didn't get too caught up in what a happily ever after with Danny might look like.

But no sense in pretending—it already was caught up, no doubt. Each time Danny ruffled Kai's hair or gave him a high-five. The time he cleaned and bandaged Kai's skinned knee before I even knew what happened. The time Kai had asked Danny to tuck him in—and since then, each time the request came, which was every evening Danny ate dinner with us.

And that had certainly become a fixture in our lives. Danny ate with us twice during the week, and we usually spent Saturdays together unless he had another obligation, or we did. But now that school was winding down and summer knocked at Silverton's door, he had much more time than he'd had in winter and spring.

We went on dates together whenever I could get a babysitter, though this became more difficult as the high school let out in May and my usual sitter took a full-time job. We never had enough time alone together—I wanted him all to myself, but stealing that time with a six-year-old in the house had been fairly impossible thus far.

Frustration found me at the end of every evening we shared when he'd wander back home, leaving me at the doorstep with a sweet kiss. I kept waiting for him to ask to stay. I worked out how we'd swing it, how I could explain it to Kai, even, but he never asked. I pushed away the doubt that crept in at those times because Danny had never been anything but honest with me. I knew he liked me, wanted me, wanted time with me. He must've felt he *couldn't* ask, maybe out of respect for Kai. I'd been working on the guts to talk to him about that.

We spent even more time the three of us—at Kai's baseball games or on hikes now that the trails were clearing on the lower mountain. We ate waffles together and played board games.

We felt, more and more, like a family.

It was amazing.

It was terrifying.

As I wandered up Main Street during my lunch hour on a delectably warm late-June day, I thought through how I could invite him to stay without pressuring him or making him feel anything but desired and cared for. Loved, if I admitted it to myself, and I had, in the secret part of my heart I wasn't sure I could share just yet.

"Mia Parker!" Leo Morrison hollered from across the street, then jogged to me. I hadn't seen her since *kinderski* ended months ago.

"Hi, Leo. How are you doing?"

She patted my shoulder.

"I'm well, thanks. I've been meaning to hunt you down. I wanted to invite you to a girls' night dinner. My girls and I get together every few weeks for dinner, and we've been meaning to invite you but the last month or so has been..." Her eyes cut to the sky, then found me again. "Dramatic, to say the least. But all's well, and we would love for you to join us."

Very unexpected. Warmth flooded my chest, and I felt a little like hopping. "I—I'd love to."

Leo nodded as though she'd known my answer all along and wanted to reward me for giving the correct one. "Great. We're meeting Friday this week. That work for you? We'll do *Guac* and have ourselves a little solstice fiesta. Sound good?"

"Perfect."

"Are you sure this is okay? I mean, if you're not sure, then I'm happy to text Leo and—"

"Mia, honey, please go. I'm glad she invited you, and I know you'll love Wells and Bel. And they will definitely love you." Danny's blue eyes held calm with a spark of humor.

I let out a deep breath, wishing my nerves would collect that calm he offered and run with it. I felt nervous out of my mind, which made me angry and a little sad. I wanted to run back to my room, lock the door, pull on sweatpants, and watch an old episode of *The Office*.

"Yeah... no, sure. Yeah. I just..."

His hands came up to cup my cheeks. "Mia. You're amazing. Leo wouldn't have invited you if she didn't already like you—she's really not someone who spends time with people unless she genuinely likes them."

His warm hands on my cheeks soothed, but my doubt wouldn't release its grip. I'd lived here over a year, and aside from Danny, this was the first time I'd been invited to do anything social. In fact, it was the first social outing with a group of women I'd had since high school.

"Really? How could she even know if she likes me? That's absurd."

That killer half-smile of his popped up, then he bit his lip.

"You are adorable." He pulled me in and touched his lips to mine, then leveled me with a stern look I'd only seen once or twice before. "You're going, and it will be great. Kai and I are having pizza and brownies and playing video games and he'll stay up a little late because that's what he gets for having a stand-in instead of his awesome mom. When you come back, you can tell me all about how insane my sister is and I'll happily listen, okay?"

I swallowed, willing the nerves away. "Okay. I can do that."

"Yes you can. You raised Kai. You've got a master's

degree. You relocated your life *by yourself.* You're a freaking miracle and you can do whatever you decide you want to."

That familiar feeling I got whenever Danny talked to me like this—like he not only liked me, but had faith in me, curled in my chest, and this time, my smile didn't wobble. "Okay."

"Say hi to Miss Leo for me, Mom!" Kai yelled from the living room.

"Be good for Danny, bud. Don't hassle him about bedtime, and make sure you brush your teeth really well."

"Mooooom."

Danny cracked up, and I couldn't resist joining him. Kai found it supremely frustrating when I gave him reminders, especially in front of Danny, and especially lately.

"Go. We'll be fine. I'll text you if aliens invade." He pulled me to him and kissed my cheek, my temple, the top of my head.

"Okay. I'm going. If your sister decides I'm awkward and she hates me after this, I'm blaming you."

He shut the door behind me, still laughing as I went.

CHAPTER TWENTY-FIVE

Danny

Man, she was nervous.

I'd never seen Mia like this. She'd gone pale about a half-hour ago when I first arrived. She'd raced home from work and changed into what could only be described as a delectable pink dress that made her golden-brown skin look darker and, forgive me but there was no other way to say it, lickable.

Yeah. I had her on the brain. Fully embedded in my mind. I suspected also in my heart, maybe even in my soul. But that's a conversation for another time.

I had no outlet for those desires, and maybe that was for the best. The possibility of losing myself completely if I had more time alone with her was high.

Clearly, Mia's social interaction had been minimal over the last few years. I'd failed to put together the obvious considering what she told me about her life—she'd gotten pregnant, been abandoned by he-who-shall-not-be-named, and worked her perfectly sculpted butt off getting her degrees and raising the best kid in the world. When would she have had time to make girlfriends and go out?

"Did you order the pizza, Danny? I got TV on and a few options ready for us to choose from."

Kai's voice shook me from my thoughts, and I looked up to see him holding a remote above his head as he hopped around on one foot.

"I'll call right now and be in. Which movie did you pick?"

Kai's eyes widened. "No no no. *You* get to pick. You're my guest, so you get to choose the movie and I get your dinner and dessert and everything since I'm the host. You have to call the pizza place because I'm too young. As long as you get cheese pizza for me, you can get whatever else you want. Also, I need some help with the brownies because I can't do the oven by myself."

I tucked my lips between my teeth to hide my smile. Kai wouldn't be offended, but the earnest look on his face and the tone of his voice told me he meant every word. He took his hosting responsibilities seriously. I wondered if Mia had talked to him about that, or if it was just *him*.

"I'll call now. Then let's get the brownies in the oven before we start the movie so they're done by the time we finish dinner. Come help me find the ingredients while I order."

Kai tossed the remote into the living room then scuttled into the kitchen and banged around in the cabinets gathering ingredients while I called in our pizza. On a Friday night, it'd take at least a half-hour to get here, if not a little longer, so we had plenty of time to get the brownies ready.

By the time I'd paid with my card and hung up, Kai had

emptied out the baggy of brownie mix, cracked eggs, and measured out the oil and water. From what I could see, he'd done it all correctly.

"Aren't you a little young to be this good at cooking? You planning on a career in the culinary arts?" I watched as he focused on carefully pouring the oil into the bowl, then took a spatula and shifted the glop around until it looked fairly well-mixed.

"You might wanna go over that and get the bottom. I never get it all off the bottom." He hopped down from the little stool he'd stepped up on that helped him reach the sink and countertops better and rummaged around while I stirred. "I cook all the time with my mom. She said no one really taught her to cook so she wants to make sure she cooks with me so I don't have to figure it out all by myself."

That had me focusing in on the batter, beating it a few times and clearing my throat against the crush of emotion that crept up my throat. That happened too easily at times like this—when Kai would say something so matter-of-factly that hinted at the hardship Mia had endured growing up and then again raising him on her own.

I'd learned at Ma's hip in the kitchen. She'd insisted we all know how to make the basics, and as I got older, I took a special interest in breakfast foods. Some of my favorite memories were helping her on a Sunday afternoon after we all got back from skiing or working. We always had an afternoon brunch because Sundays, especially during the season, were insane. The time moved to after church in the off-seasons.

I wondered if Mia would like Ma. I wanted to ask her to come to dinner at the house while my folks were in town— they were back for the summer now and would be here until after Sommerfest in August. It felt like I had all the time in the world to get around to that introduction, but we had about eight weeks until the fest, which meant I better get serious.

There lay the rub: asking her to meet my parents *was* serious. It wasn't something she'd ask me since she didn't have family. So that step would fall completely to me. And if I asked and she said no? Or made an excuse so she wouldn't have to say no?

That same thought had shut me down more than once in the last few weeks since my parents had arrived back in Utah. But tonight, I had Kai all to myself, and Mia was out with my sister and her friends, and that meant something. Me watching Kai without her—that held significance.

She trusted me with her son. I could certainly trust her with my family. I knew they'd like her because she was supremely likeable—just like I knew Leo would like her. And I suspected she'd like the family, but all of us together could be overwhelming. Maybe I could arrange for a family dinner with just us and my parents. That'd cut down on the insanity, and on Liam and Leo's bickering, for sure.

"Did I do something wrong?" Kai's small voice interrupted this flurry of thoughts.

My head jerked up to find his eyes wide, his hands clasped together in front of him. He could read me well enough to see something was heavy on my mind.

"No, of course not. You're awesome. I'm super-impressed by your cooking skills. I just feel bad that you didn't make any brownies for you."

His head cocked to the side. "What?"

"Yeah. I feel bad we didn't make any for you. These are clearly all for me, right?"

CHAPTER TWENTY-SIX

Mia

I focused on breathing normally as I wandered the ten-minute walk to *Guac*. Danny's pep talk had calmed me, but each step I took toward the intimidating group of women I barely knew made the pressure in my chest build.

When I crossed the street, I saw Leo standing on the sidewalk. She had on a cerulean blue sundress that ruffled in the warm summer breeze, her hair pulled away from her face in a half-up braid that trailed down over the hair that spilled over her shoulders to her mid-back. She would've looked like a summer goddess had her posture not been rigid and her arms crossed at her chest. A towering man stood next to her, his jaw obviously taut even from this distance.

A spike of alarm raised. Was this man harassing her? I hurried my pace and called out, "Hey, Leo."

She turned to me and offered a genuine smile, her back fully to the man, who watched as she held her arms out to me. I wasn't expecting a hug, but maybe she needed one after... whatever it was that happened with this man, so I took her embrace. She pulled back and beamed at me, and in that moment, the Morrison genes were on full display. Eyes that matched her dress, gorgeous smile, and even the shape of her face, so like Danny's.

"So glad you could come, Mia."

"Thank you for the invite." My eyes flickered to the man, who remained nearby, but hadn't spoken. Odd.

"Bel ran in to get us a table. Wells should be here any minute."

"Wells is here *this* minute," a voice came from the other side of the street. A tall woman with flippy, stylish blond hair trotted across the street and held out an arm to Leo, who happily folded her into a hug.

"Wells, this is Mia Parker." Leo gestured grandly to me, and I chuckled. Leo had a lot of flair, that's for sure.

"So glad to meet you. In fact, I'm sorry we haven't met before now. I've been settling in too, and well, there's no excuse but I'm glad to meet you now."

I took the hand Wells held out and shook. "Likewise."

Wells then swung back and tilted her head as she spoke to the man who still stood there, conspicuous and kind of giant and awkward in our midst. "And Jonas? Did you introduce Mia to Jonas?"

Leo's voice defined curt. "No."

Wells widened her eyes at me and blinked rapidly. I might've laughed except Leo seemed genuinely bothered by this guy, who looked more and more familiar as I stole glances at him.

"Ooookay. Well, Mia, this is Jonas Bauer. He'll be

taking over for Liam as mountain manager, and he's got irons in a few other fires in the area too, from what I gather." Wells patted Jonas' arm.

"Ms. Parker. Lovely to see you again. Congratulations on your successful transition to head librarian."

The voice did it—I had indeed met him before. I shook his proffered hand, the shock of his obvious perfect recollection of me causing my voice to falter a bit. He stood out at six foot however many inches and with his stony demeanor, but I wouldn't have thought he'd remember me from the passing few words we'd exchanged, when he'd insisted Leo was the best ski instructor at Silver Ridge—his severe assessment out of nowhere was something that had struck me and though I hadn't seen him since, I'd never forget him. "Thanks. Uh, nice to see you again too, Mr. Bauer."

"Well, that's enough of that. Let's head inside." Leo marched inside without a backward glance.

Wells spoke with a grimace. "We better get in there. Nice to see you, Jonas."

"And you, Ms. Bryant." He then nodded to me. "Have a nice evening."

I watched him go for a moment before Wells tugged my arm and I followed after her.

Before she opened the door, she stopped and turned to me. "I'm sure you're wondering what that was about. I am too. All I can say is if Leo doesn't bring it up, I wouldn't say anything."

I forced a laugh. "No problem here. I won't say a word."

I couldn't deny curiosity since Leo's open hostility and blatant ignoring of Jonas surprised me and seemed extremely obvious—no way he could miss that—but I didn't know any of them well enough to ask about it. Plus, the one and only other time I'd spoken to him, he'd made a point to compliment Leo's skills as a ski instructor which I'd assumed meant they were friends. Evidently not.

"Ladies, right this way," a high school-aged boy said with a gesture to follow him as we walked in.

Wells and I wandered behind him to the booth where Bel and Leo sat, one on each side of the table. Wells took a seat by Bel, so I swallowed down my nerves and lowered onto the bouncy red vinyl next to Leo.

Leo turned to me. "Sorry you had to see that."

I raised my eyebrows in question, as if to say *what could you possibly mean?* But before I could actually say the words, she spoke again.

"Jonas Bauer and I don't get along."

"Oh."

Wells chuckled from across the table. "That's putting it lightly."

"Not my fault, that's for sure," Leo harrumphed with crossed arms, then uncrossed them and took a sip from the water in front of her.

"Hey Mia, so glad you could come. Sorry about... all this." Bel smiled sweetly and waved her hands to encompass the table, evidently meaning Leo, and Jonas, and who knew what else.

"Thanks for having me." Or, I hoped I'd be thankful.

Leo grumbled audibly.

"I'm shaking it off. Three. Two. One." She closed her eyes, blew out a breath, then opened them to look straight into mine. There were those Morrison blues again. "I'm fine. Everything's fine. So tell us your story, Mia."

"Leo! You can't just demand someone's life story like that." Bel shook her head.

"That's pretty much what she did to me..." Wells said, dipping a chip into a small salsa bowl.

I took a moment to appreciate that there were four small bowls and a little carafe of salsa. While I wasn't much of a germaphobe, I appreciated not having to have a communal dip bowl of salsa. I'd only ever been in with Kai, and he didn't like salsa, so I'd never tuned in to the fact that they did that.

"It's fine. The quick version is I had my son Kai about a year after my last surviving relative and my guardian at the time, my grandfather, passed away. The man who fathered Kai left us when Kai was born, and has since been incarcerated for all kinds of fun stuff like distribution of illicit substances and other things that will keep him in jail for a few decades. I got my degrees, somehow got the librarian job here, and we moved into the apartment under Danny's house a little over a year ago."

It all came rushing out in a rote, emotionless kind of way. I didn't feel much emotion for Mason or his leaving me and Kai, nor did I feel the sting of my grandfather's death the way I had the first few years, but laying bare my life wasn't something I did often. Though I'd done it with Danny not too long ago, so I'd had practice lately.

Wells' mouth hung open a moment before she snapped it shut.

Bel chimed in before anyone else. "You got your undergrad and graduate degree while being a single mom?"

I pressed my lips together in a thin smile and nodded. "Yep."

Next to me, Leo began what I could only describe as giggling. I suspected she didn't do a lot of giggling both based on the bit I knew about her, and the aghast expressions on Wells' and Bel's faces.

"She's lost it." Bel shook her head.

"Care to share what about Mia's life story just knocked you off your rocker?" Wells asked.

I tucked my hands under my thighs and worked to ignore the flush as Leo *kept* laughing. Finally, probably a full minute later, which elapsed in a weird kind of emotional slow motion where each breath I took brought me a bit closer to feeling like I might lose my lunch, Leo set a hand on my arm, leaned down to capture my eyes, and spoke.

"I'm not and never would laugh at your life. You are an astounding human being and I am so happy you're here with us. I'm laughing because I have had a few moments lately where I've thought *man, my life is hard* or something like that, and hearing you say what you just said throws my miniscule problems into sharp relief."

I blinked, absorbing her words.

"I'm sorry, Mia. I shouldn't have laughed. Please know I was laughing at myself and how utterly ridiculous I am." Leo squeezed my arm for emphasis, then let go.

"You really are amazing. I can't imagine how hard it must have been to go through college and raise a kid like Kai. He's so sweet," Bel added.

"Thank you. I don't look back and think of it as hard, even though I won't pretend it wasn't. What I can say is that I'm really glad to be here in Silverton, and I'm happy to be here with you tonight."

We all smiled at each other for a moment before the waiter came to take orders. I sat closest to where she stood, so I went first. As I watched the other women order, a sense of amazement clung to me. Whatever I expected, the warm welcome I received by these three alarmingly beautiful women wasn't it.

Clearly, it'd been too long since I'd spent time with

other adult human women outside of work. Did I expect them to laugh at me like high schoolers or ignore me like... what, a cliché mean girl from a B movie?

"So Wells, catch us up on you. When is Liam proposing?"

I laughed at Leo's bold question and Wells' reddening face in response. Just like that, they'd folded me in, and a sense of joy I'd not had in years filled me to the brim.

CHAPTER TWENTY-SEVEN

Danny

I woke to the sound of the door shutting.

I'd carried Kai to his bed over an hour ago. He'd passed out on the couch next to me while we watched our movie, bellies full of pizza and brownies. The strangest sense of peace had settled in my chest as I carried his body, all elbows and knees, to his space-themed room. He woke as I set him down and ran to the bathroom. After a few minutes, he returned, toothpaste foam at one corner of his mouth.

"Thanks for a fun night, buddy." I ruffled his hair as he snuggled into his bed.

"You're welcome."

His eyes were already drooping as I tucked the covers up next to him. As I stepped over a pile of discarded clothes and a tower of Legos, I wondered at the feeling still filling me.

"Love you, Danny," a drowsy voice said from the darkened room.

I hesitated at the door, wondering if he was even conscious. "Love you too, Kai."

And after I said it, I knew that was it. The feeling. The peace. I loved this kid and wanted to be around him. I'd never felt strongly about a kid like this, maybe because I'd never had one in my life that meant something to me. My siblings hadn't given me nieces and nephews yet, and my jobs didn't put me in the path of little kids very often. The little ones at storytime were cute enough, but I didn't actually interact with them all that much.

But Kai had been coming around my door for about a year now. I'd seen him happy, sad, sick, excited, disappointed, and everything in between. I loved him, just like that, without warning.

"Hey, how'd it go?"

Mia's smooth voice interrupted my thoughts as I straightened on the couch. I'd slumped down there and decided to sleep since I normally turned in early.

"It was great. We had fun. I took him to bed about an hour ago though I'm pretty sure he fell asleep about a half-hour before that." I patted the cushion next to me. "Come sit."

She set her purse on top of a bookshelf just inside the room and rubbed her hands together as she approached. Good grief, she was lovely. Her dress highlighted the perfection that was her skin, her long hair twisting in loose curls down her back, the shape of her. Her dark eyes sparkled, though I could see they were tired.

She plunked down next to me, but not as close as I might have wanted, though there was no amount of closeness I didn't want with Mia. I wanted it all.

We sat in quiet, the space silent except for the low hum of the air conditioner outside. The day hadn't been all that hot compared to what it would be in another month, but the night hadn't cooled as it normally would have. Must be rain coming, which would be great since Utah got so little rain.

"So, it's Bel?"

The heaviness in the room, the stillness of her body, spelled it out for me, but I couldn't offer her more without knowing what she was asking for sure. "You mean…"

"Who you were hung up on for all those years." She beat me to the punch.

"Yes. She moved here when I was eight. We were pretty much best friends from then on, until the summer before senior year of high school. We reconnected in college and dated for a few weeks before we realized it wasn't going to work."

Her brows pinched slightly in the middle of her fore-head, and her mouth turned down. Not quite a frown, but not the usual sweet smile that played there. I wanted to kiss the expression from her lips. I wanted to shake her.

I dropped my head to catch her eye. "I'm over Bel, Mia. I told you that before, and I meant it. I've been over her for years, but I didn't realize it until last fall when we finally talked and cleared the air. I am thankful for who she was to me, and I'm super happy for her and Jamie. I don't want her."

Her chest rose and fell visibly, like her breath came hard and fast in a way that didn't match our cozy scene on the couch with the sun dimming the sky as it set on this longest day of the year. Her lips parted, and I almost had to close my eyes against the desire to tell her the truth.

The truth that I only wanted her.

The truth that I'd never wanted anyone like I wanted her.

The truth that I loved her.

"I don't mean to make this a big deal. It just caught me off guard. I kind of wish you'd told me—given me a heads up so I wouldn't have felt so blindsided. But I see how in love with her fiancé she is, and I believe you when you say you're over her." She brought her knees up to her chest and wrapped her arms around them.

"I'm sorry. I should've let you know. I didn't realize it'd come up, though I guess I should've anticipated that."

She pressed her pink lips together and nodded, still holding herself in reserve, not even giving me a hand to hold. I fought against the impulse to haul her to me and cover her, smother her with my wanting. Not an attractive thought, not a good move, but man, did I want to.

And maybe I hadn't been clear enough. Maybe I let her think I didn't feel much for her. I didn't press things physically between us because I honestly didn't know how to manage that. She couldn't come to my place. I didn't want to mess things up by pushing and having her ask me to leave so Kai wouldn't be confused, or even because she didn't want me that way.

Flat out, I was scared of her rejection, which only circled back to creating shame for not being bold and confident.

I hadn't done all this with anyone yet. I didn't know what I was doing and feared rejection at this point would finish me off. But part of this confusion, and part of her hurt, which she wasn't verbalizing but I could see on her face, was because she didn't realize it wasn't just that I *didn't* want Bel. It was that I *did* want her, regardless of Bel or anyone else. None of them mattered. Only she mattered.

"I want you, Mia. I'm afraid I haven't made that clear. I don't care about Bel—not that way, and I haven't for years. I care about you. I—" I stopped short of the real feeling, the full reality of what I felt. I couldn't make that confession just yet... not yet. "I think you're amazing, and I want to be with you all the time. I want you to believe me, so please tell me what I can do to make sure you do."

She bloomed then—straightened her legs and dropped her hands to her lap, her chin lifting and her demeanor lightening.

I closed the distance between us. "Do you understand what I'm saying?"

Her deep brown eyes stared back into mine for a moment before she reached out and hooked a hand at the back of my neck. She pulled me to her and our lips met. We'd shared countless kisses in the last few months, but this one felt like something more—hungrier, wilder, almost rough.

We pressed closer to each other, lips crushed together. I tilted her head, adjusting the angle so we fit and connected deeply, all sensation. My hand fisted in her silken hair, a fire in me burning hotter than I'd ever let it. My lips moved along her jaw, behind her ear, down the column of her neck. My breaths came fast, each inhale full of the scent of her.

And she responded in kind. Her hand moved from my neck to my shoulders, then slid along my chest. If I hadn't been otherwise occupied, I might've swallowed my tongue at the feel of her exploration. She clutched my shirt at my sides and let out a groan that served to melt my mind.

"Danny." She nuzzled into my neck as I kissed along her shoulder and dragged a hand down her spine. "Danny."

And then, like lightning, the realization hit. That wasn't *Danny* as in she was lost in the moment but *Danny, stop*. I did, immediately, pulling back so abruptly, she teetered where she sat. I searched her face, readying for the worst—the rejection I'd been bracing for all along. The very reason I'd kept a little distance between us, always pulling back before we could get to even this place.

There it was. On her face. Her lovely dark brows pinched, her eyes wide. "I think we should—"

"Come to dinner with my family." It came out, interrupting the let-down she'd no doubt been about to hand me. I couldn't bear it, couldn't hear it. I knew she wouldn't say no to meeting my parents, even though that was a step forward for a relationship. Her kindness would keep her from saying no, and I evidently embraced the wretched part of me willing to capitalize on that.

"What?"

"My family's having a big dinner. My parents are only in town another month and a half, until right after the Sommerfest, so they... anyway, I'd love for them to meet you and Kai." I stood up, pulled a hand through my hair, and backed up a few steps, knocking into the overstuffed chair on the way.

"Of course we'll come. But you don't have to leave..."

She came after me, but I'd already made it to the hallway, already slipped my sandals on my feet and grabbed the keys I'd left on a hook. "No, I've gotta run. But I'll see you Sunday, yeah?

Bewildered, she answered as I practically sprinted out the door. "Yeah."

CHAPTER TWENTY-EIGHT

Mia

What just happened?

Danny shut the door and had probably already settled in at home before I fully came out of the haze his kisses had created. I'd said his name, both in supplication and exclamation. I'd said it because I wanted him to know I wanted him too.

Then he disappeared.

In retrospect, I wouldn't have been surprised if he had apparated like a character in *Harry Potter*—just disappeared from right there in the living room and reappeared somewhere else—anywhere I wasn't, I guessed. But no, first he tossed out the invitation to his parents' house and then bam, gone, no more glorious lips and hands at work in a way I downright longed for.

Needed, it seemed.

I exhaled slowly, not sure I could make sense of him or

even the night as a whole, so I resolved to allow myself some autopilot activity before bed. Clean the kitchen, maybe fold Kai's laundry, then surrender to bed and hope my mind wouldn't spend the night obsessing over why he ran away just as I was about to ask him to stay.

No such luck, I realized as I took in the kitchen. No dishes in the sink. No empty pizza box anywhere to be seen. A tin of brownies covered with plastic wrap and tucked in the corner of the cutting board. The kitchen floor that looked suspiciously clean considering a six-year-old had eaten not only pizza but made brownies hours before.

Clean counters. Spill-free table.

He'd cleaned my kitchen.

"Aarrrghgh." I let it out, the very real frustration Danny conjured in me every time we were together these days.

He set me on fire, then left me to burn on my own. And I always had a moment after the fact, when I wanted to get mad at him for being a tease or at the very least being unwilling to talk to me about being more physical, but I'd find something like this. Something adorable and thoughtful and downright dangerous to my ability to keep my feelings to myself.

Fine. *Fine.* Laundry then.

I flipped off the light in the kitchen and made my way to the living room, wishing the evening was cold enough to justify a fire in the fireplace. I welcomed summer gladly, but I needed consoling, and nothing like a blanket and a fire and menial tasks did that.

Then I spied the basket, formerly sprouting clean and unfolded laundry in all directions.

My jaw dropped. He'd folded Kai's laundry.

Danny had taken care of my son, gotten him to sleep, cleaned my kitchen, and folded my laundry. Well, thankfully not *my* laundry or that might've been a little embar-rassing at this point, especially since he kept running away before he ever saw my unmentionables on me much less in a laundry basket, but still.

He'd folded my son's laundry.

I slumped into the couch and succumbed to the tears that had threatened since earlier tonight when I discovered it was Bel Paxton who Danny had loved all those years.

I believed him when he said he'd moved on. I believed she had no interest in Danny. I really had no concerns that they were anything but friends, if that, at this point. But I felt so *silly*. I felt so new. Leo said it like she assumed I knew, and she obviously knew we were dating, so she must have thought Danny had told me.

He should have. That's where some of the hurt came from. Some of the nagging fear. I'd been left once—not for another woman, but still. I didn't want to get more and more invested in someone with an unavailable heart.

That thought paired with the way he held us at bay, so to speak, had me scrambling. And he allayed my fears completely—I knew he'd tell me if he still had feelings for Bel. He would. Danny was honest, and I trusted that. But he *still* kept me at a distance. And just when I decided to take a chance and move us forward, he jumped. *Literally*. He jumped up and ran away, tossing the invite to his parents' house as some kind of smokescreen.

I crushed the heels of my palms into my eyes and sucked in a watery breath. I didn't want to cry about this. I didn't want to feel like crying at all. I'd had a great night with new friends, all of whom I really enjoyed. Despite the blip about Bel and Danny, I'd genuinely loved my time with them and looked forward to the next time we got together. I got a glimpse of real, adult friendship and I wanted more.

And Danny had done everything and more I could have wanted tonight. He'd showed caring for Kai came naturally to him, and he cared for me, too. He'd taken some of the million things I do as a single mom and he'd lightened the load. He did that constantly, now that I thought about it.

He did everything but love me physically or say the words.

"He invited you to meet his parents. That's something," I said to the empty room. I needed to focus on that because that meant something. I knew it did, and even though I didn't understand the timing or why he wouldn't talk to me about it instead of staging his disappearing act, I could recognize it wasn't a step back.

I fell asleep that night with Danny on my mind, much like I had many other nights. Before I knew it, the weekend had flown and the time for dinner with the Morrison family arrived. Danny texted on Saturday with the time he'd pick us up on Sunday. No other word. No apology for escaping. No flirty texts or asking what we were up to.

So, when he knocked on my door exactly when he said he would, I had no idea what to expect. Would I find the sweet, solicitous Danny who seemed to fold in perfectly with me and Kai, or would it be the runner?

"Come on in for a sec. Kai's just picking up his room, which he promised to do earlier but then confessed he hadn't done." Entirely unnecessary information, but nerves had choked out any ability to be calm and smooth and left me frazzled.

"No problem."

His subdued smile told me he didn't feel comfortable, which immediately created a pit in my stomach. I tried to ignore it as he stepped inside and shut the door. He reached out to me, then dropped his hand and tucked it into his pocket.

I couldn't stand it. Not when we were going to meet his parents, which I hadn't even allowed myself to get nervous about, but I knew I couldn't avoid the feeling for too much longer.

Instead of words, I stepped to him. Relief shot through me at the widening smile as I leaned my head to his chest and wrapped my arms around him. "Is everything... good?"

A little puff of air into my hair where he exhaled, then what felt like a small kiss there on the top of my head. "Yeah, I'm okay. Are you?"

I pulled back to look at him but kept my arms around him, unwilling to sever the connection before we made some progress. "I don't know. I'm nervous to meet your family, but more than that, I feel upset. I don't know why you left like you did the other night, and I don't know what to do about it. So I'm asking, rather than feeling weird the entire time I'm at this dinner with a bunch of people I don't know but want desperately to like me."

His shoulders sagged, and he hugged me tight. "Ah, Mia. I've messed this up completely."

CHAPTER TWENTY-NINE

Danny

Her face held the question, but all I could see was this woman coming to me asking me to explain why I'd been such a spazz and run away from her when all I wanted was to stay.

Stay. Stay. Stay.

Stay for good. Not leave. Never leave.

And here she was, bold enough to ask when she'd been left before. I'd been so selfish and stupid, so cowardly and insanely misguided in my thinking, and her open questioning of my idiocy brought that into sharp relief.

"I'm sorry," I said again, shaking my head in frustration.

"It's... it's okay. Or, I think it is. I guess I'm not totally sure what you mean so if you could possibly tell me a bit more what you're saying, that would help."

Red rose to her cheeks, and she began to pull back a bit before I caught her hands at my waist and held her there.

My heart threatened to beat out of my chest as I prepared to explain, pressing her hands to me, willing her to stay close and imbue me with some of her bravery. "I've been stupid. I've been... scared, honestly, and I hate saying that because I don't think that's the kind of man you want."

The change in her face barely registered before she crushed herself to me and held me tight. I hugged her back, savoring her closeness and praying this meant she understood, in some small way, what I felt for her, even though I was nothing but a confusing wreck when it came to expressing myself. I sucked in a shuddering breath, her warmth and the silken brush of her hair against my cheek both comforting and thrilling.

"Let's go. I'm starving." Kai skipped down the hall, right past us, and pulled open the door, evidently unconcerned about our embrace.

Mia tightened her grip, then let go and backed away completely, ducking her head as she wiped her eyes. Was she crying?

"Hey, let's stay—"

"We should go. But I want to come back here after, and put Kai to bed, and keep talking about this, okay?"

"Absolutely."

I'd never been someone whose parents embarrassed him. My parents were awesome. They were loving and supportive and challenging and a little much sometimes, but generally, I loved them.

Except tonight.

Tonight, I maybe didn't love them like I thought I did. They evidently set out to humiliate me and test my ability to stay quiet as my mom trotted out every possible "wasn't he sweet?" story.

For example, the one where *Danny lined up all of his GI Joes and made them sleeping bags out of toilet paper that he sewed together with yarn—wasn't he sweet?*

Or, *Danny grew his hair out to be shoulder-length in fifth grade, and cried when he got it cut and they told him it was just a little too short to donate to cancer survivors—wasn't he sweet?*

And for good measure, *Danny scrapbooked everything he and Bel did from the time he met her until... oh.*

YEAH. That one was just great. I hoped Mia took me at my word and believed I was over Bel, but reinforcing my obsession-level love for her via my scrapbooking habits was less than ideal or timely. Fortunately, my mom realized it and rapidly changed the subject.

Leo also had my back, bless her. The conversation switched and Liam, Wells, my parents, and Bel and Jamie chatted away about something while I kept my attention glued to Mia.

Leo leaned over to Mia and said, "You know I think all that devotion to Bel made him ready to recognize when he found someone he really cared for."

Of course then I had to pretend I hadn't heard Leo or I would have gone up in flames of embarrassment, but she was absolutely right. All that time loving Bel had prepared me to love Mia. I felt more sure of that than anything I'd ever felt before.

And I'd tell Mia that. Soon. Maybe tonight, if I could summon the courage.

"So Kai, what do you like to do for fun?" Liam asked from across the table.

He and Wells sat at the far end next to my da. Jamie

and Bel were across from me and Mia, then came Kai, then Leo, and Grandpa Will on the end. I wondered if the set up made Leo feel her singleness more acutely, but she actually seemed to be in a good mood.

"I like sports. Swimming. Reading. Skiing in the winter, of course." He wiggled his brows, and everyone laughed. If there existed a cuter kid, I'd have a hard time believing it.

"Sounds like a good mix," Jamie put in.

"It is."

"He's picking up skiing very fast, aren't you Kai?" Leo turned to him and held up a hand.

Kai's face burned with a blush at Leo's words, but he met her hand with his and gave her the biggest, mooniest smile, and I had to reach over and ruffle his hair.

"Only because you're the best teacher, Miss Leo."

More than one audible *aww* sounded around the table.

"Oh man, this one's a charmer." Grandpa Will laughed.

"Kai is Leo's biggest fan," Mia explained.

Kai just nodded and finished chewing some salad as a few other comments sounded. Then, "Yeah. I'm her biggest fan, but I'm also going to marry her when I'm bigger."

Everyone chuckled, and my ma clutched her hands to her heart like the moment hurt to watch. The sparkle in her eye told me she found the exchange exceptionally endearing, which wasn't unusual, but I knew at some point soon, I'd be on the receiving end of a heart to heart from Alice Morrison.

I smiled at her and nodded, already acquiescing to the motherly advice and insights she'd no doubt offer very soon. She tipped her head to the side and squeezed her eyes together for a quick moment, a gesture she often made during my childhood. My chest warmed at the sight of her so happy, here presiding over the growing family. No longer just four kids, but now four kids, two women who'd be joining the family soon, and hopefully another if I had any say. That, and a little boy who had no grandparents, or aunts and uncles, and who'd be so very loved here at this table.

Excitement ran up my throat and nearly choked me. I wanted that. I wanted this picture, for good.

"And Mia? Tell us about your family."

Da worked to draw Mia out, though she wasn't exactly shy, but she clearly deferred to me and the others before speaking up. I could only imagine how overwhelming my family could be, especially now that we'd added Bel and Wells.

Mia responded, giving details about how her parents had met when her father was stationed in the Philippines. I dipped my head to whisper in Mia's ear. "Sorry they're in your business. They just want to get to know you, but I know they can be a lot."

She patted my leg, and her eyes caught mine. A swooping sensation flashed through me, and if I'd been standing, I would have stumbled. I wished I could read what she'd written there in that gaze. My body seemed to recognize the look packed a punch, though my mind scrambled to understand.

CHAPTER THIRTY

Mia

Danny's attention shifted around my face, studying me, and the intensity there made me lose my breath.

"I don't mind," I managed, my voice breathy.

He stared back at me, and if we'd been alone, nothing would have kept me from showing how much I felt for him. *Nothing.* I wouldn't let him run away.

He'd started to explain himself when Kai burst in earlier and we left the apartment. But I'd said what I wanted to say, and he'd responded beautifully. Not cagey or angry by my confrontation, but penitent. I didn't fully understand what he meant, but I knew his frustration was aimed at himself. As enjoyable as this evening had been, and it really had been lovely to be with his family and get to know some of the members I hadn't met yet, I couldn't wait to get back to that conversation.

It felt like something big was coming, and I wanted it.

"Good," he said, the word low and rough.

That sound, that look, that face... I exhaled slowly through my nose, feeling my belly clench at his nearness.

Leo burst into laughter next to me and shook me from the Daniel Morrison forcefield. I took another bite of the delicious grilled vegetables and watched the scene unfold like it had all evening.

Leo's laugh cut off when she spoke. "You're insane if you think Bayern Munich isn't winning next year. They'll fire the coach and—"

"This'll be good. Go ahead and tell us how we're all wrong about everything." Liam cut in, though his tone sounded playful rather than genuinely irritated.

Leo shot him a glare, though I didn't see much playfulness there. "I will. *I will* tell you, because you are. I'm the life-long Bundesliga fan. You and Danny are just posers."

Danny held up his hands. "I will not dispute that you got me into European soccer."

I smiled at him, appreciating his peacemaker tendencies. It didn't surprise me he tried to smooth things over between the two siblings.

"Correct." Leo nodded at Danny in approval.

"Oh whatever. I started watching Euro leagues long before you even knew what they were. There's no shame in admitting I had a hand in—"

"You can pretend you inspired my love, but you'd be wrong," Leo argued.

Liam sighed dramatically and seemed liked he might respond, but Wells' hand grasped his wrist and she turned to him. Something in her look or that touch must've stopped him, because he clamped his mouth shut and turned his attention to his food.

"We all love soccer. It's great. Why is this a thing?" Jamie asked.

I watched as Bel bit her lip and ducked her head while Leo huffed next to me. Grandpa Will brought the odd little volley to a close.

"I've loved the leagues since I was a kid. I taught your dad, and he taught you all. You were raised playing the game, so makes sense you like to watch it. I'll take full credit for developing this family's devotion, and we can blame your mother's half-German roots for the devotion to the Bavarian team."

He raised a brow at Leo who dropped her head to his shoulder in a sweet, warm way I wouldn't have expected.

"Well said, Will," Alice said with a broad smile. If the bickering bothered her, she didn't show it, though she did seem relieved to have it come to an end.

"Is Jonas a fan?" William, Danny's dad and the second William Morrison at the table, asked.

The energy rolling off Leo changed from irritation to what I'd call fury. Not a surprise after what I'd observed when I saw them speaking before dinner on Friday, but still confusing, particularly considering the warmth with which others had spoken of Jonas this evening.

"He doesn't strike me as someone who's a fan of anything other than himself." Leo scooted one remaining piece of her grilled chicken around on her plate.

Liam, as I'd come to expect based on the evening's conversation, countered her. "He actually grew up with the striker. He's a huge fan, never misses watching a game."

Leo cocked her head to the side, frustration on her face, but I could swear she seemed intrigued more than anything else. "Seriously?"

Liam nodded. "Yep. It's a whole thing for him. We had

a long conversation about it a while back when I told him I was going to meet Danny at *Craic* to watch a game. I invited him along, but he declined."

"Shocking," Leo mumbled.

"I know you have your reasons you think you dislike him, but he is a human. He's got likes and dislikes, fandoms and interests, just like everyone else. Right, Wells?"

Leo cut in.

"I have legitimate reasons. He's slowly but surely working his way into every part of our family business and sooner or later, he's going to make a move for it, and I'm the only one who won't be acting surprised." Her cheeks flushed deep red.

"Come on. He's nearly single-handedly saved the family business. I'm not going to fault him for being a bit stern and unusual if he gets the job done. He's worth it. Right, Wells?" He looked to Wells and seemed to ignore Leo's unimpressed stare.

"Um, well, can I abstain from contributing to this discussion?" Her smile appeared uneasy as her gaze surveyed the table, most closely looking at Jamie, Bel, and then Leo.

"He's not all bad," Bel offered uneasily.

Leo scoffed. "How can you of all people say that?"

William cleared his throat. "All right, let's forget about all that. Who's ready for dessert?"

Danny took my hand as Kai trotted out the Morrisons' front door.

"Mia, do you have a moment?" Alice asked just before we left. We'd already said our goodbyes.

"Of course. Danny, can you make sure Kai gets buckled?"

He nodded, shot a look to his mom, and left me there just inside the Morrisons' home. The rest of the family still chatted in the living room since no one else had a six-year-old to get to bed.

Nerves fizzled through my chest as I studied Alice's face.

"I just wanted you to know how precious your son is. You've done an amazing job with him. He said please and thank you, and he's just lovely." She touched her hand to my wrist and squeezed, all her motherly warmth and kindness just shining off her.

"Thank you. I can say the same about yours."

She chuckled. "I'm glad you think so. He seems to feel strongly for you."

The crow's feet around her shining eyes accentuated her beauty—clearly, this woman had done her fair share of smiling, and the years had made her all the more beautiful for it.

"I hope so," I said lamely. I couldn't wait to get home and talk with Danny, but now that we were leaving, I felt sad to say goodbye. "Thank you again for such a great evening. I—I know Kai loved it too."

"Of course, honey. Come back and see us again soon."

With that, I let myself out, longing, hope, and a painful kind of joy swirling in my chest.

CHAPTER THIRTY-ONE

Danny

We drove to the tune of Kai's excitement ringing from the back seat.

"Now Miss Leo knows I'm going to marry her."

"That blackberry cobbler was amazing. Mom, you should learn to make that. It was so good. I'll help you."

"I should probably start watching soccer more so I can know what everyone's talking about."

I kept quiet, letting Mia respond when his comments called for it, but this one had me saying, "When the season starts, we can watch together. I'll help you get up to speed."

I smiled over at Mia, only to find her staring at the dash, weighty thoughts filling her—or, I assumed, because her whole demeanor had changed as we drove the short five-minute drive from my parents' to our house.

Our house. I liked the sound of it. Too bad it actually meant two different living spaces in one building.

As soon as I parked in my garage, Kai started in, and I had to smile.

"Please, Danny."

Mia broke from her intense stare-down with the dashboard. "Kai honey, Danny is not going to carry you every time—"

"I'm happy to." I touched my hand to her shoulder to reassure her.

Ever since we came back late from a baseball tournament Kai had in the valley and I carried him to bed, he asked for me to repeat the performance of personal chauffeur. I couldn't be sure what he liked about it, but I didn't mind. I'd gotten to know him well in the last year, and especially the last three months since Mia and I had seen each other several times a week. Having him trust me to tuck him in, or even just deliver him to his bedroom for the evening routine, felt like a gift.

I trudged down the little sidewalk between my garage and their front door. Mia unlocked, and I took Kai to his room. He affected a dead-weight posture, though his continual sleepy chatter confirmed he hadn't passed out like he had other times.

"I like your family," he said quietly as I flopped him on the bed.

"They like you too." I ruffled his hair. "Go brush your teeth and get your jammies on and I'll read to you."

I moved to Mia who stood just outside Kai's door and kissed her cheek. "I'll tuck him in and be right there."

She nodded and went to kiss Kai as he brushed his teeth, then disappeared down the hallway into the kitchen. Kai scampered back, all ready for bed in Spiderman pajamas as usual. All through reading to him, I thought of what I'd say to Mia, and wondered what'd been on her mind in the car. Maybe she'd found my family abhorrent and couldn't wait to dump me.

I didn't really worry about that. My family was amazing, even with Leo and Liam's bickering. But still. She had something on her mind, and I needed to be as honest as I could with her.

I wanted to tell her everything, but I'd been so foolish. I'd been so scared, and that wasn't something I could just turn off after years of running from moments just like this.

Finished with the book, I set it aside on Kai's bookshelf and pulled his comforter up to his chin as he snuggled down into the bed. His eyes had grown heavy. I ruffled his hair.

"Goodnight, buddy. Thanks for coming to dinner tonight." I moved to the door and shut off his light, both eager and dreading what came next.

Mia sat at her small kitchen table, a steaming mug of tea in front of her, her gaze vacant. She didn't look up when I walked in, so she must've been circling whatever she'd had on her mind in the car.

I pulled up the chair next to her and sat, then ducked to move into her sightline. Her eyes fluttered, and she smiled—small, but not tight like when she was upset, so that seemed good.

"Everything okay?" I hated to ask—to start a conversation that way, but she'd gone somewhere I couldn't access and I needed her to talk.

"Did he go down okay?"

I nodded. "Yes. He knocked out before I turned the light off."

Usually, I remembered to report back on how things went with Kai, whether I had him to myself or we went on a little adventure or I tucked him in. She monitored everything about him, and it'd been the two of them for so long, I understood she wanted to hear. It wasn't in a controlling way, but just that motherly tendency to hoard data on her child. It only made me love her more. "He also said he liked my family."

A small half-smile curved her lips. "I could tell he did. I did too. Thank you for inviting us to go with you."

"I'm glad you came. I know they can be... a lot."

We shared a grin and then she agreed. "They can, but having met Leo, I knew what to expect there. I guess I was surprised by how much she and your oldest brother fight..."

I rolled my eyes. "Aren't we all? The weirdest part is they've always been like that. They're seven years apart and they fight like you'd expect Liam and Jamie to fight. I think it's because they are actually a lot alike, though I'm not sure either of them sees it that way."

She picked up her mug of tea, then spoke into the tendrils of steam still rising from the drink. "And you're the peacemaker."

"Sometimes. Or Ma, or Da. Bel has been in the past, and Jamie when we were kids and now that he's around again. Wells obviously has a calming influence on Liam. Now we just need to partner off Leo and find someone who can wrangle all her rage."

She burst out laughing. "Her rage?"

"Or whatever it is. I don't know. I love her, but whoever she ends up with, she'll need someone who's ready for her... *all* of her."

She moved to pour me a mug of tea and set it in front of me, then sat back in her chair.

"So..." she prompted, though her soft voice sounded kind and lovely.

"So, as I said, I'm a coward." Good grief, how I wished I could transport myself to a time when that wasn't what I thought of myself. When that wasn't how I acted—the title I'd earned.

She studied me a moment. "You said you weren't the kind of man I wanted."

Inwardly, I flinched. Hearing her say those words came like a blow, even if she was quoting me.

"I wish that wasn't true. But I'm afraid I've been acting in a way that can't possibly be what you want. You don't want someone scared. And I'm sorry I've been that way with you. I don't mean to be. I never plan to run away. I just..."

I pulled at the back of my neck, sure my cheeks were flagged with red. I ran out of words, the fear crawling up my throat as I sat there at her kitchen table, looking into her dark brown eyes.

"Please, Danny. Please talk to me."

The pleading in her voice had me pushing back the fear, busting past the shame for being so afraid, and going for it. "I like you, Mia, and that's putting it mildly. I *want* you. Only you. I've never wanted anyone like I want you."

A slow smile spread across her features, starting at her eyes and moving to those perfect lips. "Don't you know? I want you too."

A rough breath escaped, and rather than say any more words, I stood and pulled her out of her chair, crushing her to me. I held her pressed there, one hand around her back, the other at her head. Her hands clutched around my waist, and I relished the pressure of her against me.

"I hoped you did. Thought maybe you did. But the only other time I've felt anything like this, it didn't go so well. And you've got so much going on, I just.. it's hard to believe you'd choose to be with someone like me."

Her dark eyes glittered back, and her brows pinched as she shook her head slowly. "Danny, you are... you're amazing. I hate that your experience with Bel made you think you're not, especially because I know she thinks you are—"

"I'm not concerned about what Bel thinks of me." The hard edge in my voice made clear I didn't want Bel to be a part of this conversation.

She set a hand on my chest, right over my sprinting heart. "Okay. Good. But you have to know that I think you are kind and generous and sweet and the best man I've ever dated, that's for sure."

I swallowed, thrill and unease chasing each other down. "Didn't you tell me you only ever dated Mason and now me?"

A grin split her face, and some of the tension in my chest eased at the sight.

"That is technically true. But just because my ex is a convict doesn't mean you shouldn't enjoy that high praise."

She pushed against me playfully, and I leaned into the pressure.

I chuckled. "That's good to know."

She sobered then, inspecting me closely, her hands still pressed to my pecs and my arms still wrapped around her, resting low on her back. "So you've been running away because you've been afraid I don't feel the same way? Haven't I been showing you my feelings—every time we talk or... kiss?"

The deluge of heat came like someone had poured red paint over my head—flushing down to my toes immediately. Now or never, I supposed.

"You have. It was definitely partly the rejection. And then there's Kai... I haven't known how to navigate—or, how you want to handle things with him. But, uh... also because I've never done this before."

CHAPTER THIRTY-TWO

Mia

I narrowed my focus, searching his face.

What did that mean?

"You mean, you've never had a relationship?"

He pressed his lips together and tried to take a step back —I could feel all his energy wanting to make space, but he was trying to communicate, even if it clearly pained him, and I wasn't about to let his poor instincts lead him to running again. I grabbed at handfuls of his shirt and held him in place.

He cleared his throat. His blue eyes bore into mine like he wished I could read his thoughts so he wouldn't have to speak out loud.

"That's true. I've never had a relationship. But I've also... uh. I've never *been* with anyone. Before."

His gaze darted around the room, anywhere but to me. I watched him flounder, clearly so uncomfortable, but I held him fast to me. I bit my bottom lip in an effort not to let myself smile, because I felt it coming. I knew something insane like a giggle was about to emerge, and that would give him the entirely wrong message.

So I said, "Okay."

Because it was. It was entirely okay and completely amazing. All the worry and fear that'd ratcheted into my ribcage over the last few days, and especially the last few hours, slipped away, and only tenderness and adoration remained. And the book lover in me had to appreciate this moment too—I had my own personal Jamie Fraser.

Back in the moment, evidently that one word had done nothing to quell his fears. He attempted to step back, but still, I held him close.

"Mia, I—"

"Can you listen, Danny? Can you listen to my words and really hear me right now? What I'm going to say is important, and I want you to understand me and believe me when I say them."

His Adam's apple bobbed as he swallowed with what looked like great effort. He nodded, and widened his stance like he was bracing for whatever came next.

Could he really believe I'd reject him *now*?

"I haven't had much relationship experience either. What I had with Mason could hardly be described as a healthy relationship, though it taught me a lot about what I do and do not want, and how I do and do not want to behave with future partners. As for the physical element, I have Kai, so obviously I've been with someone. I'd regret that, too, if it weren't for Kai. But I'm not worried that you haven't done those things. I realize it means we'll have some different things to work through as time goes on, but I want that."

His chest rose and fell under my hands. I shook him gently for emphasis. "I want that with you."

"You do?"

The disbelief in his voice nearly broke my heart. If I hadn't met and liked Bel, considered her a friend, even, I'd want to punch her in the solar plexus. She'd killed his confidence so handily, and yet he'd *let* her, too. He'd let himself stay in that hurt place for far too long. I understood that's what he meant when he said he'd been fearful and cowardly, though I didn't see it that way.

I leaned up on my toes and pressed my mouth to his. "I do, Danny. I want you to stop running away from me, and be with me."

He held me to him, a shuddering breath escaping before he spoke.

"You have no idea how much—" He pulled back, and his blue eyes practically glowed in their intensity. "I don't want to disappoint you."

I huffed a little then, frustration and love comingling to leave me with a strange frowny-smile. "The only thing you can do to disappoint me is keep disappearing on me, particularly when I'm about to ask you to stay with me, or tell you how I feel. Everything else, we'll figure out."

He shut his eyes, and his chest deflated in what I hoped was relief. "I can do that. I *will* do that."

My hands slid up his solid chest and linked behind his neck. I nudged the back of his head slightly, and he leaned down to capture my mouth. My eyes fluttered shut as my belly flipped at the contact, the warmth, the low, primal sound issuing from him.

"So will you stay with me tonight?"

His turn for fluttering lashes and a floundering search for words. "Uh... *tonight?*"

I chuckled at his immediate nervousness. "I'm not trying to compromise you, Daniel Morrison. I just want to spend a little more time with you, be close to you, and enjoy getting to *keep* you."

His brownish-red brows ducked low over his eyes as his hands flexed at my waist and pulled me even closer. "I'd love to."

At his words, my pulse raced. We abandoned our tea, which was my idea so that I wouldn't throttle him or beg him—I'd have something to do with my hands and lips when I needed a moment. It worked okay, though now, I knew exactly what I wanted my hands to do.

And finally, I could let them.

I took his hand and pulled him with me to the living room, then dropped to the couch and he followed. No need to rush now that I understood him—we could take our time, and I didn't have to worry he'd run from me again.

I inhaled a long, deep breath, and could have sworn he did the same. Another beat. Then we crashed together, lips and bodies meeting in an electric crush.

His hands were in my hair while I traced his strong shoulders and smoothed down the line of him, relishing the dip of his triceps, the rounded curve of his biceps, even the bend of his arm. I'd never found an elbow attractive, but somehow, Danny Morrison's was doing it for me.

"Your hair's so soft. And your skin..." His low whisper shimmered on my skin as he traced my neck with kisses. "Mia... your skin makes me hurt with how much I want to touch every part of you."

He slid his hands from my hair down my back and hauled me to him so I straddled him, bracing my hands on his chest, which was no hardship because he had a truly spectacular chest.

"I want to be close to you all the time. I feel like I'm going insane sometimes because all I can think about is you."

His rough confession sent a shiver through me. The switch had definitely flipped for Danny. He didn't seem to be holding anything back—not his affection, not his words, and *oh*, how delectable. He might not have had much experience, but his ability to stir me into a frenzy couldn't be doubted.

I didn't want to leave him hanging, though he seemed confident enough and I could barely summon words as his hands and lips explored.

"I know what you mean," I said, my voice breathy and high. I might have been a poetry lover, but the words didn't come naturally to me.

"You're so smart, so sweet." He traced up the other side of my neck with his nose and breath, placed a kiss just below my ear. "When I saw you on the trail, I thought you were the most beautiful thing I'd ever seen."

I let out a sharp laugh and pulled him close with every limb, my head resting on his shoulder and our bodies pressed close. "I was a sweaty mess on the verge of a panic attack."

"I felt a little like panicking when I saw you too. Thank God I kept it together."

I let go enough to bring us face to face and dove back into a kiss—long, thorough, dizzying with heat. He matched me breath for breath, tongues and lips saying as much or more than our words.

Pressure built in my chest, everywhere, the more we pushed and pulled at each other. Our movements edged toward desperation. We'd been there on the couch, pasted together, for minutes, or hours, and it hadn't been enough—

wouldn't be until it'd been days or weeks. I couldn't get enough of him—his strength and vulnerability, his mesmerizing blue eyes, and the words he kept whispering into my skin.

"Mom?... Mom!"

Danny froze in place whereas I jumped a foot in the air. I heard Kai's voice tinged with panic coming from his room. Wide-eyed, I looked at Danny, who said "go" as I took off down the hall. Adrenaline raced through my veins as I opened his door, my body switching from the thrill of being close to Danny to the fight-response Kai's worried voice stirred in me.

"I'm here, baby."

CHAPTER THIRTY-THREE

Danny

July progressed with all the heat and frustration I'd come to expect from days spent with Mia and Kai.

Don't get me wrong. I loved spending time with them—genuinely did. But ever since we'd had our talk after dinner with my family, I had a veritable green light with her that I simply couldn't heed. After Kai woke up with a nightmare, Mia settled him down, but the spell was broken. We saw the time—after midnight—and realized in that cruel, responsible adult way that made me question my choices to do anything responsible again ever, that we both had work early the next day.

And, there was no rush.

I knew this. I felt it. I believed it. But damn, the taking it slow thing got old. In many ways, we'd been taking it slow for a year. Sure, we hadn't dated, but I'd wanted to all that time—since the first time I saw her. So this crazy little world where we both admitted to liking and wanting to be with each other, but also knowing the logistics of alone time, were tricky with Kai at home... well. Hence the frustration.

But also, we were both swamped. The anniversary celebration waited just around the corner in August, and I had been making trips to Salt Lake to *lay on the charm,* as Liam called it, with the local radio, television, and print organizations. We needed everyone out in full force with this—to get them to cover the event which would, ideally, parlay into hype going into the next ski season.

So me showing my ugly mug and being of the Morrison persuasion was supposed to make a difference. I wasn't sure it did. I definitely didn't feel equipped to talk up the resort— that was the word I'd been told to use—or answer questions, but luckily, no one wanted nitty gritty details. They wanted someone to charm them into visiting, and I could do that. The only person I knew who loved the mountain more than I did, if possible, was Leo, and even though I loved her dearly, she was not the one to be the face of the mountain to these folks. Her tendency to be blunt might not serve us well.

Things at Silver Ridge were progressing on schedule. Liam's plan to leave things to Bauer and sail off into the sunset and brew beer—okay, fine, not sail off, but leave the job he hadn't wanted for years—looked like it would happen. They'd installed one new ski lift already, and the second high-speed lift should finish before the Sommerfest. We'd be able to let people take rides up the mountain, and it'd be another great publicity element to the fest.

So I'd been in and out of town, and though I saw Mia every day, whether for a good night kiss or sharing breakfast before work, I missed her.

More and more, I could see I wanted life with her, and

by that, I wanted *all* of life. I wanted her, and I wanted Kai, and I wanted it for good.

And honestly, that still kind of freaked me out. I wished I could change that about myself—that I could more easily embrace what I wanted and not feel a sense of impending doom about it. But there it sat every time I thought of confessing how much I loved her and Kai, heavy on my chest and sticky in my throat.

So I hadn't. I'd made no confessions, and I had no plans to... I decided to wait and make sure. Make really sure she felt the same before I said it. Ideally, she'd say it first, but hoping for that might've been a bit much.

Returning to town after a long day in Salt Lake, I couldn't wait to see her. We'd planned on dinner at my house. But first, I had to get through a quick—or so I prayed —meeting with the committee planning the fest. The combination anniversary celebration and summer festival would be here in a matter of weeks, and that time would fly. We had to have everything ready and make this event count and then all hold our breath for a few months and see how the next season went and pray we'd done enough to get more people in the door and keep the lodge afloat for another year.

Man, I was glad that wasn't my job.

"All hail the conquering charmer!" Liam leaned back in his chair at the large conference table and smiled at me as I slumped into the seat next to him. He patted me on the back, and even though it drove me insane sometimes, I did love the guy.

"Let's not get too crazy," I said with a shake of my head.

He grew more and more excited as the summer months ticked by. It made sense—he stood on the cusp of leaving a job he'd wanted to ditch for at least two years that I knew of, if not more. He was about to throw himself into brewing full time, and just in time for all of the fall seasonal brews and competitions, not to mention his business partner John's schedule. I hoped he enjoyed every second, because he'd certainly earned it.

"You can admit you're the charming one, Danny." Leo smiled at me from across the table.

"Fine. I'm the charmer. Golden boy Liam over here ain't got nothin' on me, and that slouch of a rockstar brother of mine couldn't charm an old lady after helping her cross the street."

"Hey now, why are you impugning my charm?" Jamie asked as he sauntered in holding Bel's hand.

They were mostly insufferably adorable, except it came as a relief to everyone who knew them to see them together, in love, and without angst. And just that response within myself should've told me, for years, how I should move on from Bel. I never realized how much I wanted for Jamie and Bel to just... get on with it.

I smirked at my own thoughts, but played it off in the moment. "'Course. Who wants some famous dude when they could have me, carrot-topped underachiever that I am."

I splayed out jazz hands, and everyone laughed.

"I'm not sure we can call you an underachiever anymore Dan." Jamie pulled up a chair next to me, and Bel settled next to him. At the far end, Jonas Bauer sat, his attention tied to his laptop.

Soon enough, Bauer started the meeting. He'd taken over leading meetings at some point during the spring and we'd all gotten used to it, though at first, even though I liked the guy well enough, having someone other than family direct our planning had grated.

But now, I could see he had the best for the lodge and the mountain at heart.

"Who's this coming in October?" Leo pointed to an item on the calendar Bauer had handed out.

"Another potential investment group."

Leo stiffened in her seat. "Why do we need more investors?"

Bauer pulled his thin frames from his face. "Because, Ms. Morrison, we can always use more capital. We can take this lodge even farther from small-town lodge to major resort destination."

I didn't have to look at Leo to know her jaw was clenched shut.

"No harm in letting them have a look around and see if it's a fit." Liam's cheery voice sounded in the room, and I couldn't have been the only one bracing for Leo's response.

But, Bel to the rescue. She set her hand on Leo's wrist and said so quietly I almost didn't hear, "Leave it for now. It'll be okay."

Bel had always had a calming effect on Leo. In truth, Leo'd grown out of needing that so much until the last year or so when things with the lodge had spiraled out of control. I hadn't figured out exactly why all of this bothered her in such a fundamental way, but it clearly did.

"If that's everything, we'll convene next week. After that, we'll move to bi-weekly shorter check-ins and then we've all got our assignments for the fest weekend." Bauer nodded once, then sat and returned his attention to his computer, effectively dismissing us.

"Are you off to see your woman?" Liam asked as we shuffled out the door.

"Yeah. Haven't gotten to see her as much as I'd like lately. She's got some evening events going on at the library

—book clubs and a knitting club and something else, plus with me running around... anyway, yeah. Off I go."

Liam stopped me just outside the hulking lodge doors with a hand on my shoulder, that affectionate, brotherly move so familiar even though it had, over our lifetime, come with both good and bad news.

"I'm so happy for you, Dan. She seems like a great woman, and you seem to be very happy."

"Thanks, Li. She is. And I am."

Mia

Danny didn't run away again.

We just hadn't had time together. Well, we had. We had lots of time. Time barbecuing. Time swimming with Kai at a little pond Danny and his family used to go to when he was growing up. Time fishing with Kai or on hikes the three of us. Occasionally, we stole dinner by ourselves and a few hours after Kai went to bed. But other than falling asleep watching a movie once a few weeks ago, we'd not spent the night.

I chose not to obsess about that. I chose to rejoice in going slowly, in not jumping into bed together, though that wouldn't be what it was at this point anyway. But I couldn't pretend I felt confident it was just accidental or circumstantial and not that Danny wasn't ready. If he wasn't, I could respect that, but frankly, it made me wonder if maybe he just wasn't that into me.

Tonight, he had plans with his brothers. Leo, Bel, and Wells had invited me to join them for dinner again, and we'd eat at *Guac* once more because all of us had been craving Mexican.

"Oh good, you're here." Leo grinned when she saw me following the host to the table.

"Yes, finally. Sorry I'm a few late—the sitter was running behind." I plunked my purse down on the booth next to Bel.

"Don't worry about it. One of us is always late, and it seems to rotate depending on whatever life has going on for us. We won't kick you out of the club." Bel smiled reassuringly and nudged a bowl of salsa to me.

"Thanks."

"So, two weeks 'til Sommerfest. Is everyone ready for this madness?" Leo asked before scooping salsa onto a chip and chomping down.

"It's going to be insane, isn't it? Based on the reservations I have, plus the calls I keep getting begging for a room, the town is going to be packed." Wells' eyes shone brightly, full of excitement at the coming event.

"Yes. It will be utter madness, and I'm guessing this year it's going to be even more insane than usual. Sadie is already baking like a madwoman and preparing everything she can to freeze doughs or starters or whatever else she does just so we don't run out, and that'll happen anyway. She'll work like a dog the entire time *with* an assistant she hires for these busy times, and we'll sell out everything every day." Bel shut her menu just as the waiter arrived.

"Ladies?" he asked, his face expectant and ready for our order.

We gave it to him quickly. I suspected that, like me, they

were all starving too. *Enchiladas. Fajitas. Chimichanga. Tacos.* We'd covered good ground with our order.

"Could we also get a large guacamole for the table?" I requested since I'd been dreaming about their guac for days leading up to this meal.

The waiter left with a nod, and Leo sat beaming at me. I tipped my head to the side in question. "What?"

"I knew I liked you, but then you go do a thing like that, and it cements it."

We all laughed at that, then extolled the virtues of *Guac*'s guacamole and how it enhanced the Silverton quality of life quotient significantly.

"So how are you and Danny?" Leo asked as soon as the waiter set down our entrees.

"We're good. I really like him."

I couldn't keep the cheesy grin off my face, but I'd come to realize I didn't need to with these women. They supported each other, and though I'd only gotten to interact with them a handful of times, they'd already done that for me. Since our first dinner, each of them had stopped into the library. Bel dropped off pastries one day, Wells delivered some wildflowers, and Leo brought coffee. All unnecessary, and all incredibly sweet.

Leo narrowed her eyes. "I'm glad. Is he... stepping up?"

I sat back in the booth, my back stiff against the cushion behind me. "Uh... what do you mean?"

Leo winced. "You know he's never had a relationship, right?"

"Yes."

"And you know he's never shown much... ambition?"

I swallowed, a sick feeling invading my gut. "We've talked about both his relationship and work history, if that's what you mean."

She nodded, decisive. "Good. I just don't want to see you disappointed."

"Leo, that's not fair." Bel gave her friend a hard look.

Wells ducked her head, suddenly intent on her enchiladas.

Leo blew out a long breath and set her fork down. "Maybe not. But I've been thinking about it, and I don't feel right not saying something. So this is me, just saying... you know, go easy. He's one of my favorite people on the planet, so I'm not going to tell you to stop being with him. I'd *never* say that, because I love him and I like you more and more every time I see you. But you have Kai, and Danny has never been one for commitment. I hate the idea of any of you getting hurt when he decides it's all too much."

My heart beat in my ears as I nodded in what felt like slow motion. I could hardly breathe, so I didn't—I held my breath in and let the air scratch and claw at my lungs until I had to let it out. If anyone at the table spoke, I didn't hear them. Then, Bel's hand on my arm got my attention.

"Leo's constantly concerned about people getting hurt, and she's not always wrong, but in this case, I think her worries are misplaced. I've seen you two together, and I've seen changes in Danny in the last few months I never would have expected. That tells me only good things."

Her sweet face and warm voice and gentle touch soothed the riot in my chest a bit, but I could only force a smile.

"So when is Liam totally done with the lodge? Should be any day now, right?" Bel asked, deftly shifting the conversation away from me and Danny and bless her, I could've kissed her. If I'd been able to think past the end of my own nose, which I couldn't do.

Because all I could really hear were Leo's words. "*I hate*

the idea of any of you getting hurt when he decides it's all too much."

The conversation continued without me. "After the fest, Jonas will be doing the job full-time. Liam's already working a little more than part-time with John for the brewery. I swear he's like a kid at Christmas every time I see him after he's been there. He's so happy."

Wells' joy-filled words shook me from my self-focus.

"I'm so glad. He definitely seems happy, but I'm not sure it's all because of the job." Bel raised her brows meaningfully at Wells who glowed at the comment.

"I may have a little to do with it. But with things going well at the lodge and finally getting to do the work he's wanted to for years, I think he's got that soul-deep satisfaction of the work he does becoming meaningful. I've experienced the same thing in the last year, and I wouldn't trade it."

Leo cleared her throat. "That's great. I just wish it didn't come at the cost of handing the family business over to a man we may or may not be able to trust."

Bel dropped back against the booth with an eye roll while Wells tutted and turned to Leo. "I know you're not convinced Jonas is the right person for the job. I wish you could tell me *why*."

Leo's jaw pinched, and I watched in fascination as her cheeks reddened. "I can't explain it. But he's not family."

Bel rested her elbows and captured Leo's gaze. "You know I'm not an unreserved fan of Jonas', but you have to admit that at this point, we're long past keeping it in the family. You know that, right?"

Leo stretched her neck to one side and rolled her shoulders. "I acknowledge that the financial piece can't stay within the family. Liam and I made peace on that front months ago, and I see the benefit. What I'm not convinced of is Bauer being the pied piper of skiers and acting in a role that makes him the primary decision-maker when I am wholly unconvinced he has the lodge's best interest at heart."

"Wow." Wells' face displayed her shock.

"This can't be news to you."

"I guess it's not... not entirely. But I didn't realize you had that much of a problem with him. That's got to be really difficult."

Wells' compassion for her friend shone from her eyes and declared what a lovely person she was. I would've expected criticism, maybe even an attempt to correct Leo's assumptions based on her previous comments and apparent familiarity with Jonas Bauer, but here she was, simply empathizing.

Leo cleared her throat again. "Thanks. It's not great. But I don't plan to let him have the run of the place without oversight, and if that means me looking over his shoulder, then so be it."

Bel and Wells shared a look I couldn't decipher as the waiter came and set down a tray of shot glasses brimming with golden liquid.

"Ladies, from the gentlemen at the bar."

Our heads turned to the far end of the restaurant where Danny, Jamie, Liam, a hulking man with dark hair and the largest hands I'd ever seen, and another I knew as Wyatt Saint all sat watching.

"Well that's an astounding little lineup," Bel said with a breathy quality I could relate to.

"Eh. The two on the end aren't bad," Leo said, then turned back to the table and shot the liquid like it was nothing.

Wells shook her head. "I fear some of the effect is lost on you since you're related to three of them. Two of them are my cousins, and even I can admit I'm staring at the makings of a calendar."

I sipped the tequila, enjoying the heat and tang on my tongue, my eyes locked with Danny's, feeling ever so grateful I wasn't related to him.

CHAPTER THIRTY-FIVE

Danny

Head-turning.

The women at the table were nothing short of astounding. I could admit my own sister was beautiful, and Bel and Wells were too. But Mia, sitting there in her bright white summer dress with little ruffles on her straps and a vee-shaped dip to the line of the top...

I died.

I'd had no idea they'd be here, and supposedly neither had Liam or Jamie. I hoped not. I'd begun to understand their desperate, sappy, anxious-to-catch-a-glimpse situations, but I knew girls' night had a purpose, as did guys'. But here we sat, five buffoons fawning over a table of women across the restaurant.

"Dudes. The Morrison genes make strapping men, sure, but damn if Leo isn't nearly painful to look at tonight."

Jamie's, Liam's, and my head snapped from the table to eye Warrick.

The giant man held up his ridiculous hands. "What? I hate to say it but—"

"Then don't say it." Liam's face held no humor.

"Are you seriously going all overprotective big brother on her?" Warrick crunched a chip.

Jamie shook his head. "It's not overprotective. It's that we can all mentally ascent to the idea that Leo is beautiful and all grown up, but hearing dudes we've known all our lives drool over our own sister is a little..."

I finished for him. "Creepy. Icky. Something. I mean, good for her and all, and best of luck to you if you want to give it a go, but..."

War's head jerked sharply to the left.

"Nope. My brother here already made a play." He patted Wyatt's back.

My eyes widened, and I had no doubt my brothers' did too. "You made a play for Leo?"

Wyatt had the shy, manly cowboy thing going on since he'd developed a boutique cattle ranching business that'd taken Utah's beef industry by storm—he'd grown the small family business and kept his sanity and humility, which earned him mad respect from me.

Wyatt's eyes on Leo, he toasted the air in her direction, and she winked back at him. "I did. We had a good time, until we both realized we're about as suited to one another as ketchup is to filet mignon—her being the filet mignon, of course."

"Uh... other than you likening my sister to steak, you're hardly ketchup, old friend." Liam waited for Wyatt's response.

Wy had always been quiet, humble, and probably the

best of us, even counting Liam. But he'd lived fairly isolated up at the Saint family ranch which was located even farther in the mountains. In the last few years, he'd made it known he wanted to find a wife—not a girlfriend, but a straight-up wife. I wasn't surprised Leo didn't go for him, only because I didn't think she'd want to live up there, and that wasn't something Wyatt could flex on.

He chuckled low into his beer. "Yeah, sure. It wasn't just that. We have very different ideas on a lot of things, and I guess I knew that, but had to see for myself. I'm glad I did, and now we're friends. She's already told me she'll help find me a wife if I want to enlist her."

We all laughed at that.

"I'm sure she will. That's Leo's favorite secret pastime." Jamie smiled to himself, then shot me a sly look. "Though Danny dabbles from time to time too."

"Just the once," I said, genuinely feeling the joy of having helped him find his happy ever after.

"And who'll help you, man?" War asked as the bartender set our plates in front of us.

I let my gaze rest on Mia for another minute, just until she let me have her eyes one more time, all sparkling heat and a little flush up her neck. Heat raced in my veins, and I wished I could find a minute alone with her, just to revel in those dark eyes and plush lips being all mine.

I shut my eyes against the crush of longing that hit me. Man, did I want her to be mine, and only mine, forever and ever, amen.

Not since high school had I had such certainty, and that'd been naïve and though not entirely misplaced, but just ultimately wrong.

I'd never learned to trust my gut again about these things—I'd never had reason to, and I'd made a concerted effort to shun my instincts and keep my eyes on the mountain, quite literally, until Mia caught me by surprise. Maybe because she'd been on the mountain itself—maybe because she'd taken me by surprise there where I literally couldn't get around her on the path.

Whatever the case, I wanted her. I wanted us. I wanted Kai and pancakes on Saturdays without having to walk outside and knock on her door. I wanted to wake up with her sheet of black hair tangled on a pillow next to me. I wanted it all.

"Earth to Dan," Liam said as a hand waved in front of my face to break the spell Mia cast.

"What?"

"Warrick asked if someone was going to help you with the whole match-making set-up." Liam's lips curled up as he watched me.

"Me? Nah, I'm all set."

Everyone chuckled.

"Yeah, man. We got that."

Wyatt spoke next. "So Liam. When are you going to make us family?"

Liam's smile could've been seen from space. "Give me a few weeks and you'll have your answer."

Jamie held his beer up at an angle, and Liam met it with his own with a clink. "Cheers to that."

"What will we be? If my brother marries your cousin..." I wondered aloud.

War shook his head. "Basically nothing but friends, still, but we can pretend."

"Then it's just down to you and Leo. Ma and Da will be so happy to double the numbers." Liam wiggled his eyebrows obnoxiously, and Jamie sniggered beside him.

"I'm fully aware they'd like to see us all settled down with the right person. I've found my person, I just..."

What could I say to them, these men who'd known me all my life? That for the first time ever, I knew exactly what I wanted, but I had no idea how to get it?

That I'd fallen in love with a woman and her child, and though I hoped I was wrong, I feared I wasn't anywhere near good enough, smart enough, ambitious enough for them?

That I'd wanted a family of my own since I could remember thinking of life after high school, and the thought of it starting with Mia and Kai made me want to weep a little with how perfect it seemed?

Liam reached around Jamie and set a hand on my shoulder as the other guys looked on. "If she's smart, and by all accounts she is, then she'll be elated to have you."

The bartender brought something else out, or maybe someone changed the topic, but my mind swirled around Liam's words. Soon enough, we all said our goodbyes, Wyatt and Warrick heading to their truck to get back up to the ranch, and me, Liam, and Jamie wandering slowly toward my house where they'd branch off to get home.

"You really set on this girl?" Liam asked softly as we wandered through the cool summer evening air.

"Yep."

"Congrats, then." His voice held a note of... something.

"Got something to say about it?"

Jamie stayed typically quiet while Liam came to a stop and focused all his brotherly, wisdom-imparting energy on me. "Listen. I don't want to sound like I know what I'm talking about—"

"Then don't." My hackles raised. Just the tone told me

whatever he planned to say would more than likely piss me off.

He sighed, and next to him, Jamie ran a hand through his hair, clearly uncomfortable, though I couldn't tell whether it was on my behalf, or Liam's, or the whole conversation at large.

"I've just got to say this, okay? I know you've been making changes. You've been taking on more, and I'm hoping any day now you're going to tell me and Jonas that you're stepping up and accepting Rod's job. But you're with a woman who has a kid, and that means—"

"Liam, come on, man. He knows full well she has a kid—"

"I know he knows. I just have to say, before you go jumping off the ledge, make sure your parachute is intact, okay? Make sure you've got a plan for how you're going to support this woman and her child. What about insurance? What about a job, for that matter? Taking the managerial position gets you to salaried work if you choose to accept the year-round job, which Rob never took, but with that, you'd have insurance and other benefits—"

I cleared my throat to stop him, to cut off the deluge of advice that felt like he was piling up a cairn to mark the passing of my old life with each stone. Pressure built in my chest, but I couldn't let them see that—couldn't admit that I hadn't thought at all about insurance. What an idiot! You can't marry someone, let alone someone with a kid, without that in place. You needed money and a reliable schedule and sick leave and...

Jamie spoke before I could. "You don't actually have to have every detail worked out. Not to mention Mia's been taking care of herself and her son for years, so that's not going to suddenly transfer fully to you. I think he means well—" he nodded to Liam who'd ducked his chin and studied his feet, "—and he has good reminders, but only *you* know how to move forward, and it shouldn't have anything to do with insurance policies."

The hand at the back of my neck dropped in a small show of surrender.

"What if I don't know how? How do I know if this is right, or that she thinks it is?"

"You talk to her." Jamie's confidence held no small amount of irony considering he'd run away from the woman he loved for nearly a decade, and he'd run away from me for nearly as long, but okay. *Sure.*

"And this is one thing I will say, and I won't apologize for it." Liam crossed his arms over his chest and nearly glared at me.

"Okay..."

"If it doesn't work out—not that I'm assuming it won't, just... if it doesn't, we'll be here."

Jamie nodded his head. "Absolutely."

My lips pressed into a thin line, I tucked my hands into my pockets, the slight summer breeze giving me a chill as we stood there under the mountain moonlight. I'd take their offering of support, but the familiar frustration of being underestimated, and perhaps also the irritation with myself that I'd given them years of evidence that justified that underestimation, reared its head. Could I really change—take a "real" job, be in a relationship, be a parent?

"Thanks."

"Liam, go ahead. I'll catch up with you in a minute." Jamie nodded to Liam, who jerked his head back a bit, but cooperated by turning up the street and wandering slowly in the direction of his place.

I braced for whatever Jamie had to say, hiding my fisted hands behind my back.

Jamie studied me, eyes shifting back and forth between mine, before he set a hand on my shoulder. "You know you've got this, right?

My brow furrowed. "I do?"

One shake of his head in agreement. "You do. Liam may have his heart in the right place, but he's not as clued into where you are with life. You own a house, man. You work hard. You love that woman. Based on what I've seen of Mia, she's all about you, too. Don't doubt yourself on this... just talk to her."

I swallowed, wishing it was that easy. Just stop doubting myself... sure. "Wish I could."

His face hardened. "Take it from someone who failed to communicate time and time again... nothing good comes from it. Go to the source, lay it all out, and trust this person you've fallen for to know what she wants."

My head bobbed to show him I was listening, hoping he'd settle for that instead of words.

He patted my shoulder, then released me. "And Dan? It might be time to stop worrying about what everyone has always thought of you. Give yourself a break. You're not perfect, but you're a damn fine man, and Mia and Kai would be lucky to have you."

CHAPTER THIRTY-SIX

Mia

I wandered home slowly, content to be alone on this walk. Funny how I'd grown so used to being alone in the years since Kai was born, and in truth, even before that since my grandfather wasn't much of a conversationalist.

Kai provided excellent company, but when he was at school or asleep or off playing, it was just me. And sometimes, the loneliest times were in the throes of parenting, wishing I had a partner to bear the load. Not just the laundry and groceries and bedtime routines, but emotional roller coasters and navigating his cognitive development, the appropriate boundary pushing and deciding how to respond so he didn't turn out to be a sociopath when he grew up. Then, there were the fevers and coughs, the time he got strep throat and wouldn't drink anything for hours until I finally plied him with popsicles. Those were, bar none, the darkest hours I'd lived on my own.

But tonight, I took pleasure in weaving my way slowly, ruminating on the evening. We'd had a great time, staying to chat over rounds of drinks, then a belated dessert. Beyond the discussion of my relationship and Leo's dislike of Jonas Bauer, we'd covered broad ground—books, movies, exercise routines, relationships with parents, and the realization that of the four of us, only Leo had siblings. We'd talked about our professional goals too, and in reality that had taken up most of the latter part of the evening, once we all loosened up so there were never any pauses and we all exclaimed happily over each revelation any of us brought out.

Bel was growing her marketing and design business. In the last few months, she'd gussied up her website and had decided to work on drumming up more work online. She promised to continue doing the library's projects pro bono, and I couldn't refuse her, but did pull her to me and give her a hug in thanks. Wells had grand plans to expand her inn and build a hotel, plus add cabins, which Bel and Leo assured me were gorgeous since she apparently already had one completed that she lived in.

And Leo was surprisingly coy about her plans, saying only that she wanted the lodge to grow and she was working on how best to do that. She wanted to grow the *kinderski* program and the adult ski program as well, but the impression I came away with was that she wanted far more than just the education portion of the lodge to be her purview.

Happily, I put Leo's words about Danny finding it *all too much* out of my head after the guys sent a round of shots to the table.

Funny, that. Seeing him there across the bar—he never came to say a word—had calmed me. It didn't make much sense considering it should have only exacerbated my fears to look them in the eye, but instead, seeing him planted on that bar stool, staring me down with his eyes practically flaming with want, I'd felt remarkably good.

I found it too easy to doubt him when he was out of sight. That had to be linked to the harsh reality that Mason had left me—he'd shuttled me and Kai home from the hospital, run out on an errand, and never come back.

Obviously, Danny wouldn't do that—he was a better man than Mason by about a thousand measures. But Danny had always been upfront with me about his resistance to commitment. And now, there sat Leo, confirming I had good reason to be concerned that though everything seemed to be going swimmingly, that didn't mean he'd become a totally different person. After all, that was unfair of me to expect.

Earlier in the day, I'd spoken to Mrs. Stanton, who'd become a kind of surrogate grandmother, which was lovely but also intense because she had no qualms about speaking her opinion, good, bad, and ugly. She'd mentioned that the most foolish thing we can do in a relationship is expect the other person to change. That didn't mean people don't change naturally, but *expecting* them to radically change to suit our needs simply because we want that is a recipe for failure.

It made sense. If he wanted me to suddenly shun all reading materials and hate books, I'd have a hard time even pretending I'd do it for him. If his condition for being together was that I couldn't work at the library anymore, I couldn't even entertain the idea of him. Wasn't me expecting him to become a creature of commitment exactly like that?

And yet, no, it wasn't. Because at some point in the near

term, I'd need a commitment from Danny if we were to continue on the path we'd set out on months ago. I didn't want to date him indefinitely. I wanted stability and guarantees. I wanted a ring on my finger, and on his. I wanted someone Kai could rely on.

But being with Danny had me convinced maybe he had changed—especially now that he'd stopped running away from me. The look on his face as we stared each other down in the restaurant told me not only that he wanted me, but that, if I dared admit it to myself, he might love me. The intensity there, the heat, and yet not just attraction but a kind of surrender, for lack of a better word, had me finally looking away and coughing to hold back tears.

I'd moved on and enjoyed the time with the girls, but all I could think about as I walked through the summer night was Danny. Maybe my wishful thinking had conjured up shadows of all those emotions between us. Maybe I was insane to be thinking about marriage with a man who'd never had a relationship, or even a real job before. Maybe I—

Danny sat on a large rock that marked the corner of the path between the sidewalk and his front door. The moon lit the cloudless sky and gave the mountains an eerie, otherworldly glow. His head looked frosted, almost, thanks to the way the light shone off his hair.

"Did you guys have fun?" I wandered up to him, taking stock of his appearance, my stomach tightening into a knot at seeing him in the middle of all my swirling thoughts. Was he drunk? Hurt? Just waiting to catch me before I went inside and relieved the sitter?

He raised his head slowly, his brows heavy over his glittering eyes. No blue there in the shadows of his face, but they still reeled me in. He spread his legs, and I stepped between them and brought my hands to the sides of his face.

"Are you okay?" My words came out in a whisper.

Though the August night was alive with crickets, the rustle of the wind, a distant motor running, his posture and energy made me want to gentle everything around us—smooth the stone he sat on, block the breeze that ruffled his hair, turn down the glare of the moon just a bit.

His gaze toured my face before the sides of his mouth tilted up, just barely. So uncharacteristic of Danny, my already fast-beating heart accelerated, rushing now.

"I'm fine. Are you?"

His hands came to my hips, and his thumbs swept down along my hip bones in a move so familiar and intimate, my response caught in my throat.

"Yes. Are you sure nothing's wrong?"

He dropped his head forward so it rested against my belly—again, a physical gesture that normally would've sent my pulse racing with thrill, but now I only felt concern. Danny carried an energy with him—buoyant and fun, maybe a little restless and eager. That hum of sweetness and excitement and easy smiles was nowhere to be found.

"Danny, honey, are you okay? You're kind of freaking me out." My voice quavered.

He shook his head against me, then pulled back and looked up into my face. "I'm sorry. I know I'm being weird. It's just an off day, and I wanted to see you—to be close to you."

My pulse echoed that desire, downright racing now, but it couldn't be that simple. The way he'd looked at me just an hour ago—had it even been that long? There had been no trace of this version of him at *Guac*.

Of course, everyone had off days, but I'd seen Danny on

an off day, and it didn't look like this. Whatever he felt, he wasn't ready to share with me. Or maybe it was something with his brothers and he didn't feel he could share. Either way, I didn't need to keep pressing him for more if he couldn't tell me yet. But I could offer him comfort, love, and hopefully a little peace.

I let my hands slide to the back of his head, into his short hair, stepped closer and leaned down to set a gentle kiss on his lips. "Come home with me."

CHAPTER THIRTY-SEVEN

Danny

The night ended in an unexpected way.

Understatement.

I woke in Mia's bed. I breathed in her sweet, fresh scent before I ever opened my eyes and felt so rested and at home, I narrowly avoided tearing up. When I did take in the visual scene next to me, my heart beat wildly at the sight of the woman laying by my side, hair swirled into a bun at the top of her head and face relaxed in sleep.

I wanted to kiss her awake. I wanted to hold her to me and feel every part of her.

The night before, we'd walked quietly inside her house. She'd thanked and paid the babysitter, and we'd readied for bed like we'd done that together, side by side, more than once. She'd lent me a spare toothbrush, which should have seemed like a waste since my house was literally on top of hers, but I wouldn't have left her for anything.

When it came time to go to bed, there had been no fireworks. She'd changed into a T-shirt and shorts. I'd shucked my pants and button-down for my boxers and undershirt. She'd turned down the covers of her double bed and we both got in, then she'd reached for my hand and had taken it with her as she rolled away from me, nesting us together my front to her back, my arm over her. I'd pulled her closer and kissed her below her ear, ignoring the thrum and excitement that had built at the prospect of climbing into bed with her.

This new territory should've lit me on fire. It could have, easily, if I'd let my mind wander over the soft curves of her body wedged against mine, but I'd focused on the larger atmosphere—my heart had felt like it was being pressed between slabs of stone. Though I wanted her and often thought I might become addled from it, this night had nothing to do with the physical. She'd offered me comfort, accepting my lack of detail and excuses for my mood. She could've sent me home with a hug and it would have been enough. Instead, she'd kept me with her, and I couldn't find words to express what I wanted to say.

Actually, that's a lie. I did have words.

Words like *I love you.*

Words like *I need you.*

Words like *I'm afraid I'm not enough for you.*

I couldn't say any of them, so I said nothing. Not one word until she wrapped me up in her bed and I kissed her, and just before I fell asleep, I found something worth saying. *Thank you.*

As we got ready for bed, I'd wondered if the morning would be awkward. How often had we wanted to spend the night together, doing a little less sleeping, and we'd never managed it. Had that all been excuses? And would she regret inviting me into the intimacy of her bed—would she worry I assumed that meant more, or too much, or…?

Then it came, interrupting my tumbling thoughts before I fully grasped the situation.

"Danny? DANNY! You're here!"

Kai bounded into the room, up on the bed, and did a full-on body-drop between us.

"Mom, did you see Danny's here?"

Kai's energy apparently started upon waking. Mia swiped the hair out of her face and she squinted at Kai, but didn't speak. Her head whipped to me, then back to Kai, and I could hear her breath catch.

"Mom. Mom. Moooooom. Did you see Danny? Why's he here? I'm so glad you're here! Let's have pancakes. Will you make pancakes? I'll get the bowl out." He stood up in the middle of the bed, shuffled to the edge, dropped and bounced off his bum and onto his feet. As he ran out of the room he hollered, "Wake up sleepy heads! Pancakes!"

With no hope of covering, I let laughter roll out. The kid was pure energy and adorability and there was no point denying it.

"Well, that wasn't quite what I would have expected," I said as I eyed her, my heart stuttering at the sleepy look on her face.

"I'm not surprised by the energy because that is all Kai, but I'm kind of shocked he didn't get hung up on you being here. And not just here but *here* here." She smoothed an escaped strand behind her ear and then bit her lip as her cheeks reddened adorably.

Suddenly, I lost myself. I lost that calm and the sense of rightness I woke with and I could only say "yeah" in a scratchy sham of a voice.

She sat up and crossed her arms over her chest. "I guess

we better go get started on the pancakes or he'll be back. His pile-drive is ruthless."

I chuckled, because the image of him taking us both out with an elbow played vividly in my head, but also because I needed to make a sound, force air out of my chest since it'd been locked there since she'd bitten her lip. I swung my legs to the side of the bed and inhaled long and slow, willing my body to calm, my mind to revert back to the man who knew who he was, where he stood, what he wanted.

But the only problem there? I didn't know where I stood, especially not now that we'd shared a bed in one sense, but not the other...

"I'll be out in a sec," Mia said, skittering into her bathroom before I could say a word.

I scrubbed a hand down my face and shook my head to get the foggy thoughts clear. I pulled on my clothes and headed out to see how Kai was doing and found him on a step stool dumping pancake mix into a bowl.

"Need any help there?"

"I got it." He hunched over the box, curving around it so he could watch the mix fall into the clear bowl.

"Okay. I'll get the eggs and milk."

We worked together to crack eggs, measure milk, and add a few dashes of other things. Mia made excellent pancakes from scratch but the boxed kind allowed Kai to do much of it himself. She'd explained this to me as though she needed an excuse for having boxed pancake mix in her house, which she certainly did not.

"Everything all right in here?" she said as she glided in, face still clear of makeup but looking freshly scrubbed, the hair framing her face just a touch darker in places.

"We've got it, Mom. The coffee should be ready now." Kai's tone held all the authority in the world.

I chanced another look at her, and when our eyes met, I could see she clearly found his assurance adorable, just like I did.

"You know how to make coffee?" Kai always amazed me with what he could do. Granted, I didn't have close contact with many kids his age, but he still always struck me as particularly capable.

He giggled. "I know how to push the button."

"Ah, I see. So you're not going to apply for the new barista position at *Rise and Shine*?"

He doubled over with laughter in true exaggerating six-year-old form. "I can't work there! I'm only six."

I kept at it. "Are you sure? I think you'd really like it there. My friend Bel gets free bread and pastries, plus all the coffee she can drink. She'd be a nice boss, too."

His eyes widened and looked at me like I was crazy. "I can't drink coffee, and I can't have a boss! My mom's my boss."

No point in pretending—this kid had me. I bent so our faces were even where he stood on the stool. "You're right. What was I thinking?"

Mia looked on with a grin and shook her head at us. "You two are crazy. If anyone's boss, it's you, bud."

Kai propped his hands on his hips. "I'm the kid. You're the mom."

We kept joking like that as Kai stirred the pancake batter, doing a remarkable job of keeping the mix in the bowl. Then he enlisted me to help with the griddle and stove, as he'd done in the past. The morning sped by in a happy haze of syrup and coffee and the delights of Kai's little brain.

"I've got to take him to a birthday party in about an hour."

We'd migrated to my backyard so Kai could run around. We were tossing frisbees and had played a short round of frisbee golf. Now Mia and I sat in the loungers on my deck while Kai scampered around playing some game only he understood.

"Thanks for letting me hang with you guys this morning." I waited 'til she gave me her eyes. "And for letting me stay last night."

She shared a close-lipped smile. "Are you feeling better?"

I crossed my legs and rested my hands behind my head. "I think so. I mean—" I shot up, and set a hand on her arm. "I felt better waking up next to you than I have in a long time. That was great. I don't want to take away from that."

Her smile grew.

"I feel like I'm at a crossroads. I'm gonna take that job and embrace what comes along with it. It's taking the next step in my work life, but it also means I'm more of an... asset in my personal life."

Our eyes were locked, and I wouldn't have looked away for anything. She focused intently on me as I finished my thought. "I'll be ready for the next step in the rest of my life too."

CHAPTER THIRTY-EIGHT

Mia

I couldn't look away from him, but I couldn't find words. My belly tightened and my lungs emptied, which didn't make sense since I was breathing. I must've been, because my chest rose and fell.

The sun shone high above us. Logically, it should've been too hot to be outside, but Danny's back yard was an oasis from the summer heat. Mature trees lined the property and created a kind of fence. The grass was miraculously green, likely thanks to the trees' protection. And he had a large patio pergola that lent shade to the deck where we sat.

Why had my mind taken a detour to admire the yard?

Because I couldn't fully process his words. Just yesterday, Leo had mentioned Danny finding our relationship, and life with me and Kai, to be too much. And now, he'd basically said he was ready to make a real commitment.

That to him, this job signaled the next step professionally but also, soon after, an opening to the next phase with us.

I should've been thrilled.

I was thrilled?

I couldn't tell.

I just couldn't tell what I felt. Kai's bounding pronouncement in my room this morning had thrown me into consciousness with a cruel suddenness I should have grown used to in the last six years, but alas, I hadn't. In that moment, I'd registered him, then Danny, then him seeing Danny, then the fact that though Danny and I had slept together, we hadn't processed it. We hadn't even really acknowledged it except in this quick moment where he'd insinuated that he liked the nearness and waking up next to me very much.

Fluttering little birds zipped through my stomach. I couldn't decide how I felt other than knowing I was glad he was glad. I suspected his taking the job might be a show of commitment in and of itself, and that gave me hope, which I immediately wanted to squash.

"That's.. uh... Danny, that's exciting. When does that start for you, if you take it?"

His little smirk might kill me. He looked so happy, and yet unwilling to unleash it on me, so he kept it hidden. Maybe I was totally off, but he seemed genuinely ready for this step.

"I think basically next week. I mean, nothing serious yet, but I'll work on building the roster and Rod does a bunch of stuff in the fall to gear up. Plus Liam and Bauer have mentioned there are other duties I can take on as a part of a contract that would give me year-round work, so I do think I'll start this next week since they're ready for some of that to get going, even before the fest next week."

"That's so exciting." *Ugh*, repeating myself. "I mean, I'm happy for you... that you've come to this decision. That you're ready for this."

His eyes flitted back and forth between mine, the expression on his face serious, but happy. I thought I could detect happy there, maybe even excited. I hoped he felt that way and didn't view this as some kind of concession he was making for me. I couldn't believe that would be the case—not something of this magnitude when we'd only been seriously dating for a few months, but the way he said it...

"Well..." I sat up and rose to standing. "We better get going so we can get to the birthday party."

"Right. Yes. Thanks for spending the morning with me." He cleared his throat. "And the night, I guess."

That adorable blush crept over his cheeks as he stood and reached for my hand. I let him take it. He pulled it to his lips and pressed a kiss there just as Kai ran up. "Let me know how the party goes, okay buddy?"

Danny held up a hand that Kai jumped to high-five.

"Definitely."

Kai ran off toward the back door as Danny and I made our way to the house.

"So, I'll see you..."

"Are you around tomorrow?" I asked, knowing the week would be insane with the fest coming up so soon.

"I've got lunch plans with my grandpa, but other than that, I'm good until about six. Liam asked me and Jamie to have dinner with him tomorrow night. I think he's proposing soon and he's getting nervous... needs a good brotherly talk-down."

"Wow. That's so exciting." Somehow, my voice didn't sound like I really thought that, but I did. Wells and Liam went together so well. They genuinely seemed to love and respect each other. I knew they'd be happy.

He nodded, flashed a grin, then pulled me to him in a hug. Holding me close, he spoke quietly into my ear. "I'll miss you. Is that stupid? Even if I see you tomorrow, I'll miss you until then."

I turned my head to kiss his cheek, then captured his lips with mine, closing my eyes against the flood of affection and love for him. So, so sweet.

The town's population had doubled... it must have. With the fest beginning tomorrow, and his recent acceptance of the new job, Danny had been running like a dog to help get the event set up. While his managerial position didn't demand that, the job would add in some of the other things he'd been doing to prepare for the fest like publicity, which he was strangely good at despite his lack of formal training. Come to think of it, I had no idea what his degree was in, though I knew he had one since he'd referenced dating Bel in college.

So long story short, the jam-packed town hummed with excitement. The local campsites were crammed with RVs and tent cities, the Silverton Inn had booked out long ago, and everyone with an Airbnb listing had filled their rooms. The efforts the Morrisons and Jonas Bauer had undertaken, along with many volunteers from the town, had clearly worked.

The library even had busier days leading up to the fest, which didn't make a whole lot of sense, but it worked for me. By Thursday night, I'd spent exactly two hours with Danny since the weekend. I missed him, and so did Kai. But as soon as things actually started tomorrow afternoon, his role would be to stroll around and chat with people and troubleshoot if Liam and the others needed help.

Friday afternoon, Kai and I walked into town. The August sun shone from high in the sky, but fortunately, the day wasn't too horribly hot. I'd noticed that even the hottest days up here were nothing like the heat down in the city—there was always a breeze, plus the added altitude naturally cooled things a bit. The biggest issue was sun protection since we were *that* much closer to the sun. Kai and I were slathered with sunscreen and I'd packed more in my purse.

The city closed Main Street and merchants propped their doors open. White tents lined the actual roadway where local sellers had set up a farmer's and art market. A giant twenty-foot archway with wildflowers sprouting in all directions created by a new florist in town, *Bloom*, framed the far end of Main Street which led up to the lodge and the mountain. Danny had mentioned it'd been a challenge to make it stable, even though the rental company for the metal frame itself had assured them the setup would be quick and easy. This structure would also serve as the start and finish for a triathlon scheduled for the next morning, as well as a 5k run set to happen on Sunday morning. Kai was registered to run the kids' race that morning.

The official fest tent had been set up in the plaza area at the base of the mountain behind the lodge, but the festivities began here in town and lined the road all the way up to the main event.

"This is crazy!" Kai said, skipping along into the fray.

I held his hand tightly, nervous about losing him in the crowd. People were already packed into the street, milling around the vendors and chatting happily. Considering it

had only opened a few hours ago, the number of partici-
pants was huge.

We'd planned to meet Danny at the lodge itself, so we
had some maneuvering to do before we could get there. Kai
weaved in and out of small groups of people, stopping at a
display of hand-carved wooden toys and then again at a tent
featuring old-timey candies.

When we passed *Rise and Shine*, Bel waved from
behind the register. The door and windows were all open,
plus tables full of people peppered the sidewalk in front of
the shop. I shouted a "hello" at her and Kai and I continued
on, knowing Bel didn't have a spare minute and wouldn't
until the store closed later today. Hopefully, we'd see her at
the fest in the evening.

Kai smiled and chatted to nearly everyone he passed,
skipping and hopping down the sidewalk, then the street, as
we made our way to the lodge. The crowd thinned out a bit
as the grade of the road up to the lodge steepened, but there
was still a startling number of people here.

"Miss Leo." Kai pointed, then ran to Leo, who stood in
front of the lodge greeting people. Once he reached her, he
flung his arms around her waist and she bent to return the
hug while looking around until she spotted me and hailed
me with a nod of her chin.

"Glad you made it," she said as I reached her.

"Me too. Somehow, I've never walked that stretch of
road. I should be in better shape than this." I puffed out
some air, my lungs constricting. I'd had a touch of altitude
sickness when I first moved here, even after living in the
valley, but I hadn't been this breathless in quite a while.

"It's surprisingly steep. That's why we have shuttles
running for the elderly and people who can't make the
walk." She patted Kai's head.

"This is amazing. I had no idea it'd be this big," I said, gesturing to the food trucks parked all around the plaza and the people gathering by what seemed like dozens.

She beamed at the scene and clapped her hands together, then held them there. "I know. It's better than I thought it'd be. It's usually about half this size, maybe. With it being the sixtieth anniversary, we went all out, but even better than that it seems like we have a ton of community support. We usually only have the fest tent, vendors, and the triathlon on Saturday, but so far adding the 5k race on Sunday seems to be going over well based on the buzz I'm hearing and the registrations coming in today."

"I'm so glad. Have you seen Danny?"

She gave me directions to find him in the fest tent, which meant going around or through the lodge.

"I'd join you, but I just spotted an issue." Her face clouded—she glared behind me, all her sunny ease vanishing with whatever she saw.

"Oh, okay. I'm sure we'll see you later."

I chanced a look behind me and saw Jonas Bauer standing off to the side of the plaza with a tablet in hand. Somehow, he'd made himself an *issue* for Leo to deal with, and I almost pitied the man, except he had such an imposing presence, I doubted anyone could ever pity him.

The building's various entrances and exits stood wide open, letting people feel free to explore the space as they enjoyed the food trucks and other vendors. Inside the huge white fest tent, traditional German fest tables sat in neat rows and columns. At the far end of the space, a local band played covers of classic songs.

"There he is," Kai yelled as he ran, wrenching his hand out of mine and bolting across the tent to where Danny stood.

I could tell something wasn't right the minute I set eyes on him. His cheeks were pale, his normally smiling mouth turned down in a tight frown, his arms crossed over his chest. He stood facing two men, one of whom reached out to clap him on the shoulder.

"Sorry man," one of the men said over his shoulder as they walked away, leaving Danny to intercept Kai's bullet of energy with a quick move.

Danny's face relaxed, if marginally, when he wrapped his arms around Kai. My heart did the usual *thump thump* at the picture of this muscular red-headed man bending to pull my all-elbows-and-knees boy into his arms. I relished the moment Danny closed his eyes when he hugged Kai to him, like my son brought him some measure of comfort in the midst of whatever frustration he experienced.

"Hey," I said as I reached them, concern clear in my voice.

He stood and pulled me into a hug, one arm still around Kai. "Hey. You look great."

"Thank you. Is something wrong? Did something happen?" I sounded more than a little alarmed, but Danny's demeanor spelled out that everything was not all right.

He released us from the hug, then ran a hand through his hair and gripped the back of his neck with one hand. I made myself focus on his face rather than admire the good things this position did for his biceps, pecs... *no.* Just because I'd barely seen him lately and felt more than a little starved for him didn't mean it was acceptable to stand there and objectify him by ogling his gorgeous arms when I knew he was upset.

But my lizard brain couldn't ignore the little thrum in my blood at the sight of him, his event T-shirt stretched over his chest, his serious face focused on me.

Why, hello there, lover.

"Not really." He laughed, though it sounded forced, not at all like his usual laugh. "Chris and Javi just told me they aren't coming back. They're two of the best patrollers we have. They're team leads and without them, I'm going to be up a creek without a paddle unless I can find replacements..."

I held onto his hand. "Is that unusual? Isn't there a fair amount of turnover in this industry?"

He blew out a breath slowly, eyes skating around the tent, before answering. "Yes. Yes it's fairly normal, except those two have been there nearly as long as I have. And it feels a little like a confirmation I shouldn't be doing this."

CHAPTER THIRTY-NINE

Danny

The day had deteriorated from exciting and hopeful to frustrating, disappointing, and embarrassing.

Not how I saw it all going, but then again, I should have known it wouldn't go perfectly.

Nothing anyone saw would have tipped them off to the fact that the local band we hired ended up playing all day because the bigger name band that was supposed to show—who I'd talked into coming and had promised a huge turnout for—had bailed on us. Of course, people wondered where they were, but mercifully, the local band was good enough and everyone seemed to take it in stride and have a great time.

And then, the news that Chris and Javi weren't returning to the ski patrol team. Not awesome news, to say the least.

But what made that worse? My awkward conversation

with Mia. I couldn't help but feel like she didn't understand why I was so frustrated. I could step back and understand she really *didn't* know the job or the industry, nor did she understand how hard it might be for me to find guys I trusted like I did them. But more than that was the way my frustration made me feel so silly and small. Like having that reaction to this news of losing two of my best and most reliable employees pointed to my inexperience and inability to handle the pressures of the job.

I hadn't been sleeping well—hadn't slept well since the night I'd spent in Mia's bed, ironically enough. I would have returned there and never left if she'd let me, but after that one night, we hadn't had much time together, and I wasn't about to invite myself over for that.

Though I wouldn't have minded if she'd felt like extending the invitation herself.

The new job had kicked into gear basically the second I accepted it—chalk that one up to working for the family, and for starting work at a time that defined the term "high pressure." This was the sixtieth anniversary celebration of my beloved family business, the success of which would likely determine future investor interest, my brother's ability to step fully away and pursue his brewery without guilt, our acting manager's level of calm and willingness to stay in the position, and oh, also, potentially influence the numbers of our upcoming ski season which needed to be epic for the whole place to stay in business.

So... mildly pivotal.

Fortunately, the interminable day did come to a close. I managed a few hours of sleep before I was up with the race organizers helping with the triathlon. Normally, I wouldn't have had much of a role in this except Jonas Bauer wanted to compete and couldn't manage the event in that case.

Shocked the hell outta me, but I loved races and the energy of a competition, so why not?

Turned out, dude was a beast. I mean, I could tell he had a high level of fitness. I'd taken him and his partner at Bauer Group for a hike last fall when we first met them and he had been entirely unfazed by the altitude, distance, grade of the mountain... all of it. Ms. Ritter had killer endurance too, but Jonas Bauer had looked like he was on a Sunday stroll.

So the fact that he won his age bracket, particularly because he worked like a dog and I couldn't imagine when he had time to train for the race, impressed me. He didn't need to impress me, but he did anyway.

And thankfully, watching all those racers run across the finish line never got old. It boosted my spirits, got my mind off myself and the stupid personnel problems I'd have to start dealing with the minute this weekend ended, and brought me back in the *now*, my favorite place to be.

The best part? Mia and Kai had signed up to volunteer, so I got to see them on and off all morning. They manned an aid station for the run, so they weren't there at the end until the last runner came through and then they moved up to the finish line with me.

Watching Kai celebrate each and every athlete crossing the finish was like someone pouring cool water into a parched mouth. It was truly a balm, and that wasn't really a word I used. But that kid brought so much joy—he added to and multiplied the buzzing, celebratory atmosphere around him. He cheered for each person relentlessly, jumping and screaming for joy every time someone ran or jogged or hobbled across the line.

And Mia? If Kai was water, she was sustenance. She was beauty and light and everything good.

Great. My love for them both was becoming unwieldy. It'd become something I knew wouldn't be containable much longer. I needed to tell her—needed to deal with whatever fallout came, and even though it made me want to shrivel up in a corner if I thought through all the things that could potentially go wrong, I also sort of thought it might go right.

I'd thought through Jamie's comments about me cutting myself some slack. I was trying to do that, but it didn't come easy. I wanted to believe it would go right.

That might've been even more terrifying. Hard to say.

But with Mia and Kai screaming and cheering for the last competitor, right along with the rest of my family who'd filled different roles during the morning and all loved a good triumphant ending, I felt so full of hope and joy, I nearly burst.

Gone was the sense of failure and embarrassment and shame. No, those feelings likely wouldn't stay gone, but I relished the complete bliss of the mountain air, the August sun heating the late morning, and the people I loved most surrounding me.

"That was amazing! I can't wait for my race tomorrow." Kai bounced along next to me as we walked to my car.

With the tri today and the 5k tomorrow with the "kids' k" tacked on, there was something for almost everyone who wanted to compete.

I had driven up to the lodge that morning because at three a.m., I wasn't about to walk that early. I offered to give us all a ride home so we could get changed before the fest tent opened this afternoon.

"I'm excited to cheer for you. You're pretty speedy." He really was, and he loved to run. I'd taken him on a few jogs and had been surprised how well he kept up with me.

"Yeah. I am."

Mia's chuckle had me glancing at her.

Damn, she's glorious.

She'd pulled her dark hair through the back of an event-branded hat we gave out to all the volunteers. The bright green should've been garish on her like it was on everyone else, but instead, she just looked... I don't know, perfect, all right?

You're fighting with yourself about how good your girl-friend looks... dude. Get a grip.

I felt generally unhinged. The last few days had thrown me off with stress, exhaustion, and negativity, and now countered with the elation and almost giddy post-race high, even without having raced myself, I felt strangely volatile. Like I might drop to one knee and start asking questions I didn't know the answer to.

"Are you guys coming to the tent later?" I knew the answer, but for some reason, in my oddly fragile state, I needed reassurance I'd see them again, even after we parted to clean off the sweat and grime from the morning.

Mia reached over from the driver's seat and slid her fingers into the short hair at the back of my neck. "Of course."

Kai chattered away from the back, rejoicing at how amazing the race was, how beautiful Leo was—the kid had devotion down—and how elated he was when Jonas Bauer stopped to give him a high-five. Unexpected, for sure. I'd never seen Bauer interact with kids, but he gave Kai a star-tling, happy smile and a high-five and thanked him for cheering him across the finish.

The aforementioned sister at my side, who'd held Kai's other hand, had been notably silent. She didn't like Bauer, and she had her reasons. Apparently, her grudge knew no bounds and didn't decrease just because Bauer's athleticism proved shocking. It turned me into a bit of a fanboy, so I was surprised when everyone didn't fall all over themselves when he wandered over, hands on hips as he recovered from his final push. And pretty much everyone did, except Leo.

She never let anyone off easy, so I shouldn't have expected her to do so with Bauer. But frankly, it made the lodge look fantastic to have our new mountain manager racing, and not just racing, but *killing*. It showed we were not just offering a place for mountain life, but partaking in it.

The end of the night led to me carrying Kai to the house. He'd passed out on the drive home, hadn't said a word when I pulled him from the car, and hung in my arms as a dead weight while I walked him to his room.

I regretfully roused him so he could brush his teeth and change clothes, which he did in a sleepy state I imagined was similar to sleep walking.

"Today was the best day of my life," he said, his words slow and sleepy.

"I'm so glad, buddy. I had a great time with you." He'd been with me nearly the whole day, cheering in the morning, helping in the afternoon, dancing away in the fest tent tonight.

He yawned and flopped back into his bed. I patted his back and he yawned again, but he grabbed my arm before I left. "Love you, Danny."

I looked down at his small hand resting on my wrist, now relaxed and no longer holding me there. His breath evened out just as my heart pinched in my chest. "Love you too, Kai."

I sat there, watching him sleep, his face slackened, dark

lashes resting against his cheeks and mouth open just slightly. *God, help me love him right.* All my mind and heart focused on the prayer. I wanted to be good enough for Kai. For Mia. I wanted them to know how much I loved them and, I hoped it wasn't too selfish to admit it, I wanted their love in return.

Tonight, Kai had given me a reminder that I already had the first piece and a chance to tell him how I felt too. Now I needed to figure out how to tell Mia.

CHAPTER FORTY

Mia

Danny's face looked a little pale when he came back from tucking Kai in. He'd recovered from his frustration and spiraling about the personnel changes for his work pretty quickly yesterday, which was definitely something I loved about him. He hadn't let that bad news ruin the day or weekend. But I could tell he had a lot on his mind, and he needed to bring whatever it was up on his own time.

But the expression had me concerned. "He go down okay?"

He pulled at his neck... something I learned he did when upset or thinking about heavy things.

"Yeah. He did great." His eyes flitted around the kitchen, but wouldn't land on me.

"Is something wrong?" I pressed, coming to stand right in front of him so he couldn't ignore me.

"No, no. Not at all." He placed a hand on each of my arms, the touch soothing the nerves that had cropped up in the last few days. "He told me he loves me."

His cheeks flushed, and his eyes studied me.

"That's very sweet. I know he does." I kept my voice calm, despite my pounding heart. Fear and hope curled in my belly.

When he should have spoken, when it looked like he'd say something more, he hesitated. I wanted to close my eyes against the intensity on his face or crush myself against him, but I couldn't. I wouldn't run away from this moment, whatever it would be, because I was scared.

But he still wasn't speaking. I'd go insane before he said another word, I just knew it. My pulse pounded at my temple, in my neck, and anxious energy piled up in my chest. "Danny…"

He slid a hand around behind my head. "I told him I love him too. We've said it before, actually."

Not exactly better than saying it to me, but something about him telling my child, my whole world and the person I'd loved with my heart, soul, blood, sweat, and tears these last six years, crushed any defense I might have had against him.

"I—that's wonderful." Tears gathered in my eyes, but I cleared my throat, unwilling to cry just yet.

He nodded, the intensity still there, but a small smile curved his lips and wrinkled at the corners of his blazing blue eyes. "It is."

My throat had gone dry at some point in the last few minutes. I forced a swallow as I held him at his waist—when had I grabbed him there?

"Mia…"

He'd kill me. I'd end up dead on the floor if he kept

using that low, serious voice and looking at me with such… *intent*.

"Danny…"

Wavering and weak, his name sounded strange to my ears, which were so attuned now. No longer a rushing sound crushing my mind as my heart galloped, but unusual stillness, like I'd been waiting for this moment for longer than I could remember.

He shook his head, just barely, and his smile grew to that gorgeous, all-consuming one that made me feel like someone had finally turned the lights on after days of darkness. He stepped closer, both hands in my hair now, and lowered his face so he looked directly into my eyes from just inches away.

"Mia, I love you." Another flashing smile. "I love you, so much."

I'd sensed it was coming, of course. I knew it. That had to be the reason my body had reacted the way it had—raving, then stilling; galloping, then calming. But hearing it from him, no question or doubt, easily qualified as the most beautiful thing to happen in my life since Kai's birth.

The words welled up in my throat, but before they escaped my mouth, he pressed his lips to mine. All the love he spoke of weaved into our kiss, and I thought he must feel how I returned it. He must know.

But in case he didn't, I pulled back and pressed my palms to his cheeks. "I love you too, Danny. Very much."

Instead of a smile, a flame lit in his eye, and then his kiss returned, heat and love and joy and hope, all circling us there in my dimly lit kitchen.

"You should stay," I whispered in a quick moment when our lips had parted. "Stay tonight."

~

I woke slowly, mercifully not at the jostling of Kai's jumping on the bed and loudly celebrating Danny being here. Instead, the summer morning light filtered in through the blinds, and I stretched my body long, arms above my head and toes pointed, feeling life crawling back into my limbs as I came to full consciousness.

"'Morning."

The gruff sound rumbled next to me, and a strong arm wrapped around my waist and pulled me a few inches to the right until I was nested with Danny.

"'Morning," I said, lacing our fingers together and hugging his arm to my chest.

I wondered how long we had until Kai bounded in, but before I could get that thought completely out, there he came. The chorus of *Mom!* and *Danny!* and *Race time!* pinging off the walls of my small master bedroom.

Not much time to spend snuggling and reveling in the morning together, but that was life with Kai. Plus we had the race this morning, and so we needed to move out. I wouldn't soon forget our night of being together... hopefully the first of a lifetime.

Soon enough, we were loaded into Danny's car on the way to the race. Kai talked a mile a minute, and by the time we parked—no more than a ten-minute drive including parking, but maybe not even that—Kai and Danny had made plans for the following weekend to go on a boys' hike.

We'd gone on a few hikes the three of us, and Danny had asked if I'd be okay with him taking Kai sometime. That, among so many other things, brought bright little tingling sparkles to my fingers and toes. Watching him interact with Kai as he drove us in the wake of our confessions and all the night had held hours ago... my heart threatened to climb out of my chest and dance around from the hope and happiness there.

When we arrived at the race starting line, the same one the tri had used as its finish, Leo sat next to Wells at a table checking people in. Leo manned the kids' race, and Wells must have been doing the adults'. The kids' race would happen just after the adult race ended, but since it was only a 5K, it would be quick.

"Welcome, welcome. Last name? Oh, duh." Leo winked at Kai and sifted through the race bibs in a large box, then pulled one out and handed it to him. "There you have it, Mr. Parker. I hope I get a post-race high-five."

Kai gifted her a broad smile and then we shuffled along to get a bag of racer swag so the next person could check in.

The set-up, yet again, impressed. I knew they'd been working on this weekend's events for months, but they'd thought of every detail—things to keep kids occupied like bouncy houses and tables with crafts, right next to snack areas and great shaded seating for parents.

Liam hustled up, clipboard in hand, and patted Danny on the back. "Dan, bro, awesome job this weekend. We've got all the TV channels coming out later today, and a few here this morning, along with the Trib, the Examiner... everyone's here. You're awesome."

Danny smiled, but pulled me close with a hand at my waist. "Bel gets some of the credit, but I think most of it goes to you, man. You've made an amazing weekend, and people know it. This is going to do good things for us."

"Agreed. The weekend has been a success already. You can be very proud, Mr. Morrison." Jonas Bauer's serious, almost stern presence, loomed at our left.

Danny stepped back to let Jonas closer into the circle of conversation and nodded heartily in agreement with him.

"Well, I should get this guy warmed up for the big race... we'll see you later. I'll be over after he finishes to help the rest of the day."

Though initially we thought Danny would be too busy to spend much time with us, things ran so smoothly, he was able to leave when we left and not be chained to the events like we thought he would. That was largely to do with the hard work of Liam and Jonas and all their meticulous planning, and Leo and her management of the volunteers.

The morning rushed by, complete with Kai winning third place in his age group for the kids' run. He was practically vibrating with excitement and triumph as he launched himself into Danny's arms after the race.

I guess I didn't rate a hug. I got a high-five as Danny lifted him high in the air and plunked him on those strong shoulders. My sold-out little heart fluttered yet again at the way Danny celebrated Kai, made it all a huge deal that he won third, that he finished at all, and made my boy feel special.

Danny had a gift for that—for making people feel special. I gave myself a moment to breathe the warm August air thick with the scent of wildflowers and sun-warmed grasses, and thanked God we were the ones who got to have him.

More and more, I saw that clearly. I loved him, Kai loved him, and he loved us. I could hardly stand the welling elation and sense of awe that brought me.

"So this weekend? I'll clear my Saturday if you do. I know you start school this week so I might not see you as much. But eight o'clock Saturday, you're mine, buddy."

Danny caught my eye and winked, then leaned in for a quick kiss before he had to go.

Kai's smile blazed only slightly less bright than the sun. "Saturday."

Danny

The exhaustion from the weekend threatened to flatten me.

"Seems like you had a pretty good weekend too," Liam said, handing me a frosty beer and slumping into the chair next to me.

He never missed anything. Of course he could tell things had progressed with me and Mia, especially now that he tuned in to the world around him and wasn't drowning in the stress of the family business going down in flames.

"I did."

We sat on the plaza behind the lodge looking out at the towering Silver Ridge and surrounding mountains, staring into the night sky dotted with twinkling stars. We would have to finish the take-down of the event space tomorrow—the rental companies who provided the barricades for the race, the people we rented the stage from... they'd come by tomorrow. All bar tenders and employees had been paid, volunteers thanked profusely and sent home with any extra food we had, and the band, including the lovely Quinn Darling, invited back whenever they wanted to play.

We collected the trash, separated out as many bottles and plastics as we could for recycling as we went. We wiped down tables and folded them, loaded them up. Fortunately, we owned our fest tables and benches, so we powered through and packed them into the lodge before the volunteers left and it was one less thing we'd have to wait around for contractors to come pick up tomorrow.

I loved the events we put on—so many of them were rooted in the history of the lodge and the town. But the aftermath often left a crazy anti-climax that bummed me out. That said, I had little to be sad about tonight.

"I'm beat." Liam swigged his beer, then set it on the table between our chairs and let his hand drop down, lifeless.

"I forgot how tired these things leave me. I mean, I know they do, but especially being more involved..."

Liam sniffed, chuckled. "Yeah, being more involved is pretty draining. I'll give you that."

I eyed him, and maybe he could see the little streak of hurt that crossed my face. I thought we'd gotten past the whole *Danny doesn't do anything* thing.

He shook his head, a chagrined smile on his face. "You know I'm grateful for you. I always have been. You did a great job, and you should be proud. I didn't mean that to come out like it did."

"Don't worry about it. It's true that I've never done this much." I took another sip, then set down my bottle, my body losing the will to even hold the drink.

"It's worse during the season—you know that, right? I

mean, the events are grueling, but taking Rod's job... it's going to be exhausting. Paired with the other stuff in your contract, which I have no doubt Bauer's going to hold you to, you're going to be a zombie from November to April." He rested his head against the high back of the wooden chair and watched me.

I swallowed the jump of anxiety at his words. Obviously, the job would require more of me. That's what I said I wanted, right?

"Yeah. I figured as much. I already have a personnel headache after two of my senior patrollers told me yesterday they aren't coming back this season." I scrubbed my face, working to bring back a sense of calm and accomplishment rather than slip into that puddle of anxiety and dread that threatened.

"That's tough. There are lots of good people though, and hopefully, we'll have a nice influx this year as word gets around we're expanding. The new lifts should help draw staff, don't you think?" he asked like he didn't know.

Nice of him to try to make me feel like I knew what I was talking about.

"In theory, maybe. People like decent pay, and we have a good reputation in terms of the business culture. Rod obviously provided a draw that I don't, but then we have the influx of money, the new lifts, and the other stuff going on in the area like Jamie's development... we should have some new blood soon." I hoped. Desperately.

He groaned as he sat forward, sounding old and pained, but also exactly like I felt, so I couldn't laugh too much. He set a hand on my shoulder and gave me that look he got when he planned to give me advice. "It'll be okay, Dan. I'm pretty sure you told me the same thing not even a year ago. You were right, and now I'm right. This is a good thing."

I pulled a hand at the back of my neck, restless and out of fight for the night. "Hope so."

The week labored on. The tear-down Monday bled into Tuesday after we discovered some damage to the plaza from the stage and in another place where a vendor had done something insane with his gigantic truck and torn up a whole section of the cobblestones.

Then there was an emergency up at the site of one of the new lift towers that ate up all of Wednesday. We had our after-action review meeting on Thursday, which I wanted to believe Liam tried to keep short, but even he seemed bedraggled by the end of it.

At that point, I hadn't seen Mia for more than a stolen kiss when I got home. I hadn't seen Kai at all since I was getting home after he went to bed and didn't see him in the mornings because, though I'd spent the night twice now, it wasn't exactly open season there. I wasn't moving in with Mia and Kai, and though I'd felt like the world lay at our feet on Sunday when I woke, the after-glow of the event— maybe of the whole weekend—set in on me like a shroud.

When I finally poured myself into bed Thursday night, I prayed I'd find the strength to snap out of this bad mood, or whatever it was. It wasn't like me, that's for sure.

I was scared. It wasn't simple anxiety—not that anxiety was all that simple. But it was a kind of fear I hadn't felt before. I'd jumped off cliffs on skis, I'd blasted avalanches, I'd done really insane stuff. But this required personal bravery, and the fear sat squarely on my chest in the form of doubt: could I do this? Could I do *any* of this?

Could I be a boss, work a job, manage people well, keep

people on the mountain safe, manage a balanced work life *and* have a family of my own?

I didn't want to stay here, didn't want it to slip over into the weekend and cloud my time with Kai on Saturday morning and hopefully the time I'd spend with him and Mia the rest of the weekend.

So I prayed for strength. Prayed for courage. Prayed my commitment to grow up and be a functioning human fully engaged in the world and with people he loved wasn't a fool's errand.

CHAPTER FORTY-TWO

Mia

Mrs. Stanton glared at me through false lashes.

"Are you about to tell me you've fallen madly in love and you're running off with a man?"

Her usual warmth had fled when I started talking about Danny.

"No, ma'am. Why would you say that? I have a son, and I just started a life here. Plus, Danny's from Silverton. Where would we go?"

Her thin, dark brows arched, lips pursed a moment like she wouldn't deign to respond, then, "I haven't the slightest, but the question remains. Are you about to quit?"

I searched the room for clues. Had I said or done *anything* to indicate I might do that? No. "No, I'm not, and I'm not sure why you'd think that. Has something I've said given you that impression?"

She exhaled dramatically, like she'd run out of patience, but her shoulders relaxed in their stylish, shoulder-padded summer weight twin set. "No, in fact, you haven't. That Will Morrison is a chatterbox, you may or may not know, and I overheard him telling Ella Paxton not a week ago that his grandson Danny was head over heels for you and he expected he'd be gaining a granddaughter and have his first great-grandson by the year's end."

I opened my mouth, found it empty, then shut it. A giggle leapt out. "I—wow."

The imperious look again. "Well?"

"That's very kind of Mr. Morrison to be so—"

She waved a bejeweled hand. "That's not what I'm talking about. What's the status of your relationship with Daniel Morrison?"

I hid a small smile. The way she said his name—I could almost hear her reprimanding him for talking too loudly in the corner of the library, which he'd admitted she had to do often when he visited weekly during summers growing up. "We're dating. Seriously. I love him. But we haven't talked about marriage..."

We hadn't. But it felt like we had. Maybe it was the nature of having Kai in the mix, or maybe it was just that I felt so happy to be with him and have things between us clarified, I didn't want to start thinking that our future was uncertain. Not already. Not yet.

"Daniel is a darling boy, Mia. Good for you. But I hope you'll remember, as I may have mentioned before, he is just that—a boy. He loves stories, skiing, hiking. He loves the mountains more than anything, and I can't imagine how that might work out for someone trying to make a life with him."

A sick feeling weighed in my belly. "You seem so certain, but that hasn't been my experience at all."

"Well, you're new. That's why I mention it. I've known the young man all of his twenty-six or whathaveyou years. The whole town has. And what we've seen is just that."

I swallowed against the thickness in my throat, the ache in my jaw. This woman wasn't my grandparent, she wasn't my mother; she was a sort-of former boss I visited with regularly. But through months of training together, though they had been short, I'd come to care about her, and I knew she cared about me. Hearing her opinion of Danny hurt.

"We've talked about his past, and where his focus has been. He seems to think it's time for a change for him, and I think Kai and I fit into that." I wished my voice hadn't been so shaken as I said it.

Her gray eyes watched me, flitting to my mouth, no doubt noting the down-turned tilt. "You're a smart girl. You'll figure it out."

"One last dinner before everything changes," Leo said, her tone surprisingly glum.

The Leo I'd come to know in the last few months was either excited about something, declaring something, or planning something. I supposed this could fit into the declarative realm, but her delivery revealed a very different energy.

Bel shook her head and shot Leo a frustrated look. "We talked about this."

"We did. It doesn't mean this isn't the last dinner before everything changes. I don't mean for the worse, I just mean..." Her eyes toured around the table. "Things are changing."

Bel pulled Leo into a hug, and their eyes shone with tears when they pulled apart.

Wells cleared her throat next to me, but her voice came out watery. "We'll miss you so much, Bel."

Bel Paxton would leave with Jamie Morris in just a few days—they'd be settling in LA until they left for Jamie's next tour in late October. Bel planned to come back for the fall festival, but we all knew it might not work out once she got to LA and things there got crazy.

"I'll miss you too—you'll have to let me video chat with you during dinner every once in a while. I think there's a very good chance I'm going to get to LA, Jamie's going to start recording, and I'm going to be sitting around feeling like half my heart's still here with you all."

That got me. I'd only been a part of this little circle of friends for a few months, but I'd known Bel for a year now. And she was sweet, thoughtful, kind... she was a beautiful person, and I hated that just as we finally started a true friendship, she was leaving. That said, one look at her with Jamie and I could see she'd be just fine. His eyes lit up—no, his whole demeanor, his whole body, seemed to come alive when she was next to him. He'd take care of her, and she was strong.

"You'll probably end up being best friends with Whit Grantham and Jenna Halter and never think of us again."

Leo's voice teased, but I wondered if she really feared Bel becoming friends with famous women and leaving her behind. Whit Grantham, world-famous country star, was reportedly one of Jamie's best friends, and Jenna had been linked to him romantically, but Leo mentioned at some point that was only because they did an appearance on *The*

Tonight Show together years ago. Jenna was a hilarious actress and seemed like an awesome person, so I couldn't blame Bel if she did end up becoming her friend.

"Never. I mean, I'd love to meet them and be their friends, but I won't be replacing you."

They went on like that for a few minutes, but eventually, everyone recovered, until Wells said, "Bel's really the one whose life is changing. As far as I can tell, we're all sort of staying the same, right? I had my big upheaval last year."

Wells had moved to Silverton, taken over the Silverton Inn after her great-aunt willed it to her, and had eventually fallen for Liam Morrison.

"Yeah, all except the whole engagement thing." Leo again, but then her eyes flashed in fear.

Bel elbowed her. "Uh..."

Wells chuckled.

"It's okay, guys. I know he's taking me away tomorrow, and I'm not an idiot. We've had all the conversations, and he's been very honest, as have I. I have a good feeling about this trip." Her smile grew.

Leo fell back against the booth. "Thank the Lord. I was scared I ruined it. Liam never would have forgiven me."

Wells just shook her head. Then Leo's eyes fixed on me. *Oh boy.*

"And you? How are things with you and the youngest Morrison man?" She fluttered her lashes for effect, like she wasn't busting into my business.

Truthfully, it made my heart glow a little to be included. First, because I had a man I loved, who loved me, and I could happily report that fact. But second, and maybe even more significantly in this moment, I felt loved by these friends. Included in their ribbing and emotional reflection on the coming changes... I felt I belonged.

"We're doing very well."

Each woman beamed back at me, clearly so happy for me, and for Danny, and for us. If only I could forget Mrs. Stanton's words of warning from earlier today.

I must have broadcast that thought, because Bel asked, "What is it, Mia?"

I held a breath, wondering if I should say anything. I didn't want to admit that Mrs. Stanton's words had affected me. I didn't want to be thrown off course by someone who wasn't family and who shouldn't have that much of a say in my life. But she knew Danny—had known him all his life. Then as I looked at these women, I realized they'd known him too—Leo far better than anyone, and in many ways Bel too, for a time.

Exhaling, I leaned back so the waiter could set down my plate of enchiladas, topped with a pile of guacamole high enough to ensure I'd leave satisfied.

"I'm happy. I love him. But if I'm honest... I'm nervous. I've never done this before, and he hasn't either. And people keep giving me these well-meaning warnings about him, like they don't believe he can commit to me or take on the responsibility of being with me. And while I get that, because we've talked about his past and his reluctance to *grow up* as he puts it, I also hate the idea that he'd be saddled with me, the *single mom*."

Wells set a hand on my leg and squeezed, but Leo spoke. "Some people are voicing concerns that might be legitimate. But they aren't saying things you don't know, right?"

Her blue eyes speared me from across the table. She held a forkful of food in her hand, but paused, waiting for my answer.

"True. We've talked about all that. No one has said

anything that has given me the impression he hasn't been honest with me."

"Then you've been warned. Great. Duly noted. Now you live your life, and live with the consequences." Leo nodded, then took her bite of food, case closed.

Live with the consequences.

As I'd explained to Kai more than once, our choices have consequences. Some are good, some are bad. We have to accept the consequences of our actions. I hoped that my choice to be with Danny yielded all positive consequences —more love, more happiness, more stability, more joy for me *and* Kai, and Danny. But what if that didn't happen?

"Can I just butt in here? I may not be Danny's sister, and we haven't been close the last few years, but I know him." Bel sat rigid, shot Leo a look, then focused her attention on me. "Danny Morrison is the most faithful person you will ever meet. He is loyal, he is loving, and he would never hurt you. I can't predict how things will go, but if he told you he loves you, you can believe him. And it's not a paper-thin kind of love. It's thick as a slab of granite and it's immovable. If you love him and feel good about him being a part of your and Kai's lives, then claim him and never let go. He won't either."

Danny

Mia's hug when she opened the door was quick, light... *off*.

"Everything okay?" I asked as I walked into the door.

She gave me a close-lipped smile. "Of course. He's been chattering non-stop since he woke up an hour ago. And I'm admittedly ready for a few hours of quiet this morning."

The twisted feeling in my chest didn't subside at that. She wasn't saying anything wrong. Normal stuff, normal news, but something about it... *ugh*. It had to be me. I hadn't been able to shake the funk all week, despite talking myself out of it ten times a day. But time with Kai and the mountains would help.

"Are *you* okay?" Mia asked, her eyes surveying me closely with no small amount of concern.

Apparently, my weird mood was visible to others.

"Yeah. I'm in a funk, I think. Probably just the post-event blues," I said, a light chuckle to follow in hopes she wouldn't think it was her. It wasn't her at all. If anything, she and Kai were the good parts—the best parts of my life right now.

"Sounded like work was really busy this week. I didn't realize it would be so crazy after the fact."

I followed her into the kitchen where she filled Kai's water bottle and handed me a little sack lunch.

"It's not usually that bad, but we had some issues with one of the lift towers, and some other stuff..." I released a breath through my nose. "It'll be fine. Kind of makes me wonder if I'm cut out for all this, but... I guess I'll get the hang of it."

I zipped the lunch into my pack and finally looked up to find Mia looking like I'd slapped her.

Then she spoke. "Maybe you shouldn't keep the job... if it's that awful."

This was where my lack of experience in relationships had to be a drawback. What did that mean? "I—"

Kai bounded in from the hallway. "Danny! Danny! Dannyyyy are you ready? Are we going? Did you pack a lunch? How long is the hike? You promised it would be at least three hours. Is it at least three hours?"

And just like that, our conversation ended.

"You'll be back before the storm?"

I nodded while helping Kai with his pack. "Well before. It shouldn't hit until late afternoon, and we'll be back a little after twelve."

I kissed Mia on the cheek before we left and asked if we could have some time together when Kai and I got home. She agreed, thankfully, and off Kai and I went.

~

Though this wasn't the first hike I'd taken with Kai, it was by far the longest. He'd promised me he could do a longer one, so we were doing one of my favorites, on the beginner side of intermediate but nice and long. There was one semi-dangerous stretch with a narrow ledge through a fairly dry area that had slid out in June, but I'd reinforced the trail and it stood solid now.

We'd passed that point a half-hour ago. We were just shy of two hours into our hike, and only about fifteen minutes from our lunch stop.

"Watch this, Danny," Kai yelled from behind me.

I whipped around, about to take off and grab him if it was another one of his "tricks" he attempted like jumping off rocks way too high, which he'd already done twice now, but instead, I found him hopping on one foot along the trail.

"Very nice. That takes some good balance."

"Yep. And strong legs. I'm working to get my legs strong for ski season. Miss Leo says that's one way to be ready for the snow." His focus remained on the dirt path in front of him.

"Well, she's the expert." If only Kai wasn't six, Leo would've found her man.

"She is. She's the best."

He continued hopping, switching feet every now and then, and by the time we got to our lunch spot, it'd taken a full forty minutes. But in the end, we weren't in a rush, and the day was perfect. Up here on the mountain, the air was several degrees cooler. We found a spot under some trees and listened to the thin streams of water trickling into the secret lake as we ate.

The lake sat nestled into a small clearing, and really, it

could hardly be called a lake except we were in Utah, and any body of water ended up being called a lake unless it was man-made. It was more a pond, but officially, the location had been dubbed, decades before I came along, Secret Lake. At this elevation, everything still grew, so wildflowers blanketed the open space surrounding the water and oaks, aspens, and pines shot up around it, creating a quiet, sacred atmosphere. Beyond the pines, Silver Ridge Peak towered along with its fellows since we were not even halfway up the mountainside.

"This is the coolest thing I've ever seen," Kai said, his voice quiet, reverent.

I patted his head. "It is. It's one of my favorite places. Thanks for coming with me."

Once we'd finished our lunches, we lay back on the little blanket I'd brought and watched clouds roll by. He called out shapes, occasionally crunching on goldfish crackers. The mountain breeze rustled in the tall grasses, summer birds chirped, and my soul began to calm.

This beauty was why I loved this place. My eyes shut slowly as my mind conjured a picture of me laying here with Mia and Kai, the three of us a family, and everything about that image settled into me like sediment into shale, the inevitability of it seeming right and true as I drifted off.

I woke with a start, the sense that something was very wrong bringing me to full consciousness in a second. Raindrops pelted my face before I could sit up completely, and a crack of thunder growled.

"Kai, buddy, we've got to go *now*."

Kai was up, shoving his feet into his hiking boots—he'd

taken them off to feel the ice-cold water, then kept them off as we ate and napped. I tied the laces securely, threw on my pack, and grabbed his hand.

Lightning shot into the sky. I counted. One... two... three... four... five... *good.* At least five miles off. We could get out of the clearing and head down the trail so we were on a steeper face. We couldn't wait or there was a decent chance that portion of trail would be trashed... These clouds had flash flood written all over them.

"We need to get down the mountain as fast as we can. Follow me close, no hopping this time, all right?"

Kai nodded, fear written all over his face.

I crouched in front of him so I could look right in his eyes. "It's just a storm, but I don't want to be way up here since the rain is coming hard already. It could disappear before we know it. But just in case, I want us to move quick. We'll be just fine... let's just challenge ourselves to getting down faster than we got up. Sound good?"

A somber nod was all I got, but we couldn't stay there and wait for his confidence to return. He was right to be scared, at least a bit, because I was too. This storm was predicted to start in the late afternoon hours. We'd slept for over an hour, but that still should have given us three or four hours until it hit—plenty of time to get down the mountain before a single raindrop fell. That, and rarely did summer storms actually materialize to be much of anything... but still, I shouldn't have risked it.

We hoofed it, and I knew I was pushing Kai's legs, but I didn't want the lightning catching us. For now, it sounded like maybe it was rolling in the other direction, not getting closer, so we moved as fast as we could.

When the trails were flat or only slightly downhill, we jogged, and Kai kept pace with me. I asked him every few minutes if he wanted me to carry him, but he said no. He promised he'd tell me when he needed help.

And then it happened. The thing I dreaded, the thing that, maybe, my gut knew would happen from the minute I felt the rain.

"Danny!" he cried out, his leg sinking into soft earth made into mud by the driving rain. He'd edged too close to the side, his foot slipped, and he toppled over, hands stuck in the mud too, grappling for the side of the trail as he rapidly sank and slid further down the slope. I dove for him, landing hard on my ribs on a slab of rock—that'd leave a mark—and grabbed his wrists with my hands. This was no towering cliff or steep ledge, but the rain had made dry, mountain desert dirt into mud on this side of the trail, and the minimal pressure of Kai's body had pushed it just enough to create what was essentially a small mudslide. He would have been fifty feet down the way in seconds, possibly buried in mud.

Just that thought sent another jolt of adrenaline through me and I pulled him, hand over hand, to me, not releasing him at any point. He was hurt, though I couldn't be sure where, and at this point, it didn't matter because we had to move. We had to get down this mountain *now*.

"I've got you." Already moving into a steady jog, I clutched him to me, my heart galloping in my chest, mind racing, my body not feeling a thing. I brought his face to mine so we were eye to eye. "I will get us home. Hang on to me, don't let go, and I will get us home."

CHAPTER FORTY-FOUR

Mia

The relief that came from an empty house and a morning with nothing to do wouldn't come.

I paced the stretch between my room and the kitchen several times before I gave up and went for a jog. The nervous energy that built rather than burned off during the exercise propelled me into the shower. I did no lingering over books like I'd planned. I'd left my sweatpants before nine on a Saturday when I had the morning to myself.

Something was deeply wrong.

Danny didn't seem quite right when he arrived, but the fact that he'd admitted he was in an odd mood helped. I should've taken him at his word and believed it was simply the post-event weirdness, but I couldn't shake that somehow, I had a hand in forcing him into this job. I didn't understand if he was trying to tell me he wanted to quit when he told me about the stressors he'd discovered this last week. Maybe he felt like he needed my permission, or maybe, even worse, he was giving me the warning.

Maybe he didn't just mean the job when he said he wondered if he was *cut out for all this*... maybe *all this* wasn't just the job. Maybe it was me and Kai too.

Mrs. Stanton's words of warning sounded in my head. She'd made it sound like his love for the mountain would supersede his love for anything and anyone... could that be possible?

But then, I thought of how he was with me and Kai. Truly nothing except his initial freak-out before we really started dating even hinted at a lack of commitment to us. And then, there was Bel's unequivocal statement that he could be trusted. For someone who'd rejected him, that seemed like oddly high praise, though I knew it wasn't a simple dynamic between them.

I ran my hands through my still-damp hair and wished the smoothing away of the clingy strands would serve to clear my mind too. I felt so jumbled and confused, and that made me mad. I didn't want to doubt Danny, not now, after making my mind up about him. I didn't want to feel this distance between us, even when we stood talking in my kitchen.

It came from me... I knew I was off when he came to the door. Not purposefully, but I was waiting for that warmth and comfort that just being with him brought me to kick in, but it hadn't. His bad mood, my waffling... it combined to make the most awkward morning we'd had in a while, but we couldn't even acknowledge it because in theory, we were past all that.

I hoped some time in the mountains would help him feel better, and that being around Kai would too—if anyone could cheer a person up, it was Kai. I smiled to myself at the thought of him bubbling over with joy as he ate his cereal this morning. He loved Danny and couldn't wait for his "boys' day" of hiking.

A sharp pang of hope and sadness speared my chest. How could I feel those things so close together? The hope came from the thought that Danny might really be the man to be a father to Kai. After all this time, had I stumbled on a man who would love my son as much as I did? The sadness came from the reality that Kai hadn't had that. He'd never had a boys' day. He'd hungered for it, and I'd never come close to anyone like I had with Danny.

I shut my eyes against the geyser of emotion—*too much*. I needed distraction, and there was only one solution for a gorgeous morning after I'd already run my guts out, showered, cleaned the kitchen, and driven myself crazy by pacing the small space.

A good book.

For the first time all morning, I let myself be carried away from my worries, my neurotic building *need* to see Danny and get this all worked out. The characters swept me from my own circumstances, and before I knew it, my stomach demanded attention and I returned to the world of my living room to see I'd read for hours.

I hadn't gotten to do that in a long time. Kai played well independently, but he rarely let me read for *hours*, and sadly, I could rarely stay awake long enough to do that at night anymore.

The morning was a salve to the raw feeling I'd been carrying around the last few days. I savored the salad I made with fresh vegetables I'd picked up yesterday from the farmer's market. I set out butter to come to room temperature so I could bake a cake with Kai once he got home and got cleaned up—another incentive for Danny to come back for dinner, and hopefully before that.

I listened to the birds chirp in the little Japanese maple Danny had planted just to the west of his house, right outside our door. I enjoyed how the sky darkened slowly, clouds sliding over the sun to shift the light. The power of the thunder rumbled through my chest, the echo through the mountains creating a megaphone effect.

Thunder!?

I hopped up, checking my phone. It was after noon, and not a word from the boys. Danny had said he planned to be back by now, so surely they'd be wandering in any minute, dirty and happy and even though they'd had lunch on the mountain, inevitably hungry.

Minutes passed. No one came to my door. No knock, no footsteps above me indicating maybe Danny had run into his house to drop his backpack before bringing Kai by, which he wouldn't do, but at this point, a mild panic grew in my chest.

I called Danny's phone. Called it again. Left a message for him to ring me back as soon as he could. Texted, but it failed to deliver.

They must still be on the mountain. They must not have made it all the way down.

Lightning brightened the sky in a jagged slash. My heart twisted under my ribs, and if the thunder hadn't sounded only moments later, I would have sworn I could hear the blood rushing in my veins.

Get home. Get home. Please get home safe.

I reminded myself—Danny grew up in these mountains. He knew his way around. He'd cut the trail they were taking. He'd hiked it a hundred times—more. And Kai was strong. Kai could keep up. And if he couldn't, Danny would carry him back. If something happened, if someone was hurt...

Oh, God. What if Danny is hurt and Kai is alone and the phone doesn't work? What if they're both hurt and can't call for help? What if the trail washed out with the rain and—

STOP.

I had to stop the spiraling from consuming me. I could feel it happening and it wouldn't help. No.

Danny knew what to do. He could help Kai if he got hurt, and he could get Kai down the mountain. Danny wouldn't fail me. Not now.

CHAPTER FORTY-FIVE

Danny

I'd never gotten down a mountain so fast, and definitely not with the nearly dead weight of a six-year-old on my back.

"Almost there, buddy." I squeezed Kai's legs gently to reassure him. He'd stopped audibly crying within minutes of getting on my back, but the whole situation had gone sour and I hated that he was hanging on for dear life, dirty, hurting, and scared.

Oh and by the way, genuinely in danger. Fortunately, the lightning had in fact stayed a ways off until right about now.

After Kai's mudslide, I'd gone at a fairly steady jog the entire way except for a few craggy parts of the trail toward the bottom. My body held up, thank goodness, though I had to force away the visions of what would become of Kai if I fell or got hurt on the way down.

What'd taken us almost three hours on the way thanks to the many small detours and side trails Kai had taken took an hour and fifteen minutes on the way down. By the time we left the trail, thanks to the adrenaline, the chill of the rain, and the exertion, I couldn't feel much of my body at all.

We made it down the mountain to find an empty parking lot at the trail head—no surprise since everyone else had probably cleared out, or not started up. Would've been great if I'd driven us there, but part of the beauty of Silverton was living so close to the mountain that you didn't have to get in a car.

If I hadn't fallen asleep, we would've left sooner. We would have gotten home and Kai wouldn't be hurt and upset. The thoughts kept swirling around in my head, jabbing my gut with guilt and frustration.

This was on me.

I took an old shortcut to get to the neighborhood and mercifully, just as another deluge of rain began and lightning cracked through the sky, I knocked at Mia's door.

"Oh, thank God." She pulled the door open and stepped back so I could shuffle in. "What happened?"

I walked past her to the kitchen and bent to set Kai down right into a chair to avoid putting pressure on his legs in case he had a break.

"I'm okay," Kai's tiny voice came.

I kneeled in front of him and started undoing his laces as Mia gripped his head and kissed him roughly through rain-soaked hair.

"How is your foot?" We hadn't spoken much on the way down because I'd truly been at a near-run most of the way, the rain had been loud, and I'd tried to focus on putting my feet in safe places so I didn't fall and complicate the issue.

"It's okay. There's pins and needles now from you carrying me."

"Why are you all muddy? What happened? Are you hurt, Kai?"

Mia's rapid-fire questions pulled the string of concern around my neck. My chest had grown tighter as the minutes passed, each step closer to this house and Kai's mom, and each step closer to having to face my complete and unequivocal failure to keep her son safe.

"I'm okay. I think I twisted my ankle. It hurts." Kai's little voice sounded watery. He was trying to be brave, not to cry. He stood slowly. "I can stand though."

I shook my head, my breath still short.

"I'm so sorry buddy. I'm so, so sorry." I turned to Mia. "We fell asleep watching clouds after lunch. It was a perfect spot. And then I woke to the rain, so we started down, moving pretty quickly. The rain came hard, and it must have softened the trail. Kai slid on the side—"

"Danny dove to save me though, Mom. Like, superhero jump. He was standing right next to me, but I slid pretty fast in the mud and he just went for it. It was actually awesome." He summoned a smile, and that little light in his eyes sparkled.

My chest constricted more, Kai's sweetness piercing my already bruised heart like an arrow. How could he see this in a positive light?

"It's all my fault, Mia, I—"

"Let's get you into the shower and see what's going on under all this mud," she said to Kai, an arm around his shoulders as she steered him toward the hallway.

He seemed to be walking fine now. Thank God for that, because the thought of him being seriously hurt... I leaned on the wall just outside the kitchen, my body starting to come down from the adrenaline rush. My bones felt heavy, my heart fluttered sickly in my chest at the thought of anything happening to Kai, and man, I almost felt lightheaded.

Mia turned to me before they got to the bathroom. "It was an accident. The storm showed up hours before it was supposed to. He'll be okay."

Her steady voice, the total lack of anything accusatory or angry, should have calmed me. But my heart seemed to be pounding again, my head fuzzy with pain now, and I clutched at my gut just below my rib cage.

"Danny?"

"I'll get cleaned up and be back," I managed to say, thinking I might have to lay down a while, until whatever this was passed. Instead of straightening and moving to the door, I hunched against a sharp pain in my abdomen.

"Danny?"

I heard her say my name, but couldn't answer. I doubled over, the ache in my left side, my ribs, and now my shoulder and back, so intense that I couldn't breathe, certainly couldn't speak.

"Danny!"

I dropped to my knees and forced out an award-winningly obvious, "Something's wrong," before my field of vision closed in and everything went dark.

CHAPTER FORTY-SIX

Mia

I paced the hallway, the living room, back to the kitchen.

"Come on. *Come on.*"

Bel and Jamie were on the way to watch Kai for me. Leo had answered as soon as I called and raced over here, then followed the ambulance down the mountain. The EMTs thought a broken rib, maybe even a punctured lung, though Danny's breathing didn't seem labored and he did wake up for a minute as they loaded him in.

I couldn't leave Kai alone, but didn't feel I could take him with me after he'd been through such a rough afternoon. He was still mud-covered and shivering until after the ambulance and Leo left. I helped him get cleaned up and in cozy pajamas, started up his favorite movie, and now wracked my brain for a dinner I could make in a matter of minutes and with shaking hands and that he would love.

His normal sitter was booked. I actually called Bel to see if she knew of anyone who babysat, and she insisted she and Jamie come over, lamenting that Liam and Wells would be upset they couldn't help since they were out of town. Kai knew Bel well from our trips to the coffee shop, and he idolized Jamie simply because he was Danny's older brother.

"Are you okay? Is Kai okay? What can we do?" Bel rustled into the house with bags on each arm and Jamie behind her carrying pizza boxes.

"Pizza!" Kai shouted. "Oh, and Danny's brother!"

Bel widened her eyes at me before she wiggled her brows at Jamie. "I like that. Should I call you *Danny's brother* from now on?"

"Uh, no." His gorgeous face gave nothing away except one small twitch at the corner of his mouth.

"We're okay, and other than a few scrapes, Kai is fine. I have a feeling he's going to pass out early after all of this." I got out plates, utensils, chili flakes—anything they might need.

"They think he broke his ribs?" Jamie asked as he gave Kai a high-five.

I blew out a breath, hoping to calm myself before I hopped into the car. Thankfully, the worst of the storm had passed so my drive down the canyons wouldn't be too harrowing.

"Broken, maybe bruised. They're worried something else is going on though, because they couldn't get him to stay awake. It was so crazy... I've never seen him like that. I mean, obviously, but..."

I felt my words catch and held my breath again. I didn't want to cry now, not when I had to drive, and I certainly didn't want to freak Kai out any more than he already was.

"He'll be okay. He's strong and he's a fighter. Don't rush

your drive, and we'll be here with Kai for however long you need." Bel wrapped me in a hug which I desperately needed, then turned to Kai. "Right, bud? We're going to have a great time."

"Can I show you guys my room?" Kai yelled, already down the hallway.

Jamie chuckled and followed, and Bel shooed me out the door. I grabbed keys, raincoat, and the small bag I'd put together in case I needed to stay the night in the waiting room. At this point, the ambulance wouldn't have even gotten to the hospital. The EMTs said they would've life-flighted him but he seemed stable enough and the storm made a flight iffy, so they drove. Leo would call me when they arrived and give me an update, and it couldn't come soon enough.

But for now, I got on the road and prayed Leo would have good news when she called.

The drive down the mountain took forever. I made a point to go the speed limit, knowing my emotions and anxiety wouldn't do anything to help me and speeding would only make all of that worse. But that meant I took the canyons at fifty-five and the distance seemed to stretch out longer each time I saw a mile marker sign.

Leo called about thirty minutes into my drive. They'd taken him into the ER and soon after arriving, they'd wheeled him into surgery.

I drove in a focused kind of daze—taking in all the necessities of the road while not allowing myself to think. I couldn't allow myself to think about how utterly terrifying it was to see this big, strong man I loved so completely slump in my hallway and pass out. I was already scared enough that they were so late, that I couldn't get a hold of them, then that Kai had clearly fallen and was covered in mud, and then Danny bent over, dropped to his knees, and passed out, only a few garbled words I didn't understand slipping past his lips before he flattened onto the floor completely.

No. I couldn't think about that.

I finally parked, grabbed my purse, and ran inside the ER. Leo met me and led me through a maze of hallways to a small waiting room with a TV mounted on the far wall and forest green seats. It must have been an interior room because there were no windows, and happily, no other people there.

"Was he awake? Did they talk to him?"

She'd kept the conversation so short when she called since she knew I was driving and insisted I focus on the drive and get there safely. It was wise, but I needed details.

"They got him to come to in the ambulance. He said he thinks he hurt something when he jumped to grab Kai—I guess he landed on his side pretty hard. They were thinking his ribs, maybe his spleen, and wanted to monitor his breathing."

If there had been air in my lungs, you could have fooled me. I couldn't find it—couldn't figure out how to breathe past this news. That all sounded so serious.

Leo put a hand on my arm and squeezed, drawing my attention back to her.

"He's okay. They started an IV because his blood pressure was low on the ride. By the time they arrived at the ER, they'd called ahead to say they suspected all that, so they did a CT scan right away, and I guess from that they could tell his spleen had ruptured. They took him right into surgery, but I got to see him before he left. It happened so fast. I mean, half-hour, maybe, and he was being wheeled back."

I swallowed against the sound rising in my throat, knowing it was something ugly and terrible—a groan or sob and something in between. "Was he okay? I mean, did he seem like he was..."

I wanted to say *did he seem like he was okay* but I kept asking the same question and what could she really tell me? He had a ruptured spleen or a punctured lung or a broken rib, or all three.

Her blue eyes leveled me as she grasped both my wrists in her warm hands. "I told him you were coming, and he would be fine. He actually seemed pretty calm considering everything that was happening—maybe it's all that EMT and patroller training he's had, I don't know."

"Thank you. I'm sorry I couldn't come with you. I had to make sure Kai was settled, but I can't—" I pressed my lips together, gritting my teeth hard to steady myself. "I can't lose him. I've just now found him."

Leo shook her head, a stern look on her face. "None of that. You'll see him when he's out of surgery, and he'll be fine. They said a few hours, depending on what they find while they're in there... He'll be fine."

CHAPTER FORTY-SEVEN

Danny

Someone had stuffed cotton balls inside my ears. And mouth. And eyes. And lungs. And brain?

"How's your pain?" a voice said next to me.

I pressed my eyes open wide and searched for who spoke, and found a super tall guy in scrubs typing into a computer.

"You're in recovery. You've been here about a half-hour. We'll keep you here a bit longer and then take you to your room. Your girlfriend and sister will be there when you get there."

He looked at me expectantly, so I said, "Sounds good."

"How's your pain?"

Pain. Pain. I couldn't think of what hurt, but something did. Something middle-ish. "It's fine, I think. Hurts, I guess. Can I have water?"

Also, could someone remove the eighty-five cotton balls from my mouth?

He pushed me to put a number to my pain, then brought me a Styrofoam cup with a bendy straw and ice-cold water, but didn't let me gulp it down like I wanted. He let me have one small sip, no more, then said I needed to go easy on it and he'd let me have another sip in a few minutes.

What could have been minutes or hours later, once my head finally cleared a bit, they wheeled me up to the room where I'd be for some amount of time—someone had told me, maybe the tall guy, but I was still fuzzy and so tired. Retaining neat factoids about the name of the place they parked my wheelie bed didn't rank high enough on my list.

I heard voices behind the door of the room, and the unmistakable sound of Leo bullying some poor, unsuspecting nurse who probably assumed she had an angelic character to match her golden braided hair. The grouchy demeanor should've clued them in.

I dozed in the room until the door cranked open and in walked Leo, her arm linked with Mia's. At the sight of her, my lovely, sweet, kind, beautiful girlfriend Mia, I let out a dippy "Hey you." If I wasn't hopped up on pain meds, I might've been embarrassed. And if not about that, then about the fact that I'd passed out in the middle of her floor and no doubt traumatized Kai for life.

She released a watery chuckle. "Hey."

I held up a hand, however limp it might've been, and she took it. Hers was cool in mine, though I was roasting in my little hospital bed, kept nice and toasty by warm blankets piled on my feet because I'd been freezing in the recovery room.

"You look like crap." Leo hid her trembling lips behind the comment as she crowded into the room behind Mia, though the words came out with absolutely no bite. In fact, it sounded more affectionate and sad.

"I know if you're on the verge of tears, I must look pretty terrible."

She whipped away from me without an answer, and I let her go, shifting my full attention to Mia, who pulled up a chair with her free hand and sat next to me. I could look in her eyes more easily, study the curve of her cheek. I reached up to run my fingers along that smooth, soft place, and she leaned into my touch.

She exhaled, and her shoulders slumped. "I'm so sorry you're hurt."

My hand dropped to the bed, the tape securing my IV pulling at my skin.

"Please don't apologize." I shut my eyes against the frustration, embarrassment, and pure exhaustion. "I might have to sleep a bit. Can you stay?"

"At least three days, if not another day or two. I'm relieved we didn't encounter any other major issues during surgery, but I want to make sure things hold steady. After that, it'll be taking it easy for quite a while. No hiking, and definitely no jumping off cliffs to save children." The doctor nodded, said she'd be back one more time before she went home later on, and left the room.

I glared at Leo. "What did you tell her happened?"

She fluttered her eyes, pure innocence. "Exactly what did happen. You were hiking. You threw yourself off the side of a mountain to save a little boy who was falling. After grabbing him, you jogged down the mountain during the thunderstorm for over an hour and several miles carrying that boy, until you deposited him at his mother's doorstep, and fainted."

Mia's face showed shock while a mixture of embarrassment, disbelief, and annoyance rushed through me. "You have to be kidding me. That is a load."

Leo stood, stretched, and gave me that wide-eyed innocent look again, like I'd ever once fallen for it. "What? You did all those things. That is actually what happened. You may not think it was heroic, Danny, but it was. You somehow *ran* down a mountain in a storm, protecting Kai bodily and making amazing time, by the way, all while you had a *ruptured spleen* and insanely bruised ribs."

"It was all adrenaline," I mumbled, not sure what else to say.

"One reason I love you is that you'll never allow yourself to be made a hero because of this. That's fine. Just don't let yourself become a martyr either." She gave me one of her very pointed *Leo looks* and then walked to the door. "I'm getting some coffee. I'll be back in half an hour."

Mia moved back to the chair beside my bed—a position she held while I slept until the doctor came in to talk with us. The doc's review of my injuries—ruptured spleen, bruised ribs—and what they'd done to repair them, was thorough. I thanked God it wasn't ski season, because I wouldn't have been able to ski at all like this. I'd have to take it easy for a good six weeks, and I'd be in the hospital for another few days at least.

But what Leo said rang in my ears, and part of me believed her. *Don't become a martyr.* Sure, *martyr* was taking it a little far, but this was a mess of my own making. I needed Mia to know I understood this was my fault. I could take responsibility for my own actions, and she could trust me.

The whole way down the mountain, I'd kept vacillating between two thoughts—what if I lost Kai? And what if I lost Mia?

Either one felt like an ending I didn't want to read, but the combination—truly a horror. I couldn't face that ending, so I needed her to know I didn't take what happened lightly. I'd been waffling and nervous about the job. Our last real conversation had been tinged with my moodiness and a sense that things weren't settled on her side. I wanted to clear the air and make sure she knew exactly how I felt.

The intensity of the experience—seeing Kai hurt, fearing for his safety, losing consciousness and learning how badly I'd been injured... these things calcified something in me. Confronting just how easily accidents happen, I couldn't stand the thought of her not knowing how much I loved her, how sorry I was, how much I hoped for a life together if she could forgive me for being an idiot.

I took both her hands in mine—she humored me by bringing her body close and leaning up since I was still laid out fairly flat in the wake of the surgery. It'd only been a few hours, and soon, she and Leo would have to get back to Silverton.

"I am so, *so* sorry. I can't tell you how much. I—"

The shake of her head stopped me.

"Danny. Please stop."

CHAPTER FORTY-EIGHT

Mia

His big blue eyes blinked back at me, waiting.

"Please don't apologize for an accident."

He swallowed then reached for his little cup of water and took a gulp before speaking. "I messed up. We fell asleep and the storm rolled in. I should've started us back down the mountain right after we ate."

"Danny, honey." I pressed my hands to his. "Nothing about that is wrong. You had a great time. I know because Kai told me five hundred times before I got in the car to come here, and that's even with slipping in mud and having to race down the mountain during a rainstorm. Before all that, I'm sure you were making his dreams come true by just *being* with him. You do that so well—you aren't rushing him or pressuring him to get to the next thing. That is so rare, and I don't think you understand how much it means to him."

His face crumpled, but he clenched his teeth against that tide of emotion and spoke again. "I'm so glad he had fun. I'm so sorry he got hurt."

I leaned closer to him, getting right in his face so he could see I really meant what I said. "You have nothing to be sorry for. None of this happened because you did something wrong or weren't responsible. Everything that went wrong did so accidentally, and I know that. Plus... look at yourself."

His brows dipped, and his eyes skated over the hospital bed, then slid back to me.

"You risked your life for him. What more could I ask for? You literally threw yourself down on rocks and nearly killed yourself to save him, then hauled him down a mountain in record time, and had absolutely no concern for yourself. If anything, you need to apologize to me for not taking better care of yourself."

His head dropped back to the bed, and he winced. "I don't know how you can forgive me so easily."

This man was determined to make himself feel terrible. No wonder Leo said what she did as she left—she must've known what was coming with all this self-blame. "Honey, I don't have anything to forgive you for, don't you see that?"

He took a moment before responding. "I get it on one level, but on the other, I know what it felt like to carry him down the mountain and feel the insane fear that he was really hurt. You know how energetic and sweet he is, and he was so quiet the whole way down, just clinging to me. He did a great job, just letting me carry him, but it's probably the most scared I've been in recent memory. I was terrified he'd broken something or had a terrible gash we couldn't see under all the mud, and I didn't have time to stop and check him out because we had to get down the mountain."

My heart would have tripled in size if it were possible. My whole body ached with how much I loved him, this sweet strong man who'd risked his life to get my son home safe. And who loved Kai so much. "Danny honey, I hate to tell you, but that's what loving a kid does to you. It's the most terrifying thing ever."

He gave me a sad smile. "Really?"

I smiled, wiping tears from the corners of my eyes. "Yeah."

He looked to the ceiling. "Then I'm doomed."

We chuckled together, which made him press against his incision and grunt a little. "Laughing is terrible. We can't do that anymore."

I turned my head away to keep him from seeing me laugh again, then turned back, and he sobered. Something in that look made my stomach drop.

"Mia, I love you and Kai so much. And I want us to talk about—"

"No, please… let's wait. Okay? I don't want to have this conversation while you're on pain killers. I don't even know how much of these conversations you'll remember, and I don't want anything this… important… to be something you could forget."

He frowned at me, his lips pulling down and his forehead wrinkled in disappointment so much, it would've been comical if I hadn't just shut him down and made him feel that way. I ran my hand over his head and through his hair.

"I love you too, Danny. I do want to talk about whatever is on your mind. But right now, I want you to rest, and get better, and come home."

∽

Danny stayed in the hospital four days. I didn't get to visit him again because by the time I made the drive to the hospital over an hour away, it was too close to visiting hours ending. I thought about going that very next day, but Kai didn't feel great even though his leg looked fine, and honestly, I was too exhausted to drive all that way safely.

The hours at the library crawled by. I couldn't wait to have him home.

And then, there was that. He wouldn't be coming home to *me*. Leo would stay with him at his place, which was annoyingly *on top of* mine, but I couldn't be the one to take care of him. He needed someone with him at night for a few days, and I needed to be with Kai. I still had to work, and yet I kept thinking it was all so stupid.

Why wasn't I the one he leaned on? Why couldn't Kai and I both care for him, and all of us be together? My heart wanted that closeness; my mind did too. It felt like we were waiting for some outside force to give us permission to fully invest in each other, except that outside force, in the shape of a thunderstorm and a busted spleen, insisted on pushing us farther apart.

He was on the verge of telling me what he wanted for our future. I could feel it. That moment in the hospital when he looked at me, and everything zeroed down to the two of us, I knew that's what he wanted. And yet, I couldn't stand the thought of it being fuzzy for him. I also hated the thought that he might be feeling protective and wanting to be with me in order to take care of Kai.

That sounded awful, but I wanted him to want us both. I thought he did. Most of me believed he did. But we'd had such a weird few weeks, and I didn't want that big discussion happening in the hospital hours after a major surgery while he blinked at me with sleepy, mildly intoxicated eyes.

So I shut him down, and then drove myself crazy waiting for him to get home.

Leo texted to say she was on the way back to town with Danny in tow, and they'd arrive right around the time I got off work. I'd grab Kai from the after-school program and zip home so we could greet him and help get him settled.

And once I knew he was settled.. maybe tonight if I couldn't stand to wait and his eyes were clear, or maybe tomorrow if I could steal a long lunch and grab some time alone with him, I'd bring up our future again. I'd wait for him to feel better and be ready, and then I'd let him know I was ready, too.

CHAPTER FORTY-NINE

Danny

The canyon zipped by as Leo drove like a bat out of hell—her usual setting.

Seriously, the woman drove the way she skied. Only problem with that? She was an expert skier, but not as much an expert driver. But I wasn't about to say anything because she'd spent almost every waking and many sleeping moments by my bedside and I couldn't feel anything but thankful.

And terrified.

Thankful and terrified. But that could be a pairing often used to describe the way one felt in Leo's presence. A confusing and yet surprisingly accurate mix.

"So why are you weird?" she said, busting into my odd train of thought.

I'll blame the pain meds on that.

"Uh... am I weird? Could it be I've just spent four days

in the hospital recovering from major surgery and am on a fairly decent dose of pain killers?"

She scoffed. "I'd take that as an excuse, except I know that's not it. You've done well in the hospital, charmed all the nurses and became best friends with the docs, and yet every time I turn around, you've got a rain cloud over your head."

I considered making another excuse. Something like *isn't being sentenced to minimal physical activity and having my sister babysit me for a week enough?* But instead, I came clean. "I tried to bring up the future with Mia, and she shut me down."

"'The future sounds ominous."

I sighed. "I hope not. She's it for me, and I want her to know that. I don't want to continue pretending we don't both know it. But she wouldn't let me even say that much."

Leo hummed, shifted gears, rocketed forward, and nearly gave me a heart attack as she weaved in between two huge trucks. "When was this?"

I gripped the arm rest with one hand and pressed back into the seat. "That first night. After that, I didn't dare bring it up over the phone."

"The first night like right after your surgery when you were high as a kite on pain meds?"

The nerve. "Yes, the first night. And I wasn't *high as a kite.*"

She glanced over at me with raised brows. "Uh, yeah ya were. Do you not remember how emotional you were? I think you cried three times in the span of ten minutes."

"Hey. Real men cry." I didn't need to defend myself.

"Of course they do. But not over the nurse bringing grape juice, and not over Jamie texting you to check in."

"What's your point other than to point out what a basket case I was?"

She shook her head but didn't look away from the road again, for which I was thankful. "My point is, I can understand Mia not wanting to have you say those really big deal things while you were coming down from surgery in the hospital. And my guess is she's eager to have that discussion, just not in those circumstances."

She had a point. I knew she was right. Mia had even said that she wanted to talk, but just not right then. Part of me understood that, but that urgent, desperate part, the me that wanted her to know I loved her and I wanted her to be mine and for me to be hers... I didn't want to wait.

"I get it to some degree. But did she really think I'd essentially propose to her and then forget about it?"

Leo turned, a huge wide-open smile on her face. "*Propose?* Daniel David Morrison, you cannot propose to a woman while in the hospital just after surgery. But more importantly, congratulations! Mia is awesome."

I nodded. "She is. She's amazing. So you can see why I have the sense of urgency I do. I screwed up, endangered her kid, and the thought of losing them both feels about a million times worse than a ruptured spleen."

Leo cackled.

"How eloquent. You should include that in your proposal." She chuckled to herself, and I shot her a dirty look before she kept talking. "But seriously, you guys do need to get on the same page."

Something about that struck me. "What do you know?"

"Mm mm, no. I'm not saying anything more, but I do think you have some conversations to muddle through. I promise to give you space to do that in the next few days—I can run errands or just get out of dodge if you need privacy."

"Good. Yes. Thanks."

"Does it hurt?" Kai asked, sitting gingerly next to me on the couch.

"I'm sore, but I'm doing fine." I gave him a big smile, hoping to reassure him. "Are you hurting?"

He shook his head adamantly. "No, not at all anymore. I'm sorry I slipped and you had to carry me."

The little frown on his face killed me.

"Kai, buddy, you know it's not your fault, right? That was a crazy trip down the mountain, and I'm so glad nothing worse happened. I'm so glad you're okay." I ruffled his hair.

"Yeah. But now you can't hike anymore, right?"

"Not for a few weeks, but after that? You and me are back on that mountain... maybe a shorter trail to start out, deal?"

His eyes literally sparkled at me as he nodded enthusiastically. "Deal."

Mia and Leo chuckled from behind him. Then Leo stepped up to Kai. "Any chance you'd show me your room downstairs while your mom and Danny have a minute to talk?"

And just like that, she gave me the opening. Mia moved to sit in a chair next to the couch. At least I was able to sit up more, so I could look at her eye to eye from my spot.

"I'm glad you're home," she said, gently touching my arm.

I took a slow, deep breath, releasing some of the stress

that had built over the last few days. The experience in the hospital had gone as smoothly as it could have, but I missed home, I hadn't slept much at all, and I missed her.

"Listen, I'm not sure if I'm allowed to talk about this yet, but I really need to say some things to you."

She reared back a bit with a small smile pressed between her lips. "Of course you're allowed."

"You sure? I'm still on pain meds. And it is in the wake of an accident."

She leaned against the back of the chair and crossed her arms, giving me an unimpressed look. "Point taken. I trust that despite your drug-induced stupor, we can have an important conversation."

I shot her a dirty look, and her face broke into a gorgeous smile.

"Good grief, you're beautiful." I set a palm on her leg, then took her hand when she gave it to me.

"I'm sorry I didn't want to talk in the hospital, but I'm ready when you are."

"I'm ready now. I've been ready, and I should have brought this up weeks ago." My heart would've set off all kinds of alarms if I was still hooked up to the machines at the hospital. It raced in my chest, almost making me light-headed. But no excuses, no more delaying. "I love you, Mia, and I want you to be my wife. I want you and Kai to be my family."

Her lovely mouth opened, closed. Opened again, then, "That's... a lot."

My turn to stutter. "Uh... yeah?"

She bit her lip, but I could've sworn her eyes were smiling. "I mean, that's a lot of responsibility. Commitment. Marriage is something I'm only going to do once, so you shouldn't say that unless you really mean it."

"I wouldn't say it if I didn't." I grabbed her hand with both of mine. "I know our relationship has been a lot of me learning how to handle more responsibility, but at no point have you and Kai felt like a burden or some challenge I have to overcome. I admit the job thing, it has been stressful and a big change for me. I've had my doubts..."

"I've been worried your concerns over the job were exacerbated by our relationship."

I gripped her hands a bit harder, praying the pressure would make clear what I meant. "Never. Not at all. My only concerns over you and me have been feeling like I had nothing to offer you and thinking you shouldn't want to be with me. But if you want me, I'm yours. I've never been more certain of anything in my life."

Her lashes fluttered, then she grabbed my head with a hand on each cheek. "Daniel Morrison, I want you. I want to be your person. I want us to be a family."

CHAPTER FIFTY

Mia

We weren't officially engaged, but we might as well have been. I was fairly certain Danny would ask as soon as he could walk around for more than ten minutes at a time without getting winded.

My goodness, I loved him. The concerns I had over his ability to be certain about us were gone entirely. The whole ordeal with his surgery had clarified things for both of us, and though I hated he'd gone through surgery and so much pain during recovery, I was so very thankful for the push to express ourselves and get past the miscommunications we'd been having.

A week after the hike that changed our lives, we gathered at Danny's for breakfast. There were too many of us for just the four-person table in his kitchen, so we spread around his cozy living room, all seats on couches spoken for, and the chairs from other rooms pulled in. Danny sat in his usual spot on the couch, Kai and me next to him.

Jamie and Bel had delayed their move to LA by a few days in order to help with Kai and be able to keep an eye on Danny. I heard that meant Jamie had to rearrange his recording schedule, and Bel said he had an all-out debate with his manager over the phone, but luckily for Jamie, he had enough clout he could swing it. Bel's admiration for her fiancé had shone in every word as she told me how he'd stated in no uncertain terms that family was his priority and he wouldn't be back in LA until his brother was stable.

Liam and Wells had returned just a day or so ago, but I hadn't seen them. They'd planned to come home when Leo told Liam about the accident, but Danny had reassured Liam he didn't need to rush back because between Leo, me, and Jamie and Bel, he was well taken care of.

So when they walked in just moments ago, no one having seen them since they'd left on their trip, Leo's audible gasp stole the attention in the room.

"What is *that*?" she said, eying Wells' left hand like it might jump out and bite her.

Wells flushed, her cheeks red immediately, and Liam clutched her close. "We had a good trip, thanks Leo. And how are you?"

"No. None of that. Don't make me seem like a monster when you walk in here and I see *two rings on her finger*."

Oh snap.

"What? Two rings?" Bel chimed, setting her plate on the coffee table and moving to Wells.

"Uh, so..." Wells' attention seemed to be caught between Bel, Leo, and Liam.

Danny clapped. "Did you get engaged? Congrats you guys!"

Wells chuckled, the blush still bright on her cheeks. "Uh, well, yes we did."

"And then we got married."

I didn't know Liam much at all, but I could hear the smug satisfaction in his voice.

"You—" Leo stopped herself.

"That's amazing! This is great—congratulations you guys!" Bel applauded, then hugged Jamie, who'd stood to haul Liam into a hug.

A chorus of congratulations surrounded the couple. Danny insisted on standing up, which he was doing with more ease every day, and he hugged Liam and Wells.

"I'm sorry. We didn't mean to show up and have things be about us," Wells said to Danny.

"Are you kidding? This is awesome news. I'm *so* glad you didn't come home for this. But I thought you were going to Arizona?" Danny patted Liam on the shoulder, then urged him farther into the room and showed him to a chair.

Liam sat and pulled Wells down next to him.

"We met Ma and Da in Sedona. They were our witnesses." He looked around the room. "I wish everyone could have been there, but this was right for us."

"I'm so glad you did it on your own terms," Bel said, looking meaningfully at Wells.

"It's wonderful," I added, a little lamely, but it was.

Wells' past included an abusive boyfriend and controlling parents. She'd broken an engagement and essentially run away from her old life a little over a year ago now. I couldn't help the tears that pricked my eyes as I watched her absolutely glow just sitting there next to Liam, chatting with her friends—now her family.

Danny came back to sit next to me and took my hand in

his. A new series of books had captured Kai's attention—he may not have noticed anyone else was here.

"So thrilled for you guys," Leo said, a stiff smile on her face. "Bel, Jam, I'm not sure I'll see you before you leave later. I've got to head out to—uh, so have a good flight, and I'll see you in early October, right?"

Jamie and Bel hugged Leo, who gave Wells one last squeeze on her arm and Liam an over-large smile, waved to me and Danny, and disappeared out the front door.

Danny's lips to my ear caused a shudder. "I'll make you that happy. I swear I will."

I looked at his face and saw him looking at Liam and Wells, who seemed to vibrate with excitement, love, joy.

I turned to him, taking in those crystal-blue eyes, flushed cheeks, messy reddish hair and the several-day scruff. "I know you will, Danny, because you already do."

The end. (For now.)

I hope you enjoyed Danny and Mia's story! They're so sweet. **Don't miss Leo and Jonas in Fire and Ice at Silver Ridge, the final Silver Ridge Resort novel!** You can also keep reading for a sneak peek of their story.

Grab Fire and Ice at Silver Ridge: Silver Ridge Resort, Book 4, the final Silver Ridge Resort novel!

The Back to Silver Ridge Series

Almost Perfect, Book 1

Almost Real, Book 2

Almost Sure, Book 3

Almost Home, Book 4

The Rambler Battalion Series

Sweet Military Romance

Where You Go: The Rambler Battalion, Book 1

As You Are: The Rambler Battalion, Book 2

Don't Stop Now: The Rambler Battalion, Book 3

Home With You: The Rambler Battalion, Book 4

All of You: The Rambler Battalion, Book 5

The OCONUS Bonus Series

Sweet Military Romance Overseas

The Problem with Planning Love, Book 1

Livie Anderson's got a plan for her life and she's on track for her next step. The last three years traveling Europe and working on a US Army base helped her experience all the adventure she wanted before she settles down in one place and stops the nomadic life. Now, her deadline to return home and start a family is fast approaching and there's a wrench in her perfect plans. Colonel Eric Wolfe came into her life and it's getting hard to picture leaving this world behind—but the Army life is the opposite of what she's always planned for.

Eric can't deny his interest in Livie, which is monumental in itself considering his total disinterest in everyone since his divorce three years ago. Despite his efforts to remain just friends, he can't resist Livie's pull—her joy, love for life, and genuine way of dealing with people. But he can't see a way to be with her without subjecting her to the military life that ruined his first marriage, and Livie's leaving anyway, so why can't he bring himself to let go?

Their lives are too different, and their plans don't match. They definitely shouldn't date, and they certainly shouldn't develop feelings. Too bad neither one of them can seem to stay away.

Finding Happiness in a Hoax, Book 2

Learning to Fight after Flight, Book 3

The Bright Side of Brooding, Book 4

Holding On to Hope, Book 5

ACKNOWLEDGMENTS

Thanks to the many people who supported me during the writing of this book! Thanks, also, to you readers who message and e-mail with questions and comments. If you enjoyed the book, please take a second to review it so others can find it!

Thanks, Emma, for always alpha reading with a helpful, critical, and caring eye. I'll never ever forget the "it puts the lotion on its skin" comment!

Thanks Caroline, for joining the beta team, and giving amazing feedback. I owe you some mezcal ;)

Thanks to Jamie for continuing our chats despite the weirdness of never being alone or leaving the house.

Thanks to Julie for talking with me about everything, writing rambles and otherwise. You are the tops.

Thanks to Zee Monadee for caring about this series and helping make this book better! I love having your editing prowess at work.

To Meme Hernandez, thank you for the lovely field of flowers and the purple! What a fun surprise. Thanks for persevering with the design process despite the challenging circumstances.

Thanks to my family, especially my kids, who cheer me on and seem to enjoy that I'm a writer even if they've been disappointed to learn they aren't old enough to read my books. Thanks to Millie for being a chill baby—this book was my first post-baby #3 and I'm honestly relieved my brain hadn't turned entirely to mush. Thanks to Matthew for helping to carve out time and space to peck away at this one!

Claire Cain lives to eat and drink her way around the globe with her traveling soldier and three kids, but is perhaps even happier hunkered down at home in a pair of sweatpants and slippers using any free moment she has to read and cook. Or talk—she really likes to talk. She has become an expert at packing too many dishes in too few cabinets and making houses into homes from Utah to Germany and many places in between. She's a proud Army wife and is frankly just really happy to be here.

You can also join Claire's facebook reader group for exclusive content and fun: https://www.facebook.com/groups/clairecain/

Website: http://www.clairecainwriter.com

E-mail: Claire@ClaireCainWriter.com

Newsletter sign-up for new releases, exclusives, and freebies: http://www.clairecainwriter.com/newsletter

Read on for a sneak peek of the final book in the Silver Ridge Resort Series, **Fire and Ice at Silver Ridge!**

Chapter 1

Leo

This was all good. Everything was *great*.

No, really. All good news. Nothing about this, what had been happening in the past few weeks, could be called bad news.

Danny was healing up nicely. He and Mia were engaged now, tied by Grandma's ring thanks to Grandpa Will's generosity. I'd determined not to feel that like the blow it was—Grandpa Will's gifting of a ring I'd always thought of as mine, being the only granddaughter and all that, to a brother I'd never expected to settle down before me. If I had to guess, they'd be married and moved in together by the end of the calendar year.

And Bel and Jamie had been in LA for a few weeks. They'd extended their time in Silverton, but had had to go eventually. I'd made peace with that. They'd be back.

And Wells and Liam were married. *Married*. Not a word about it until after the fact, but yeah, fine, I got it.

I closed my eyes against the blast of cool mountain air rustling in the trees and breathed in slow, slow, filling my lungs, willing the parts of me that felt hollowed out to solidify or disappear. I didn't want this—this miasma of feeling. Sadness and self-pity and all the nastiest things a woman could feel when her best friends and her siblings were all somehow marrying each other and running off into the sunset... and leaving her behind...

Even this real, actual, glorious sunset, with purples and pinks and oranges striping the sky to the west and illuminating the entire mountain range with a kind of heavenly glow, and which would normally make me feel that soul-expanding peace and gratitude, fell flat.

I clenched my teeth, pulling in another breath, refusing to let tears for myself fall. What a loathsome creature, to feel anything but happy for these people I loved so much. How could I stand here drowning in this ridiculous sense of loss when everyone I cared about was not only healthy and happy, but whole and moving toward wonderful new adventures?

A choking, aching sensation scratched at my throat, and I gripped the railing that bordered the overlook so idiots wouldn't wander right off and plummet to their deaths.

"Ms. Morrison."

Speak of the Devil, Ugh.

Well, I hadn't been speaking of him, or even thinking of

him for once, but he'd materialized anyway, like an uninvited jack-in-the-box of ill will.

Of course I'd hear that voice. My sicko sad sack mind had probably conjured it in an effort to complete the sense of torment plaguing me.

"Ms. Morrison, are you all right?"

No.

That wasn't just my mind. It was real.

His crisp, perfect voice *would* interrupt my internal meltdown here at the top of the mountain where I'd come for privacy and a moment to myself.

And sure, it was a public place. I'd taken the gondola to the top of Silver Ridge Peak—or as high as it went—and skirted the lodge that welcomed people at the top of the mountain for lunch, bathroom breaks, and other needs, and found my way to the observation area on the far side of the ridge. From the back deck of the lodge, you might see a person standing out on the platform, which was built on an outcropping and reinforced now by steel beams and all kinds of feats of engineering, but not without really looking.

Since it was September and late in the day, not many people were up here. In fact, the gondola would close to the public in about an hour and only remain open for the workers doing various construction tasks around the lodge and on a new lift installment that led to one of the neighboring mountains.

So the fact that Jonas Bauer had found me—not just *found* me, but approached me—and was now speaking to me as I tried desperately to clutch at some semblance of calm, confirmed the Universe's decision to crap on my head today.

And unlike seagulls, the Universe crapping on one's head was not considered good luck.

Resigned to being unable to ignore him, I turned slowly. I had never attempted to mask my disdain for this man, nor did I have plans to start, especially when he exemplified everything that was wrong in the world.

He stood there, obnoxiously tall and just this side of massive, really. But it all folded into a brutally perfect dark gray suit, white shirt, navy tie. I didn't scan to his feet because he'd no doubt have some sort of annoyingly perfect man shoe, undoubtedly the male equivalent of the Louboutin red sole to showcase his wealth and class.

Or something. I didn't know. But he always seemed perfectly composed. Inhumanly so, if one had to put a word to it, and it, like everything else about him, made my hands involuntarily clench into fists before I tucked them away.

"Bauer."

His gray eyes narrowed just slightly. "Are you quite well, Ms. Morrison?"

I blinked at him, slowly, irritated to find I noticed the close crop of his hair at the sides of his head and recognized he'd had a haircut. I shouldn't notice such things. I didn't care.

"Just fine."

"Would you accompany me down the mountain?" He turned to the side, one hand pressed against his suit jacket currently buttoned once, and gestured with his other toward the small mountaintop lodge and gondola station.

"I would not."

He didn't need to know why.

None of your business! my mind screamed.

He certainly didn't need to know I hadn't gotten a grip yet, and I was banking on these mountains, this view, *this place* returning some shred of humanity to me before I ventured back down and had to face myself and an entire weekend alone in my microscopic apartment.

"The gondola closes in moments."

Twine wrapped around my lungs. He didn't have much of an accent, but times like these, when his word choice sounded just slightly different from what you'd expect, showcased his not-entirely-American heritage.

"The gondola closes in hours, which I know because I've worked here and lived here and taken rides on this gondola *my entire life*. I'll be fine." My head snapped back to the view in front of me, praying he'd find the dismissal in the movement.

"Ah, but it closes to all passengers in seven minutes. They've changed the schedule due to a crew issue. I would hate for you to be stuck here."

Defeat filled me, along with a healthy dose of disappointment, which I wouldn't have thought I had room for after everything else. Of course my time here, in this safe place, would be cut short. Of course it'd be him doing it.

He already wanted to take everything else away from me... why not this, too?

I whipped around and stomped past him, aware I was acting like a petulant child, and not remotely interested in changing my tune. I walked directly to the gondola station, certain if I got there quickly enough, he'd lag behind, or at least get the hint, and I wouldn't have to spend the full thirty-minute ride down the mountain in a small, enclosed space with him.

"Have a good day, Leo!" Ricky, the gondola operator, shouted as the doors to the bright blue car ratcheted open.

"You too. Say hey to Athena for me." His wife was on bedrest for their third child. It'd been a few weeks since I'd dropped by. I should visit her again, and made a mental note to schedule that for the next week.

I slumped down on the hard plastic seat lined with a thin layer of material—not padded, but enough to keep people from slipping and sliding into each other—and leaned my head back against the glass window, shutting my eyes. The gondola bumbled along the curved path inside the station, and just before the doors clamped shut, the car bounced from the weight of another passenger stepping in.

I squeezed my eyes further shut as my heart beat a little louder in my ears. *It couldn't possibly be him,* I thought, grinding my molars to dust since I knew it would be. I cracked a lid open, just barely, to see the unmissable form of Jonas Bauer sitting across from me.

"Do you wish to discuss it?"

Fire and Ice at Silver Ridge is available now! Grab it today!

Don't miss the release and exclusive content until then by signing up for Claire's newsletter.

www.ingramcontent.com/pod-product-compliance
Lightning Source LLC
Chambersburg PA
CBHW051218190726
48288CB00006B/2014